THE AWAN LAKE EXPERIMENT
Awan Lake Series Book III
A Frank Anderson Novel by Peter Kingsmill
Cover design by Rae Ann Bonneville
All characters are fictional and any similarity to people
living or dead is purely coincidental.
Copyright © 2020 Peter Kingsmill
The Awan Lake Series is published by the author.

I0679643

Dedication

Children. It's Fathers' Day as I prepare this book for publishing and I reflect on my children: a stepson, three daughters and my own son, all of whom make me proud and some of whom I see far too seldom, if at all. I am especially pleased that you all matter to each other, despite distances of time, space and shared memory. You might all be surprised how much I sense the touch of your presence on my shoulder as I write these books.

PETER KINGSMILL

"This means we can never have war again, because
we can no longer protect civilian populations."
Admiral Sir Charles Edmund Kingsmill, 1856-1935
*Kingsmill, founder of the Canadian Navy during the First World War and
a summer resident of Grindstone Island on Big Rideau Lake, was commenting
before the Second World War on the development of modern air forces with their
long-range bombers.*

St. Patrick's Day, 2014

Maple Falls Review, Monday March 17, 2014: The estate of former Canadian Army General the late Samuel McKinney has been settled after a prolonged and very public court battle between members of the McKinney family. Of particular note for Spirit River residents, the McKinney's summer home, a 14-room mansion on a 6-acre island on Awan Lake southwest of the Village of Spirit River, has been purchased by an anonymous philanthropist who is thought to have ties to the *"New World Mission"* society, a quasi-religious activist organization possibly associated with a pacifist offshoot of Freemasons in the western United States.

Spirit River ON, 0745: Frank Anderson and Marjorie Webster were having their second cup of morning coffee in the wheelhouse of Anderson's workboat. They were still tied up alongside the Village of Spirit River's commercial dock but the diesel engines were purring quietly in anticipation of another day of helping Awan Lake's summer residents prepare their island cottages for winter. The September long weekend and Labour Day were just around the corner and while there was lots of summer left, schoolchildren would be headed back with their parents to their city homes. Closing down the cottages and putting away boats was an annual ritual, preparing for the long Canadian winter when Awan Lake would be ice-bound and snow-covered until spring break-up.

"We're going to quit early today," said Anderson. "It's time for our anniversary dinner tonight, and a vision of steak and crab and sharing a bottle of wine at The Lockmaster's just won't leave my mind."

"Sounds delightful, but... anniversary?"

"Well, how about *monthiversary*?"

"Certainly works for me, but y'know, we hadn't even started going steady back in mid-July, let alone special details like crawling into the sack together."

"For me, we've been going steady since July fifteenth when you joined me for that afternoon trip out onto the lake." Anderson reached across the little navigation table and took her hand. "Something special happened to me that day, and it's never gone away. And let's face it, you and I have packed more living – and living together – into the last month than most people do in years. Crawling into the sack was – is – memorable, but, well..." he paused. "Will you join me for dinner tonight, Ms. Webster?"

"Absolutely. And you're right... something very special has happened to us."

Anderson stood up and kissed her left cheek. "I guess we'd better get out there or we won't get back before dark. I'll let go the lines if you take her off the dock."

• • • •

Maple Falls ON, 1005: Maple Falls is a town some 20 miles west of Spirit River, with a population of some 4,500 souls. The community came into being in the 1840s when the government of Canada constructed a set of two locks on the Spirit River to open Awan Lake to barge traffic, linking copper and nickel mines around the lake to their markets. The town boasts a branch of a regional technical college, a small but well fitted-out hospital, several bars and restaurants, a detachment of the Ontario Police Service and... a Tim Hortons coffee shop. This morning, that is where one could find local OPS detachment commander Sergeant John MacLeod, along with Superintendent George Daniels from OPS headquarters in Toronto and Royal Canadian Mounted Police Sergeant Marianna Mankowski from RCMP headquarters in Ottawa.

As they sat down at a corner table, Supt. Daniels fished a small package from his briefcase and put it on the table in front of Sergeant MacLeod: "John, I apologize that there is no ceremony to go along with this, because God knows you deserve some ceremony, but it does come with a raise." He turned to the RCMP Sergeant and said, "Marianna, meet Staff-Sergeant John

MacLeod."

MacLeod sat quietly for a moment, then shook her hand and turned back to the Superintendent. "Thank-you, George. I really am honoured... I had sort of been thinking that I had hit the ceiling for advancement, and this is very nice to have. Do I have to move?"

"Nope, not unless you want. I had assumed you would want to stay in Maple Falls, at least until your daughter is a little older. We will be adding a new Sergeant to your detachment, and that will free you up for some special assignments."

Staff-Sergeant MacLeod chuckled: "Well, the last couple of months around here have been kinda like special assignments anyway, so I should be primed and ready."

"Geez, now you outrank me and I'll have to call you *Sir John*," laughed the RCMP Officer. "In any case, you deserve this, for sure. I admired your calm situation awareness when things got tough, but I think most of all I was impressed by your intuition."

"Thanks, Marianna. But I was helped in a big way by some pretty brainy local civilians, especially by Anderson who also has really broad experience. And when it comes to intuition, he and his new girlfriend make quite a team."

"Yeah, my former Coast Guard colleague was impressive," said Daniels. "Wish I could take credit for having trained him back in the day, but actually he was a couple of years ahead of me when we served on the Pacific side. Maybe not the world's most ambitious man or perhaps he would have been sitting at this table instead of me, rather than pushing around that baby tug of his and a construction barge – but he's rock-solid and bright as hell. John, what's Frank been doing now that things have settled down? Do you see him much?"

"We get together often enough, usually for coffee at The Zoo in Spirit River. For the last week, he and Marjorie have been off on the lake most days, closing up the cottages out on the islands and preparing them for winter. It's his usual autumn gig, and this year for the first time he's had full-time help. He's pretty proud of his new First Mate."

"I'm surprised he isn't involved with getting that burned-out marina up and running... should be right up his alley."

"Well, it seems like he and Arnold – and their ladies – are at least talking about it. But I would think there are some pretty huge insurance and legal issues around that... after all it was barely a week ago when we fully released the site from its crime scene status, but that'll just be the beginning of a re-build. Seems that the lady – Florence, who manages the Spirit River Inn – may have inherited both the inn and fifty percent of the marina after her brother-in-law was murdered, but I gather the books are, well, messy to say the least. And, of course, things are further complicated because the other fifty percent of the marina was owned by the manager Jim Russell and his wife who – as you know – were also murdered and apparently they didn't have any living relatives, not close ones anyway."

"Good Grief," chimed in the RCMP Sergeant, "you folks live an exciting life around here. I've been working away trying to get some answers about the murder of that professor from B.C. who was headed this way to speak at the protest event in Spirit River, and there were some rumblings about a connection to the manager at the mine facility here, but the boys and girls in B.C. were discounting that, saying they think the kill-order came from the States somewhere, some big firm that didn't like the professor blowing the whistle on corporate water pollution. But from what you are saying, there was a bunch of killings around here too. Do you suppose they were all related?"

"Over a two-week period, we had ten homicides here, not counting your professor guy, and we absolutely figure they are all related." Daniels paused, then continued, "John, maybe you should line up a chat between Marianna and Anderson. You and he have the most complete handle on the larger picture here, and Frank also has some related west-coast knowledge, all of which could help Marianna and her gang. She'll get a better picture, and much faster, than trying to dig around through our various bureaucracies in Toronto and Ottawa. I shouldn't say that, of course, but we all know it's true."

"I'm in. John, when would be a good time that would suit Anderson, who sounds kind of busy?"

"Well, not today or tonight, I know. I talked to Frank earlier this morning and they are out on the lake, but he's planning to take Marjorie out for a dinner this evening. I think it means a lot to them so I won't barge in, but tomorrow morning early we could probably catch up with them at Frank's house if I give him a call. Can you hang around that long?"

"Sure, I was going to go to Spirit River later anyway, so I'll get a room at the Inn and stay over. You have my cell number – see what you can set up." She paused, and said, "Thanks to both of you. I can see our folks need to expand our horizons on this."

• • • •

Awan Lake, ON, 1020: Charlie Morrell had been Operations Manager at Robertson Group International's mining operation on the east shore of Awan Lake for almost ten years. Seventeen days ago, his office had been three stories up, overlooking the massive workshop that serviced the facility's surface and underground machinery, and through which all employees passed on their way to and from work. Today, his office was an Atco trailer brought in from south of Barrie, and a service crew from Hydro One was outside, finally replacing the electrical service after the entire RGI facility had been turned into a pile of rubble by a catastrophic fire in the early hours of August 13th.

I lost a really good friend and colleague in that fire. Now, all my staff except Bonnie are laid-off, and my former boss has been forced to retire. The man who had been my new boss is now sitting in jail, charged with arson and the murder of several people in connection with that fire. This has not been a usual summer.

There was a knock on the door, and his administrative assistant Bonnie called out, "Come on in." It was one of the electricians, to announce that he was ready to switch on the power but first he needed to shut down the temporary generator they had been using for three weeks. "Okay," Bonnie said. "We'll shut down the computers. Give us about three minutes."

"We'll grab our coffee and give you five." the electrician chirped.

"Cool, thanks," said Charlie Morrell, clearing his screen of morning emails and shutting off the computer before he nodded to Bonnie and followed the electrician outside to where he was leaning on the hood of his service truck, pouring coffee out of a thermos. Charlie Morrell offered the man a cigarette, and they both gazed over the hood of the truck at the blackened mass of tumbled brick, concrete and twisted steel. The fire had taken place almost three weeks ago, but occasional wisps of smoke still rose wraith-like from the ruins.

"Must have been quite a sight when that went up."

"My house faces onto the lake and I was woken up by sirens and helicopters. The red glow lit up the wall of my bedroom opposite the window, even though there's over six miles between here and my house. It was like being in a film about the apocalypse."

"Any idea what set it off?"

"Like they say, *investigations are ongoing* but people died that night. There are whispers about arson and murder, all of which I can believe but so far there is no confirmation. The main area inside the fence is still taped off as a crime scene so we get a steady stream of so-called experts parading through here every day and the insurance investigators have put Commissionaires watching the site all night."

"Anyone you know killed?"

"Yes. My best friend up here. Bob was the development officer onsite, and I have not the slightest idea why he was out here close to midnight on a Saturday."

"Jeez, that's kinda tough. Sorry for your loss."

"Mmm. Thank–you."

. . . .

Powell River, B.C., 2115: It was after nine in the evening in Powell River, British Columbia. The food had been marvellous and the conversation friendly and interesting. Maurice, it turned out, had a long career as a mining engineer and had retired earlier in the summer. He and Vivienne still had a house back east, but they had purchased their sailing cruiser a number of years before, kept it docked at a marina south of Vancouver, and spent as much time onboard as work commitments allowed. Now they contemplated selling their house and spending several years cruising on both coasts.

Ron and Carole Byers didn't come from Powell River either. She had put in twenty-six years as an elementary school teacher and he had been a land agent for an oil and gas company. Until her retirement, they had lived in rural Alberta, sticking with it until their children had made it through college, then they sold out and moved to a house and tiny acreage on the outskirts of Powell River. Five years after arriving, they were as pleased with their decision as the day when they first moved. Ron had purchased a little skid-steer to do work around the property and which he often used to help out the neighbours for pocket change and friendship. Carole put in a few days here and there as a substitute teacher and the rest of the time they both read countless books, worked in the garden and sipped wine.

The Bonners had left from Cortes Island that morning, intending to sail all the way to Powell River but the wind decided it would stay home, so they cruised down under power instead. Vivienne, too, liked to read and had read a number of articles about Cortes Island and some of the goings-on there over the years. Maurice joked that any island near Desolation Sound with a settlement named Squirrel Cove must have some weird stories to tell. It was on the afternoon of their trip into Powell River that the Bonners and the Byers had met... well, Maurice and Vivienne met Ron first, because his little fishing skiff had run out of gas a couple of miles northwest of the harbour at Powell River. The Bonners had graciously, and with a certain amount of good-natured laughter from all three, towed him home. The dinner tonight was Ron and Carole's treat, and it had been a delightful one.

Vivienne looked around the restaurant, noting that the tables near theirs were now vacant, and leaned forward, addressing Carole quietly: "We saw some strange stuff happening early yesterday evening while we were barbecuing some burgers. It was earlier than this, so it was probably around 5:30. We were anchored in the bay at Whaletown near where the ferry from Quadra lands on Cortes, and we saw a good-sized commercial fishing boat come in and land at the Whaletown wharf, which is across the bay from the ferry dock. Nobody got off the boat except to tie up, then about half an hour later a small passenger van drove out on the dock."

"I think maybe the van was an old Astro, but it looked like it was in good shape," Maurice added. "It was white, with blacked out windows."

"Anyway, the driver – we figure it was a *she* and a smallish one at that – got out and went straight to the boat. We could see her talking to one of the crew. He shouted – not in English – to someone else on the boat and less than a minute later six more very young-looking women came out on deck and were assisted immediately off the boat and into the van."

"Assisted? Or maybe forced?"

"Yes, you're right on, Carole," said Vivienne. "Maybe not physically forced or pushed, but the way they moved they seemed to be under threat somehow."

"Anyway," she continued, "the driver lady got back in the van, turned it around and left immediately. And, within five minutes, the trawler was off the dock and headed out of the bay. This was obviously a drop-off of some sort."

"Yeah, I don't think those young women were rich Asian ecotourists on their way to dinner."

"So that's not the end of strange: less than twenty minutes later the same van was driven onto the ferry. Maurice and I checked it out with our old (but very powerful) telescope and we are almost certain it was the same van."

Carole Byers had been silent, listening intently to what the Bonners had been describing. Now she spoke, quietly: "Only two weeks ago, Ron and I were having a picnic along the shore just north of here, kind of opposite Cortes Island. We had just settled into the sandwiches when I noticed something moving back and forth in the waves at the shore. I suppose I knew right away that we were looking at a body, but my mind kinda blanked for a few moments and I got Ron to go down to the water and check it out. I still feel badly that I put it on his shoulders to confirm... it was indeed the very pale and water-logged naked corpse of a very young woman – almost certainly Asian."

"God, how awful." Vivienne said as she put a hand on Carole's arm. "I can only imagine what that was like, and I don't want to even think how you two must have felt."

"Well, certainly not an experience I care to repeat. Of course we called the RCMP and they were very helpful and comforting. However, they said this was definitely not the first young Asian woman to drift onto the shore in this area, and as you can imagine, I did not find that at all comforting. In fact – and I'm sure Ron will agree – the experience left me with a crazy sort of passion to learn more, so I have spent a good part of every day since that Friday afternoon, researching and reading online and through the library, about human trafficking and the sex trade, particularly in Canada. I've even made two trips to Vancouver to interview Canada Customs and Immigration and the RCMP, and one trip across to Campbell River to talk to the

Coast Guard. I'm afraid I've become a bit of a nut."

"Were you able to even get in the door, let alone have those government types discuss anything with you?"

Ron chuckled: "Well, Maurice, you may well ask, but she's good at that kind of stuff. And it helps when she plays the *author* card. Depending on the individual in question, that sometimes opens doors."

"Author? So you've been there, done that as well?"

It was Carole's turn to giggle: "Two small books, a long time ago. One was a collection of cute little Norwegian folktales about families coming to live on the Canadian prairies. I'm sure I sold 75 copies but I ran out of cousins. The second book was more serious, and much more relevant to human trafficking: it was called *Crazy Wife, Happy Life* and was a number of true stories about male immigrant settlers on the prairies who bought mail-order brides and took them out to their homesteads. When – and if – things didn't work out to the man's liking, he could always break the contract, but that would cost, lots. Murder was illegal of course, but in those days, having your wife committed to a mental hospital was perfectly respectable. Then you just order a new bride... as simple, if not as quick, as using Amazon today although shipping took longer. The unwanted women lived out a wretched existence in the institutions and were buried in the asylum graveyards, often in numbered or unmarked graves."

"True?"

"True. Probably hundreds of times."

"That's gross, Carole. How many copies of that did you sell?"

"None, but it did attract a lot more attention than the Norwegian immigrant folktales. I was actually arrested and questioned, then released but the questioning never quit. I had just received my teaching degree and this was to be my master's thesis. I was darn near expelled from the university, and I was barred from getting a teaching job in my home town – anywhere in the province of Saskatchewan, actually. Odd as this may seem, the university didn't accept my master's thesis, but the substance of the book and much of my original text reappeared and was acclaimed as the work of one of my instructors when he took his doctorate at a different university five years later. Looking back, it all worked out for me because I moved to Alberta, got a job teaching, and met Ron. Life has picked up ever since."

"So are you about to get your revenge with this research into trafficking?"

"By now, I could care less about the revenge part, but if it helps me get the story out there so that human traffickers go to jail and the trafficking stops, I'll do whatever it takes."

"Wow."

Ron was looking fondly across at his wife. He leaned forward, put his hand on hers and gave it a gentle squeeze, then said, "I think I need a stiff scotch. All in?"

"Why not – we're not driving anywhere." said Maurice.

"Vivienne and Maurice," said Carole, "do you folks mind if I take some notes about your story? I don't need to use your names, or even your boat's name. There is a real sweetie who works for the RCMP across at Campbell River, and she has quietly invited me to lunch and a long chat, away from the office."

Maurice raised an eyebrow across at his wife, who nodded, then he looked back at Carole: "As far as we are concerned you can share whatever information you need. In fact, if it comes to that, we would certainly testify to what we saw at Whaletown. The only thing I ask is that you let us know if and when things may go public, so we can be a bit more cautious than usual."

"And," Vivienne added, "just so you know, our boat's name is *Awan Lady*. We named her after the lake where we have lived and worked for the last dozen or so years: the *awan* part of Awan Lake means *foggy* in the Ojibwe language, and we always thought it was such a pretty name."

• • • •

Maple Falls, ON, 1845: The Old Lockmaster's House restaurant by the Spirit River canal in Maple Falls was fairly full at sunset. It was getting late in the season for some of the summer cottagers, but there was still cruiser traffic on the canal so Anderson had made a reservation for their "monthiversary" dinner. The restaurant was popular with locals and stayed open year-around, but its busiest trade was in the early summer when the canal and its two locks were operating extra hours, servicing holidaying boaters with power and sail cruisers, big and small. Many would tie up along the canal near the restaurant for the night, where they could take in a gourmet dinner rather than cook in their cramped onboard galleys or on portable barbecues on deck.

Richard, who operated the restaurant with his husband Paul, liked Anderson and Marjorie and had reserved their favourite table for two in the back room. He appreciated the gentle and polite nature of the big, muscular man and his gorgeous blond lady with the dancing eyes, and tonight he would bring them a bottle of their favourite wine, on his own tab. They were good customers, after all, and had brought important and appreciative customers with them when they dined. If they were coming as just a couple tonight, and making reservations, it must be a special occasion.

Sure enough, when Anderson and Marjorie arrived, they were greeted at their table by a bottle of Bachelder 2014 Pinot Noir from Lowrey Vineyard, from which Richard proudly poured a taste for Anderson, waiting for his nod before pouring a glass for "the mademoiselle".

After Richard had sashayed off to the kitchen, Marjorie giggled and leaned across the table: "I get such a kick out of my rough tough coast guard guy, who'll pretty much drink anything that's wet unless it's weak coffee, handling the presentation of wine in a restaurant as if he had been raised with royalty."

Anderson grinned: "Mummy taught me. She worked overtime to ensure that both her husband and her only son grew up to meet her expectations. Not sure that she fully succeeded, but as I look back, many of the lessons – the little things like that – have been useful."

Richard returned with the menus, and suggested a new item – not yet on the menu – that Paul had been working on. "I know you both like Steak Oscar, but this is a little different... a filet with a fresh lobster tail, all smothered in a blue cheese and red wine sauce, topped with asparagus spears of course. I have to say Paul has outdone himself on the sauce – it is delicious."

Marjorie tilted her head and looked across at Anderson: "Wow, Steak Paul. That sounds pretty special... I'd go for that."

"Me too. Steaks rare for both. While we're on the subject of seafood, do you still have the scallops appetizer?"

"But of course, Mr. Anderson. For you as well, Mademoiselle?"

"Please. Sounds excellent... but one thing, Richard. I feel like we're almost neighbours to you, and I wish you would just call me Marjorie. And I know that Frank prefers just "Anderson" without the mister, or Frank, as you wish."

"That would be my pleasure, Mademoiselle Marjorie," he winked and left them both chuckling as he went off to place their orders.

"Damn. Mademoiselle Marjorie, I forgot to tell you that Sergeant John called while you were having a shower. We can expect visitors in the morning – probably around eight or just after. Seems like he and that RCMP sergeant Marianna want to pick our brains about the late Sebastian Horowitz."

"So much for sleeping in. Not like we ever do, I guess. I wonder if they've found out anything about who killed the professor."

"I sort of gather that Marianna's colleagues on the coast may have dropped the ball on that, and John thinks they haven't caught on about a possible connection to the Robertson bunch."

"I'm glad I'm not a cop. I can only imagine the amount of paperwork they are having to do in connection with everything that happened last month. They won't be cleaned up until after Christmas."

"And that reminds me... about Christmas, sort of. For years now, I have wanted to spend a few weeks on the Island – Vancouver Island – but it's not a thing I would particularly enjoy alone. But doing it with you would be very special. And this year in particular, if we went over Christmas, we could spend a day with Keith's widow, Suzy, who will be especially lonely this year."

"Maybe Suzy would prefer it was just you."

"Well, that just ain't gonna happen, and anyway she knows all about you. When I was out there for the funeral I am ashamed to say that I think we talked more about you than we did about Keith."

She put down her half-eaten melba toast slice and reached out to take his hand: "Actually, I think we would have a lovely time, and it's part of Canada I've always wanted to see more of than through an airplane window. And getting to know Suzy would be getting to know more about this new man in my life. How would we go, and where would we stay?"

There was a lull in the conversation while Richard brought their steaks, fussed with the peppermill and topped up their wine glasses. Anderson took the last small bite of bacon-wrapped scallop and answered: "Part of me says we should fly and avoid 2500 miles of Canada's snow, ice, freezing rain and blizzards, twice. Another part of me says we could drive, but of course that would burn up at least ten days total, which could either be easy and fun or really unpleasant in the winter."

"Someday it might be fun to drive across our country, but I suggest we do that another time. Notwithstanding how much I know you love airports, flying sounds better – cheap enough, too, even if we rent a car once we're there."

"That's kind of what I was thinking. As for where to stay, I would love to charter – rent – a small cruiser and travel at our leisure from town to town – marina to marina, kind of like the folks in this restaurant tonight, finding good shore-side restaurants every now and then and enjoying the scenery. It is the west coast in winter and it rains a lot, so if the weather gets too lousy we could tie up, rent a car, and do something else for a couple of days. Does that sound too crazy?"

"Not at all – sounds like lots of fun. That is the ocean, however... how big a boat?"

"Maybe about the same as *The Beaver* or a little bigger – but set up for people to live on, not like a workboat with a big deck and a bunch of machinery."

"Do you think you could find one?"

"Well, back to Suzy. She still lives at Campbell River, of course, and she and Keith and I used to have friends along that stretch of the island from Nanaimo north, who ran marinas and charter services. I'm sure she could make a couple of phone calls and nail down something. She would know who had the best equipment, and she could probably broker us a pretty good deal too. We'd need to jump on it, as we probably want to be there in early-to-mid December at the latest."

The steak, lobster tail and blue cheese sauce was delicious. They opted out of desert, but ordered a couple of snifters of brandy and two coffees, leaving their table in favour of the out-door fireplace to enjoy a quiet cigarette or two, and feeling the warmth of the fire keeping the cool of the autumn evening at bay.

"I love you, Mademoiselle Marjorie."

"I love you too, Monsieur Anderson. I only worry that I will scare you away... you've been your own man for many, many years."

"I am grateful those years are over. I am much happier being your problem now."

Spirit River, ON, 0830: Marjorie and Anderson were just finishing off their bacon and eggs when Sergeant John and his RCMP colleague Marianna Mankowski drove up in the Sergeant's OPS cruiser. When Anderson met them at the front porch, the Sergeant stopped and gestured around the yard: "Geesh, Frank, it looks like you're running a boat dealership here. So much for that nice open yard of yours."

Sure enough, the normally-tidy gravelled yard was beginning to accumulate a variety of boats sitting on wooden blocks, and mostly under tarpaulins. "It's not Labour Day weekend yet, so the rush has only started, but the cottagers have to have somewhere to keep their boats until the marina is operating. Your folks had the boatyard covered with crime scene tape until just a few days ago, but there's a lot of clean-up to be done and the ownership of the property has to be sorted out. Arnold and I are leasing a travel-lift so we can lift the bigger boats out. The ones that have trailers we're taking up and storing in the old curling rink."

"So you and Arnold are going to take on the marina after all?"

"Not sure about the long-term, but for now, something has to happen. We even have Adumbi working on outboard motors in my shop."

"Adumbi? Adumbi Jakande? I thought he was a environmental scientist working on a Master's degree at Ryerson."

"Well, when the Protected Shoreline Project was shut down by the feds in early August, he stuck around and helped with that public event that was supposed to host Dr. Horowitz. Turns out Adumbi had taken a certificate in small-motor repair before he went to university in England, so after the event was over he told us he loved working on small engines and said he still wanted to lend a hand. He knows his stuff and he's having a ball – kind of a break from academia, which I can well understand might be a good thing. Arnold helps out too, especially with the big in-boards, and Marjorie and I are doing the wet stuff, so it's working out fine. Come on in, the coffee's fresh, and I see you brought donuts."

Once they were settled in at Anderson's ten-foot-long dining room table, it was Marianna who spoke up: "John is never going to tell you this, but I am. The man you know as Sergeant John is now Staff Sergeant MacLeod. I am pretty sure he will require that you all refer to him as *Sir*."

Anderson was pouring coffee but immediately put down the pot and took the Sergeant's hand in both paws: "I am so happy for you... well deserved, my friend." And of course Marjorie jumped up, gave him a big hug and said, "Sir John the Dragon Slayer, eh? We'll see about that when I find you a little dragon of your very own, but yes, congratulations Staff Sergeant."

"I already had a dragon of my own, but I didn't slay her, I divorced her. Now I'm raising a little girl dragon, but that's okay. She's learning to fly, so she spits fire a lot and there are some near-crashes, but it's all good."

The Sergeant took out his notebook, opened it to the ribbon bookmark he always used, and continued: "George Daniels says *hi* to you both, and he's the one who suggested we should meet this morning. He thinks that collectively we could add some perspective around the Horowitz case for Marianna and the RCMP.

Seems that the folks out on the wet coast are getting nowhere with their investigation into Horowitz's murder, considering perhaps it was an old man's love-affair gone wrong or something."

"It would take a helluva woman to break his neck and stuff his body into a boat high up on a trailer, which is how I gather he was killed."

"Well, they are actually thinking he had been having a fling with another man, not a woman. That Toronto business a couple of years ago – McArthur, was it? – has everyone's imagination in crazy mode."

"Well, if that's where the current investigation is going," Anderson shrugged, "I have no reason to be embarrassed that my thoughts might be more screwball. Let's start with what we know." He went to his desk along the south wall of the huge open "ground-floor loft" that he had re-modelled into his one-room home, and grabbed a pad of quarter-inch graph paper, his favourite for scribbling maps, detailed construction drawings, and often – like today – for general scheming.

He settled back down at the table and looked across at the Sergeant: "First, just so I know, what have you done with Thomas Manville? I assume he is being held somewhere?"

The Sergeant nodded. "He was refused bail because – charged as a high-risk offender, as well as being a landed immigrant with American citizenship – he poses a flight risk. He is currently in remand at the North Bay institution. He's facing several charges, including murder, accessory to murder and arson, and I assume there will be more charges to come."

"One can indeed assume." Anderson chuckled. "Okay, let's see where the Horowitz thing leads. What do we know, anyway?

First, we know the professor was internationally respected and influential on the subject of fresh-water conservation, and therefore a thorn in the side of many – or maybe most – governments and a threat to the bottom line of a whole pile of corporations doing business in the agriculture, oil and gas, and especially mining sectors. From a journalist at Envirowire a few weeks ago we learned that Robertson Group International had put on a full-court press to discredit Horowitz. And, from a whistleblower at the Global Conservation Society we have learned that GCS was, to use a Trumpian term, *in collusion* with RGI on that whole affair, most likely because GCS receives massive donations from RGI and were told to play ball."

The RCMP Sergeant spoke up: "Sure, goes to motive, but how about hard evidence, like a weapon? I know he died from having his neck snapped, but without more physical evidence it's hard to find a killer."

"I think there was a weapon. I think RGI weaponized Thomas Manville and his contracted security team buddies to manage inconvenient issues at Awan Lake, as they have done in the past at RGI facilities in South America and elsewhere. Rather than manage the issues, they mismanaged them, so either out of frustration or cockiness Manville's contractors went 'way over the top for the Awan Lake project. And, you have security footage showing that Manville – together with someone further up the RGI corporate ladder – planned to burn down the facility and murder at least one of the facility managers who knew too much." Anderson paused.

"But how does that physically connect to an old man with a broken neck in Abbotsford, British Columbia?"

"Can't answer that, but I think they are all part of the same scenario. I think it's all about Manville, trying to please his RGI bosses in Washington. We already know he had spent three years overseeing operations and expansion at an RGI mine and smelter at the north end of Vancouver Island, and we can be almost certain that he engaged – probably on a full-time basis – his team of pet security contractors. It's not a stretch to suggest that he reached out to one of those gentlemen with orders to make Horowitz disappear."

Anderson paused again. "Anyway, that's my theory. Start at Manville and the ex-marine security guards who have been arrested and work back to Horowitz, and his car, on a ferry into Horseshoe Bay Terminal. Incidentally, I think that in due course the OPS will also find linkages between the deaths of our neighbour Leonard Hamilton-Dubois and his former boss (and our Member of Parliament) Garnet Cameron. Maybe not by Manville's hand exactly... I think those murders, with their government connections, may have been above his pay grade."

RCMP Sergeant Mankowski was nodding at OPS Staff Sergeant MacLeod: "Okay, now I get it. At first the connecting threads seem pretty thin, but the similarities will be well-worth investigating. Too much there to ignore and frankly, all the other scenarios that our folks out west have been considering are pretty random. Thank-you, gentlemen. You have been a great help."

"So I can have another donut?"

"Indeed. I'm leaving you the whole box."

Just as he got to his car, the OPS Sergeant paused, unlocked the doors so his RCMP companion could get in the passenger's side, and turned back to talk to Anderson.

"Before I forget this completely, Frank, do you know anything about the old McKinney estate on that big island – I think it's southwest of here?"

"Not much. I used the barge to take a shiny new big garden tractor and all it's bits and pieces out there a few years ago – maybe three years – but I never really got to talk to any of them, just the young gardener, or whatever. Why?"

"Headquarters asked me to keep an eye on it, a couple of months ago actually but as you know, we got pretty busy with all that other stuff. Seems like they've started running some kind of church camp or something, and bringing in high-profile speakers. Not particularly religious, I guess... more political."

"Well, Arnold and I may learn a little more if they need boat stuff done, and I do remember Jim saying he would often take water-taxi runs out there. Said they kept his big pontoon boat pretty busy." He paused: "Man, I hardly ever spent any time with Jim and Margaret but now I really miss them."

"Yeah, barely knew them at all but they sure seemed like nice folks. Anyway, let me know if you hear anything at all from out there, and I'll let you know if I learn any more." He looked at his wristwatch: "I'd better get Marianna back to her car, so I'll see you later."

• • • •

Kolwesi, DRC, 0930 UTC : The 2010 Toyota 4 Runner had seen many miles pass beneath its battered body and cracked windows. Priscilla Morgenstern, a generous soul who was the locally-hired SUV's only passenger, had said in an email to her editor in New York that she thought Samuel, her driver, was "enigmatic". Other people might have called him "sullen".

Priscilla, a reporter and columnist with the USA-based news service Envirowire, was on a special assignment in the Democratic Republic of Congo, looking into the regulatory record and environmental ethics of Robertson Group International, which operated a copper mine and smelter southwest of Kolwesi. The decision for her to come to the DRC had been made hurriedly and with minimal planning, just a fortnight on the heels of a series of articles she had produced about RGI's shaky environmental ethics, particularly with regard to its mine operation at Awan Lake in Ontario, Canada which had resulted in a catastrophic, suspicious and fatal fire less than a month before.

Priscilla had arrived in Kolwesi on an Air France flight two days before, after almost 30 hours since leaving New York, including stops in Paris and Kinshasa. After a cordial but rather unsatisfactory meeting at RGI's small office in Kinshasa in between flights, along with a little sight-seeing, today Priscilla was headed out to take a look at the community of shacks and trailers where mineworkers were housed in close proximity to RGI's open-pit mine, to see if she could get anyone to talk to her. She had left her laptop in the safe at the front desk of her hotel in Kolwesi, and carried only her iPhone, a credit card and her passport – along with her trademark notebook with the waterproof lined paper and all-weather pen. Priscilla loved being out in the field, travelling light.

The road was full of potholes and Samuel's SUV was noisy, so she hadn't noticed the tan-coloured older-model Renault van which had caught up with them. Apart from an open-backed army truck full of soldiers that had passed them going the opposite way, this was the only other vehicle they had seen in the last 25 miles, apart from two or three wrecked cars in the ditches. The driver leaned on the horn and pulled alongside as if to pass, and she could see the pointy end of an assault rifle poking out of the passenger-side window as it passed and pulled in front. Samuel must have got the message, because he slowed down and stopped immediately.

To Priscilla, it seemed for a moment like she was living in slow motion, caught up in a dream. In fact, the next four minutes went by at blazing speed. Three armed men dressed in ragged military coveralls got out of their van. One went to the front passenger door of the SUV, yanked it open and trained his rifle on Samuel, who kept his hands on the wheel and stared blankly ahead. The other two men came to either side of the rear seat and opened the doors. One slung his rifle, reached in and grabbed Priscilla's ponytail and shirt and pulled her off the seat and onto the ground while the other came around the back of the SUV and smacked her in the ear with the butt of his rifle.

It was then that Priscilla began to scream. The three men laughed, and the one who was holding her by the hair took a ten-inch knife out of a sheath on his belt. He used it to slice through her shirt and bra with one fast swipe which cut deep into her right breast then into her belly at her waist, where he repositioned the blade and kept slicing through her underwear and slacks. The two men peeled off her clothes like they were skinning a game animal, and threw her on her back onto the gravel.

Two men each took a turn. They made no effort to silence her screams, which must have turned them on because they orgasmed almost immediately. The third man urinated on her face before he shot her in the forehead.

Priscilla had never been a big woman, and now it was like she had never been there at all. They dragged her bruised and bleeding little body to the ditch, dumped a 20-litre can of gas on her, and laughed as one of them threw on a lit match. Before they drove away, the man who was evidently in charge picked up her phone and passport as well as her billfold, out of which he took five USA ten-dollar bills, worth 60,000 Congolese francs. These he threw on the front seat for Samuel and told him to get lost.

• • • •

Spirit River, ON, 0950: It was a good thing that Anderson and Marjorie had planned to stay around home this Saturday morning. No sooner had the two sergeants driven off up the road than Arnold and Marion Jamieson arrived. Arnold had been a close friend to Anderson since he first arrived in Spirit River, purchased the old boat works building that now served as his house and workshop, and brought in the converted Nova Scotia lobster boat that was now his trademark "ship" on Awan Lake. Marion worked with Arnold to operate the Main Street Garage where he was a handyman mechanic while she kept the books, the staff, and her husband, in order. They had no children, but their marriage of some thirty years was nonetheless one of humorous affection, deep love and mutual respect.

"Hi folks, come on in. John was just here with Marianna – that RCMP gal from Ottawa – and they left us a monster box of donuts. We need help."

"I'll say we need help," Marjorie laughed. "Ever since I met Frank I've munched down more donuts, eggs and bacon and gourmet meals – including meals at your place Marion – than this city girl would normally consume in a year. The tummy is starting to show the results."

"There's an old saying that in a happy marriage the women get fatter and the men get skinnier."

Marion thumped her husband across the shoulder: "Don't

be rude, old man. Sure as hell didn't work that way with you, did it. Anyway, they're not even married."

"We went out for our *monthiversary* dinner last night," Marjorie giggled, and now we're already planning our second honeymoon."

"So when was your first honeymoon?"

Anderson was re-setting the coffeemaker. "Don't be nosy." he chuckled, and continued: "Actually, yes, we need to talk with you folks about that. We're contemplating taking a few weeks around Christmas to go out to Vancouver Island, but I don't want to leave you stranded with all the marina stuff. It's looking like we might be in deeper than we first thought... pun intended of course."

Marion glanced across at her husband, then turned back and said, "Funny you should mention that... we've just come over to tell you that Florence wants to meet with the four of us, soon. She must have received some information about Leonard's estate."

"I expect so," said Arnold, "but I have no idea how complicated that might be. I would also guess that settling it could take years. Any lawyer worth hiring would want to milk that settlement process for all the fees he could get."

"Well, perhaps at least she will have a more clear idea of the challenges she needs to deal with," Marjorie commented. "I feel for her... it will be awhile before she gets over August 2017."

"So, you guys. I often thought the only thing that would drag Frank away from here for a holiday would be a pretty woman, and I guess I was right. The west coast would be a fun trip, even if in December it truly lives up to being called the "wet" coast. Where would you stay?"

"Thinking about chartering a small cruiser and just hanging out at marinas around the Gulf Islands. We might plan to spend a bit of time with Keith's widow, Susan, who will be especially lonely this Christmas."

"Nice. Marjorie, I see Anderson has got you roped into being around boats all the time."

"Two months ago, a motorboat was just a thing I had to use to get from A to B. I confess that now I'm hooked and I love being out on the water. Maybe someday I'll even express that in painting and photography but for now I am – literally – just learning the ropes."

Anderson smiled at her: "She's a helluva good student. And, she has a head for detail that's missing in me. So, Arnold, Marion, you wouldn't be too pissed off if we disappeared for a few weeks?"

"Hell no. And, last I looked this morning there is still internet and email, Canada-wide cellphone packages and – if all else fails – airplanes. Go and have a ball... we'll hold down the fort here and keep you in the loop. It's winter in Spirit River, there's no urgent boat work to do, and neither of you are signed up for the village hockey team."

Arnold had drained his coffee cup and stood up. "Frank, I'm going out to your shop to look at the engine on a wakeboarder that Adumbi said he was having trouble with. Won't take me long." The two men went out through the interior door which connected the loft-like single-room dwelling to the large workshop which – at the moment – housed two motorboats on trailers. As they walked over to the one with the engine hatch open, Anderson asked, "Say, do you ever hear about stuff going on out at McKinney Island?"

"Wow, I haven't heard anything at all about that place for years. McKinney seemed like an okay guy, but the bunch that took it over after McKinney died was kinda snooty, and never used any local services at all, except for Jim's water taxi. Why?"

"Sergeant John mentioned it this morning, saying that his bosses in Toronto had asked him to keep his ear to the ground. No big deal, I guess."

"Probably not. I do know that Garnet – our late Member of Parliament – used to spend time out there with the McKinneys, especially when some of their high-powered international guests were around." He pulled his head out from the engine hatch and asked, "Have you got cooling water hooked up to this one?"

"Yup. I'll turn it on and start the engine so you can listen to it." In moments there was whine from the starter followed by a rough growl as the engine started, belching blue smoke unevenly and spraying it along with cooling water through the exhaust fitting on the transom and then outside the building through a steel flex hose.

"Hey, you should put smoke and carbon monoxide sensors in here, and while you're at it connect them to alarms in the house too," said Arnold, coughing heavily.

"Did that," said Anderson. "The alarms drive us crazy when we're welding, even with the exhaust fan on, so sometimes we turn 'em off."

"I see I'm going to have to warn Marjorie you were hatched at the shallow end of the gene pool, in case she doesn't already know."

"She's likely figured that out already."

• • • •

32

THE AWAN LAKE EXPERIMENT

Douglas, SK, 10:15: In the rolling parkland east of North Battleford, Saskatchewan, Jim Lucinski was working with his crew to prepare his machinery for another 12-hour day harvesting canola on some of the rented land that made up the nearly 12,000 acres they had seeded in May. The three massive combines were new, or almost so – all of his sensitive machinery was leased to mitigate against time-wasting breakdowns at this critical time of year – but nonetheless they all required constant maintenance in accordance with manufacturers' specifications. His crew was made up of mostly full-time young workers with families who had settled in nearby villages, and who were enthusiastic, experienced and relatively well-paid.

"Don't forget to grease the inner bearings on the straw-choppers," he shouted over the rumble of idling diesel engines to a couple of men in coveralls. "We don't need those things to blow apart in the middle of the afternoon." He turned away to look across the field at a cloud of dust on the gravel road to the south.

The cloud of dust metamorphosed into a battered-looking pick-up, which turned off the road into the field and approached the cluster of combines, a couple of tractors with self-unloading grain wagons, and two B-train semi-trailers. Jim did not recognize the old green Ford half-ton, so he knew that it would likely be he who would have to talk to the driver. He walked away from the nearest combine and waved at the driver, waiting for him to pull in close, stop and get out.

The driver was over six feet tall and likely over forty years old, with a shaved head, short beard, an open-necked shirt and jeans with battered military-type boots. "Hi, you looking for me, or can I help?" asked Jim.

The new arrival had a big smile and big hands, one of which

he reached out to shake hands. "Hi – I asked at the gas station in the village and they said to talk to you. I'm looking for work. My name is Dan... Dan Millard."

"Hello Dan, my name is Jim. Depending on what you can do, you may have come to the right place. Have you had any farm or harvest experience?"

Dan eyed the machinery and the bustle of preparation to hit the field. "Was raised on my granddad's place, but harvest was never like this back then. Been logging in B.C. and working in mines... mostly in the bush, so operated cats and trucks but not much on highways. But I'm tough, careful and don't mind long hours. What do you pay?"

"New hires start at $18.50. We bank hours instead of over-time. I could use a tractor driver if you're game."

"Not quite the pay scale I'm used to but I'm not in any posi-tion to argue. I'm good to go if you are."

Jim turned and bellowed to one of the men in coveralls, waving him over: "Jeremy, could you take Dan here out on the Massey and show him how it works? Go through a whole circuit with him and let me know how it's going." He turned to Dan and shook his hand. "Let's give it a try. We'll see how well you do – Jeremy's had lots of experience, and I doubt he'll bite."

Wonder where he's from, and why he chooses a farm in Saskatchewan. He seems to know his way around, Lucinski mut-tered to himself as he walked back to his own pick-up. *Could work out for us, at least for a couple of weeks.*

• • • •

Spirit River, ON, 1115 EDT: Anderson had just stepped off the wharf onto the workboat when his cellphone squawked. He put down the carton of engine oil he was carrying and unlocked the wheelhouse door before answering: "Good morning. Frank Anderson here..."

"Hello Frank, this is Tony – Tony Barker. I know this is short notice, but Jean and I are wondering if you'd join us for a beer and a sandwich for lunch? My apologies – obviously there's something we need to talk about, and you are the only one we can turn to who might be of any help."

"Hey, Tony, give us an hour and we'll be there... you just caught me as I was dumping oil from the engines and changing oil and filters... takes me about half an hour and we'll be on our way."

"Much appreciated, Frank. This is something I only just heard about this morning, and in my mind there is some urgency."

"Absolutely. Beer with Tony and sandwiches by Jean are a cause for celebration, not worry."

"Thanks Frank... I'll be sure to tell Jean that. See you soon."

Anderson opened the engine hatch, checked the generator and main engine extractor pump discharges and turned them on before texting Marjorie: "**Just shot a cow. looked like where eaten lunch at Larkers. I'll be reader in abound 20 minuets. heS buy-in the Burt.**"

After he hit "send" he went back to the engines to check on the progress of the used oil removal and to remove and replace the filters. He heard his cellphone beep, and checked for Marjorie's reply text.

"**Margelfloop. Slimp.**"

"What the..." then he checked what he had written, laughed, and texted back: "**gleep**".

Some ten minutes later, Marjorie walked down the dock and stepped over the rail: "I assume we're headed to Tony and Jean's for lunch and they are buying the beer?"

They shared a chuckle about Anderson's texting skills, spent a few minutes preparing the boat to leave the dock, and were soon on their way, heading toward the little island where the Barkers had their cottage. Summer would soon be turning to autumn, but there was no sign of that today. A gentle breeze out of the southwest rippled Awan Lake's waters, sparkling a light blue in the light of the noon sun while the main diesel engine thrummed softly under their feet. The afternoon was away too pleasant to spend inside, so Marjorie had set the autopilot and GPS system to steer the course to the Barkers while they stood out on the deck, soaking in the late-summer sun.

"I wonder what Tony has in mind... any idea?"

"Well, not really," Anderson said as he lit a cigarettes for both of them. "He mentioned McKinney Island, that big island 'way off to the southwest. It was owned by the McKinney family until the old man died a number of years back. I guess there was a big court battle about his estate that lasted several years. Eventually I think it was sold to some private club or camp for wealthy children, or something. I really don't have any idea at all... even Marion and Arnold don't know much about it."

"Now that I think about it, I remember Wendy talking about that several years ago, when she was doing the publicity for Robertson Mines out here. They must have made a big contribution to it... seems like it might have had something to do with a church group and fighting for peace."

"Hmm. *Fighting for Peace*... isn't that a something-or-other moron?"

"Noticed that, did ya?" Marjorie laughed. "Yeah, the word is *oxymoron* and yes, *fighting for peace* fits that definition perfectly."

"*Oxy-moron* sounds like a drug addict with a low IQ. So maybe that's what this is all about – drugs and stupidity."

Marjorie rolled her eyes and shook her head in mock sorrow: "I hope we get to Tony and Jean's place soon so he can clear this up," she laughed. "I fear this is getting 'way off track."

Ten minutes later Anderson clicked off the autopilot and took over the steering. He throttled back the engine and blew a couple of short blasts on the air-horn to let the Barkers know they would soon be pulling in at the dock in the bay behind their cottage. Tony Barker came to the dock and took their lines while they docked and thanked them warmly for their prompt trip to the island.

Marjorie gave him a hug: "Tony, we'd have swum here for a Jean Barker lunch, you know that."

"She loves it when we have visitors and she can cook for more that the two of us. Not like we get run off our feet with guests out here, except for the occasional kids-and-grandkids visits. Come on up to the house... perfect day for beer on the verandah. Won't be too many of these before we actually get into autumn."

After greeting Jean, they settled – beer in hand – into the wooden Adirondack chairs that are so much a part of summer life in cottage country. "Frank," said Tony, "have you ever been out to McKinney Island?"

"Well, sort of, but only that. Nearly 20 years ago when I moved here, and once I got my boat delivered and operational, I made it my business to see everything on the lake. So, armed with a chart, an exercise book and pencil, and a little Canon Power-

Shot, I sailed around every island with buildings or docks and along every shore, making notes and taking snapshots. Nothing nosy – just to help me recognize everything – and so it was with McKinney Island. I haven't been anywhere close to it since, except once when I kept Jim company while he was doing his water-taxi thing late one night. As I recall, he didn't have much use for the owners, either the McKinneys or the folks who bought it. They just produced some revenue he was happy to have. So... why do you ask?"

"Well, for starters, and before I retired, my firm was engaged as auditors for the McKinney estate, on behalf of the executor. It was a long drawn-out affair, mostly because of the court case. I can't go into much detail, of course, but suffice it to say that the island property at Awan Lake was a pretty small line-item on the estate's balance sheet. There were lots of other investments, but as you can imagine I was always interested in the fate of the island. Jean and I couldn't afford to buy it – didn't even want to because we love this place – but we really didn't want to see it commercialized and turned into a fly-in resort either, so we kept our eyes and ears open until it was sold to a pacifist group of Freemasons from the States. So, in effect, a non-profit corporation with a social engineering mission statement and an anti-war agenda. The money for the purchase, along with an operating trust, came from an anonymous American philanthropist."

Marjorie put her head to one side: "Kinda hard to argue with the agenda – not too sure about the mission statement..."

"Exactly what we thought, and so we have contentedly watched from the sidelines for the last couple of years. Except that – and I hereby confess that I am not a very nice person – I used my company's former relationship as auditors of the estate, plus our next-door location, to weasel my way into being their *local advisor* so I could keep a closer eye on what they were doing."

Anderson was chuckling. He leaned across to Tony and clinked beer glasses. "Smart."

"Perhaps, or maybe just mean-spirited, but in any case, now I think I'm glad that I did. I've always known they put on a lot of events that ran the gamut from philosophical discussion groups and pacifist-oriented Bible studies to sessions on political lobbying and public relations, but now it seems they are taking things to another – more troubling – level. Next month – like, in two weeks – they are hosting a five-day training workshop entitled "A Christian Response to the Threat of Fascism.""

"Now that sounds a little weird."

"That's what we thought, Frank. Jean and I have attended two, maybe three, of their little seminars and most of the folks there are our age, grey-hairs and mostly ladies in long hemp dresses. Usually the presenters were senior academics (and occasionally clergy) in blue jeans and sweatshirts. Most of these folks are a long way from being hard-core street activists."

Jean was laughing: "I had to keep a rope on tall-and-tanned-Tony when we went there. All the old gals flocked around him like he was the reincarnation of John Wayne."

"That's okay, sweetie, I can handle them. As always, all I have to do is tell them I'm an accountant and they vanish. You're the only girl who ever hung around, and that's 'cause I didn't tell you until it was too late."

When they were done chuckling and refreshing their beer glasses from quart bottles of Molson Export, Marjorie and Jean went to the kitchen to set up lunch while Tony and Anderson resumed the conversation about McKinney Island. "So far, Tony, what you're telling us seems bizarre, to be sure, but I would think relatively harmless unless one of the old farts slips and hits his (or her) head on a rock. There must be more?"

"Yes, there's more. The workshop leader, a professor of sociology at the University of Toronto, has hired over a dozen guys from a motorcycle gang in the city to help him conduct a mock attack on the island, as part of the training. He's got them armour and uniforms like SWAT teams wear, and even training rifles."

"Geez. Do the folks who signed up for the course know this is gonna happen?"

"No. Christopher, the executive director out there, pulled me aside as we were leaving after a visit and told me about it. He also introduced me to the professor. He's all pumped for this, but it's a secret and he wants to keep it that way. The only reason he told me was because he wanted me to smooth it over with the local police so they don't crash the party. He also needed to know where to get some boats now that Jim and the marina are gone."

"Crap. A bunch of wealthy wish-they'd-been hippies playing on a remote island with a contingent of Hell's Angels wannabees. What could possibly go wrong?"

"Exactly. What, indeed. I did ask the professor how well he knew the motorcycle boys, and he said that was no problem because he has a Harley that he rides pretty well every weekend so he knows most of the guys."

"Why do I find that less than comforting... what did you tell him about the boats?"

"I didn't want to get you involved, so I suggested they'd need to rent three boats and trailers somewhere – maybe Maple Falls or beyond. That's what Christopher had to do a couple of weeks ago when they had another group that got stranded out there after the fire."

"When is this thing meant to happen?"

"Couple of weeks, starting Wednesday 13th and wrapping up that Sunday."

"Did you speak with Sergeant John yet?"

"Not yet. I wanted to run all this by you first so we could do some planning."

"Not sure if we need to plan, scheme, or run like hell. That whole idea of theirs is just nuts."

Marjorie and Jean arrived with two plates each of lunch, which consisted of garden-fresh salad, home-made mayonnaise, and large toasted croissants spread with a thick layer of melted parmesan and mozarella cheeses, sliced fresh mushrooms and steamed spinach mixed together with butter, nutmeg and garlic.

"Jean's gone and done it again," said Marjorie. "Who in their right mind would have thought to put all these things together, and the result is incredible."

"I know," said Anderson, taking his plate. "I could smell it out here and it was driving me crazy."

• • • •

After lunch, Marjorie begged off operating *The Beaver,* which she loved doing, so she could spend some time chatting with Jean while Tony and Anderson took a four-mile run up the lake to pay a visit to McKinney Island. "Do you suppose," asked Anderson, "...do you suppose we could land and have a chat with Christopher? You're meant to be their local contact, Tony, and hopefully they would honour your concern to help make sure things run smoothly. We don't have to show that we have worries... just being neighbourly, y'know... stuff like that."

"I was thinking about that, Frank. I agree – that'd be a good idea. We can be pretty casual. And, if he has any concerns that he didn't mention two days ago, maybe now he might share them. Christopher isn't stupid, and I think he's a straight shooter. Naïve, perhaps, but I bet you and I will probably come across to him as a pretty hard-ass pair, and this might be a good time to play that card, in a friendly way."

"What do they have for coms out here? Satellite phone, or marine radio, or was old McKinney rich enough to have his own telephone line all the way to shore?"

"Yes, yes, and yes. McKinney was rich enough to own his own telephone company, let alone a line to the shore. They've had a direct and private telephone line for many years, and they've always had a marine radio base unit and a huge antenna. But now of course they also have satellite phones as well as internet. Like most folks these days, email is likely the best way to reach them... I'll email you all their coordinates."

"Who takes care of them? I thought I sort of knew everyone around Spirit River who does that kind of stuff – used to be Jim for boats, and occasionally Arnold for stuff, and me for construction, and there are some other handyman-type guys. But they don't use any of us, as far as I know. McKinney Island is a big and well-developed place... must be someone, maybe from Maple Falls?"

"Yes, I understand they have a go-to guy in The Falls. Keeps to himself... I don't have a clue what his name is, but I remember Christopher saying he had the guy bringing out a replacement water heater awhile back, and of course he has to get diesel from somewhere. They have recently put in lots of solar stuff, but they still need their generator, and it's a moose of a thing. I saw it one day... has its own little building."

"How do they get groceries and stuff? Surely they don't take a boat all the way down the river to The Falls... that's a helluva slow trip."

"No, they have always gone back and forth to The Falls through the marina at Spirit River – until three weeks ago. They had a good-sized launch they kept in the boat house at the marina over winter, and sometimes – particularly for passengers – they used Jim and his water-taxi. But, of course, three weeks ago that all turned into a fireball. They still have the launch, of course, because in the summer it lives out on the lake so it didn't burn up in the fire, but I'm not sure where they are landing now."

They were approaching the island, perhaps less than a mile off, and Anderson cut back the throttle so they didn't seem so hurried. "I find this whole "estate in exile" thing pretty strange, Tony. I do get it, back in the day when old man McKinney was alive, clinging to some warped self-image of being part of the military elite and therefore being above the common people. But this is 2017, not 1920, and they're just on an island in a northern lake in Ontario, not on a private estate in the Mediterranean off the coast of France."

"Yes, back in the day McKinney used to get foreign dignitaries – mostly military – visiting him out there all the time. Lot's of them, apparently, were from India, and through the British government they became special guests of Canada, so they would be accompanied by Members of Parliament, Ministers, and occasionally even the P.M. of the day or the Governor General."

"Say, Tony, did you ever see our late Member of Parliament,

Garnet Cameron, out here?"

"Yes, we met him a couple of times at those events. Bugger used to flirt unmercifully with Jean."

"I guess he deserves credit for having good taste. Was he an obvious favoured guest of the management, so to speak?"

"Seemed that way. Last time we saw him there was early this summer. He seemed very involved with some of the VIPs – Eastern Europeans, I thought."

"Strange. Sergeant John asked me about him when he came by for coffee this morning. Of course, Garnet's murder is a big deal in the Maple Falls cop shop because it's a national story. As far as what I gathered from John, although the cops first suspected a link to the Robertson Mines fiasco, they are not fully convinced that there is any connection there at all and they know they may be looking at something entirely different. But I don't think they have a clue what that something different might be."

They had completed a half-circle around the rocky shore of the tree-covered island and were now opposite a deep bay that provided shelter for a substantial dock and a couple of boathouses. Anderson took the transmission out of gear and motioned to Tony to call on the marine radio and announce their arrival: "Calling Christopher on McKinley Island. This is Tony Barker with Frank Anderson, as we discussed. We are in the bay on the southwest side of the island, requesting permission to land at your main dock."

"Yes, we saw your approach. You are welcome to tie up anywhere on the dock that works for you. It has ample depth for your vessel anywhere along its length. I will meet you on the dock in just a few minutes."

Anderson put the transmission lever forward and nudged

The Beaver forward alongside the dock. By the time he had come to a stop, Tony had already placed the fenders over the side and had taken a mooring rope from the stern to one of the rings on the wooden dock. Anderson took the bowline forward and finished securing their boat when all six-foot-five inches of Christopher strolled purposefully onto the dock, dressed in military-style khaki slacks and shirt. He had blond closely-cropped hair, blue eyes and – fortunately for the moment, thought Anderson – a friendly smile. "Greetings, Mr. Barker, it's good to see you again. And this must be Frank Anderson. This is a pleasure... your reputation precedes you." and he stuck out his hand.

The handshake was firm but not aggressive, Anderson noticed, and returned a relaxed smile. "In that case, I hope my reputation is favourable."

Christopher laughed: "I believe the person telling me about you said, *You can count on Anderson but don't fuck with him,* so that sounds favourable to me. And both of you, please call me Chris. Christopher is two syllables too many."

"And I'm Tony, Chris. We brought along a beer, and some hot coffee. May I invite you to join us on Frank's little ship and have a private chat? I don't mean to burden you with my concerns, but I want to make sure we're all on the same page. Some of your, well, let's say *partners,* have me a little alarmed."

"Certainly. You have long been our highly respected local advisor, as well as our auditor in times past. Anyone who matters around here listens when you speak. I will have a beer, and listen, and hope I haven't messed something up."

SEPTEMBER 1

Awan Lake, ON, 0915: Wendy and Anita were still asleep when Wendy's cellphone started ringing, showing an unknown number from New York. She rolled over, debating whether to just let it go to voicemail, but old habits die hard... *it might be an important call.* She clicked the answer button: "Hello?"

"This is Arthur Brighton, Editor-in-Chief at Envirowire. I'm looking for Wendy Webster. Can you tell me how I can find her?"

"This is Wendy speaking. How can I help you?"

"Wendy, you, and your partner Anita developed a very close collaboration – and a close friendship as I have been told – with Priscilla Morgenstern of our agency, am I correct?"

"Yes, you are indeed correct. We think very highly of Priscilla, and she did some great work around here."

"Then I am afraid I have some terrible news. Priscilla was on assignment in the Congo last week, and was abducted and murdered southeast of Kolwesi."

"Oh my God, no. She's... she was... such a bright light, which shone not just as a professional journalist but as a friend to... to, well, to everybody. What was she investigating, and how did you learn about it?"

"The news came through Reuters, and of course I followed through on all of it. I am devastated to admit that I approved this assignment, and it was related to mining regulation, government corruption and – you will find this ironic – Robertson Group International's operation near Kolwesi. Of course, I have no leads on who was behind her abduction and murder. I have learned it was a roadside attack, and that it was brutal."

"There is no irony there. This was a deliberate attack with a deliberate message to the media. While the proponents are almost certainly a collaboration between the prevailing government forces in the region and Robertson Group International, RGI is the principal beneficiary. The message is simple: *mind your own damn business.*"

"Ms Webster, I see we share the same perspectives, as did our late colleague. I would like very much to meet with you. Priscilla spoke very highly of you and... your partner Anita, I believe? Priscilla's work on this file needs to be moved forward."

"Are there funeral arrangements being made?"

"Priscilla's body was burned beyond any recognition in the attack, so identification was by DNA, thanks to the French government. After an autopsy was completed, her remains were cremated and her ashes are currently on an airplane into New York. We are working with her family to prepare a memorial service in the very near future. I will be absolutely sure to keep you up to date on arrangements. The memorial event will be structured to focus attention on the growing trend in our country and elsewhere to call the media *the enemy of the people.* As you know, more and more journalists are dying because of what we do."

"Absolutely. Thank-you, Arthur. I fully intend to be there in support, and I look forward to meeting with you. It is just such a sad thing today... thank-you for your call this morning."

Wendy clicked off the call, and turned to Anita who – wide-eyed and with tears – was by now sitting cross-legged in the middle of the bed. "As you have probably already realized, that was about Priscilla. That was her boss at Envirowire, calling to tell us she was killed last week while on assignment in Africa – the

Congo to be more accurate."

"You mentioned Robertson... are they part of this, too?"

"It was a story about them and their mines that she was investigating. Samuel didn't say RGI was involved in her death and I didn't ask him directly but I can tell from the way he talked about it that he's pretty damn sure they were."

"It goes on and on with those bastards. I hated them when I was a little girl and they hurt my father. That's when he started drinking. Dad and mum are better now, but everything else just gets worse and worse. How many people died around here last month? Ten? More? And now Priscilla, our dear sweet Priscilla. We only knew her for a few days. Bastards."

"We'd better call Marjorie right away. She and Frank – and the others too, including Sergeant John – need to know about this."

• • • •

North Bay, ON, 1030: The North Bay Jail east of Sudbury serves the central northern part of Ontario as a remand centre. It is an Ontario Corrections Service facility, and not a large one as far as prisons go, housing some 120 temporary inmates awaiting trial or transfer to other detention centres in Canada. It is classified as a maximum security facility.

Thomas Manville was already a bit of a celebrity at North Bay Jail. He was a charismatic American, with an easy smile, a confident manner and no criminal record as far as anyone knew. He did have a notable reputation for having powerful friends in high places (including, apparently, US Special Forces) and possibly in the underworld of international espionage. Despite having arrived at North Bay as a high-risk inmate facing charges of murder, accessory to murder and arson, within three weeks of his arrival he had already earned the trust of the warden and staff, the grudging respect of the inmates in his section, and he had scored a kitchen job.

Mondays and Thursdays were grocery delivery days at the North Bay Jail, and at 10:30 inmate Thomas Manville was already in the kitchen area preparing the walk-in cooler and storeroom to receive the day's shipment. The refrigerated semi-trailer was about seventeen minutes later than usual so the guards quizzed the driver and swamper before opening the gate. There had apparently been a traffic jam on the outskirts of North Bay and they had been held up for about a quarter-hour, the driver figured, laughing at the guards and wondering what the hurry was: "Those idiots you got in there ain't goin' anywhere anyway – who gives a fuck if their lunch is a bit late."

When the grocery order was almost unloaded, Manville told the executive chef at the jail that he felt like crap and was going back to his cell to lie down. "Yeah, okay Tom, we can finish up. Go ahead, I'll mark you off. Thanks for your help."

Manville picked up a carton of bottled ketchup and turned left into the open truck instead of right into the storage room. He walked quickly to the front of the van, nodded at the swamper and put down the ketchup before settling in behind some pallets of groceries headed for the hospital at Mattawa, some 35 miles further east.

Thomas Manville never did get to experience the delights of Mattawa at the border between the provinces of Ontario and Quebec. There is a rest-stop and picnic area on the north side of the highway along the shore of the Mattawa River, where Manville had been told he would transfer from the truck to a waiting car for a dri-

ve west and south to the international border at Sault Ste. Marie, then on to Minneapolis. As he eased himself down to the ground from the left-rear door of the van, he didn't see the waiting car, but he did see the attractive spruce trees along the side of the picnic area before the 9mm slug drilled into the back of his skull and ploughed out through his left temple.

• • • •

Spirit River, ON, 1310: It was ten after one (1310 in Anderson-speak) when Arnold and Marion joined Anderson and Marjorie who were already settled at a corner table in the Spirit River Inn Lounge. "We have news this morning," Marjorie began. "Do you remember Priscilla, the pretty little reporter from the States who spent a lot of time upstairs here at the Inn with Anita and Wendy during the big public event last month? She's just been murdered, in Africa where she was on assignment. Wendy called me about an hour ago... of course she and Anita are kind of a wreck about this."

"Has Anita told her Mum yet? I see she's working here to-day."

"I expect not – this is pretty new. But you're right, Marion, we probably should tell her – and Florence too – especially since we're here to meet Flo right away and Georgina will almost certainly be working here while we're meeting." Marjorie swivelled in her seat and waved to Florence: "Could you and Georgina come here for a moment?"

Indeed, Florence had been helping Georgina as server and bartender during the lunch rush. Both women remembered Priscilla and were, of course, shocked and saddened. They, too, were a little unnerved, since the murder seemed related to that terrible night a scant month before.

"Marjorie, your sister Wendy is simply the best thing that ever happened to my Anita. This is awful for them."

"Yes Georgina," Marjorie answered. "Those two are wonderful for each other, and I really hope it lasts, at least as long as they both want it to. I've never seen Wendy so relaxed."

Florence chuckled: "Marjorie, even your sister Wendy at her most frantic would seem relaxed alongside Georgina's dear little Anita. Still, they are a lot of fun to watch."

"Different – and better – news. Florence, did you know that Sergeant John is now Staff Sergeant John?"

"Wow. Hey, that's nice for him. He certainly deserves the promotion after all the stuff that's been going on over the last two months. He truly is a nice man... I used to think he was a bit slow, but actually he's sharp as a tack. He's just thoughtful and caring."

After Georgina went back to serving the few remaining lunch customers, Florence turned her attention to the other four at the table: "Since we're talking personal stuff, I want to share some things you may have guessed but were always too polite to ask. There were only two things that my late brother-in-law truly loved: Awan Lake was one, and my sister was the other. After I was divorced and my sister died, he was good to my son, and he was good to me. And yes, we have always been good friends but we did become lovers. It was never a passionate affair, but it was pleasant, occasional, and convenient, for both of us. Sort of like we kept each other from getting too deeply involved in other affairs which would probably be far less compatible. I hope I don't sound too harsh, or selfish. I was terribly fond of him, but in public he was always my brother-in-law and I was always his general manager."

She paused while Georgina brought them beer and took their lunch orders, then continued: "So that's the personal, private stuff between friends. And it may somewhat explain the business stuff... as you can imagine, I've had more conversations with lawyers over the last few weeks than I've ever had before or hope to have in the future. I make an exception for my own lawyer and my accountant, who have both been gems to deal with. As I said a moment ago, yes, I was always Leonard's general manager, but not just that – for years I have also been his co-owner, of both the Inn and fifty-one percent of the marina. We believed in both businesses, and were sad and worried when Jim and Margaret said they wanted to retire from the marina. Frank, Jim talked to me the day before they were killed and told me that you were pretty lukewarm about taking on his share. For their sake – and mine too – I was disappointed because I had suggested to them that you might be a logical option for him and for Leonard and I, but now of course the world has changed, in the worst of ways."

"I had lots of things to think about that day when we talked." Anderson added: "I was kinda hoping he would just change his mind about retiring... I had – still have – a hard time imagining the marina without Jim, although we hardly ever talked about anything more than boats and the day's weather."

"I know, and first let me say how much I appreciate what you and Arnold have done to take care of our clients after the fire." Georgina brought their lunches – chicken salad times three for the ladies and burgers (one rare for Anderson) and fries for the two men.

After Georgina left, Florence continued: "You folks need to

know that I would like nothing better than to have you become the owners – and especially the operators – of Awan Lake Marina. Frankly, I want to make you a deal that you can't refuse if you are at all willing. Of course, because I value you above all as friends, I will reluctantly back off if you really – really – don't want to take it on."

There was a pregnant pause as they all looked around at one another. It was Marion who began speaking: "As you can well imagine, Flo, we've all been thinking a lot – a whole lot – about this, ever since the fire. At first it was just about solving the immediate problems for our boaters and cottagers, but then we started looking at options and planning for what happens next. We all know there has to be a long-range plan in place by next spring, and hopefully earlier. Our village, our summer neighbours and of course our other businesses rely on the services and trade that the cottage and tourism industry brings."

Arnold nodded: "Even our goofy mayor has been pressuring me, just about daily. He – and I guess the other guys on council – all figure that if it floats, Anderson can make it happen and if it has an engine, I can make it work. There's some truth to that, I guess, but it's easy for them to say it when they don't have to actually do it. How about the real work of running a business. And here I'm thinking about Marion... I may know about carburetors but I also know that if it wasn't for her I wouldn't even have a business."

Anderson looked across at Marion and grinned. "See, Marion, it's all your fault. Arnold could be working part-time at the Co-op pumping gas and changing oil without a care in the world. Joking aside, I guess I could be – or could have been anyway – driving a cat out at the mine, but somehow we're all doing things we love doing and are probably pretty good at. I guess the real question is, do we want to do more of it, maybe make a bit more money? Would it be more fun, or would we regret it?"

It was Marjorie's turn: "I shouldn't even be in the conversation. I haven't been part of this community – let alone been part of your lives – for long enough to really have a voice..." she waived off the anxious looks of disagreement... "no, really, think about it. Two months ago I was one of two city chicks sharing a summer cottage on an island. I was a client of Arnold's when my car was on the fritz, I was a client of Jim's at the marina where he took care of our little boat, and I was a happy client of the Inn for a cold drink on hot days and a safe and welcoming place to stay when the weather went sideways. Frank here – I didn't even know him back then, which seems like a lifetime ago because now I can't imagine my life without him."

"So Marjorie, maybe you're the best person of all to tell us old-timers if we are nuts to even think about picking up the pieces of a disaster and trying to build something new and complicated."

"Well, Florence, I do have an opinion. I'm just not sure how valuable it is." She looked across at Anderson, who just smiled, and nodded. "Okay then, here goes: I think that all of us, with different skills and experience, share two things. One is a love for this place, and the other is a deep friendship forged, in part at least, by shared and rather dramatic experiences. So if you guys are in, I'm in too. I would love to put my energy – and skills and resources such as they are – to continue building this community and re-building the marina."

"I think," began Marion, "I think Marjorie has put what we're all thinking into a nutshell. Florence, we know that the bankers and the lawyers and perhaps even the government folks have to talk and negotiate and find ways to cost us all money, but really, we are all pretty excited to do this. Between the five of us, there are some pretty useful skills to make it happen. Where do you think we should go from here?"

Florence held up a hand and paused while she collected her thoughts. She began with, "I have requested – and received – a line of credit backed by the estate to make sure we – all of us - are not out-of-pocket for all the immediate and necessary expenses – things like that travel-lift Arnold and Frank had to lease, plus wage costs, public liability insurance, that kind of stuff. Soon you will need to consider deposits for replacement docks and repairs to salvageable ones, and of course tools and supplies. Frank, your shop and yard – even your house – have been committed to becoming a boat-yard in the short term at least, at least until we can get permission to clean up the burned-out marina yard and start to re-build. You need to be compensated for that, and we should cover the Village's costs for letting us store boats in the old rink."

It was Marion's turn: "Already that's a lot of stuff to keep track of, but I find that kind of detailed reporting kind of enjoyable. Florence and I are both pretty good with financial records and Florence is obviously very comfortable dealing with banks, accountants and lawyers. I think that, between Florence and I, we could take on all that stuff if everyone agrees."

Anderson nodded. "Makes perfect sense to me. Some people even like that stuff, but I'm not one of those people. My key role is to be ever-grateful to those who do."

"You don't get away that easy, Frank. This new enterprise needs a public face." Arnold had been looking squarely at Anderson, but then he turned to the others: "We need an operations boss and we definitely need a public leader, and I think Frank's the right person. After all, publicly he's known as the boat guy around town anyway, but more than that we've all seen him in action at meetings and stuff, and we know he has serious leadership skills. Certainly, when it comes to boats and the lake, he's the person I'll be listening to."

"I agree," said Marion, "and I think Marjorie would make a great corporate secretary, partly because I'm pretty sure she actually knows what that means, and mostly because she is so, ah, smooth when it comes to dealing with people. And that makes Florence the corporate treasurer, obviously."

"Works for me," Florence answered. "Marjorie, I just hope you're game to spend a lot of time working with me on organizational planning and growth, beyond the needs of a little hotel and bar. I'm going to need all the help I can get."

"Absolutely." Marjorie looked across at Anderson, who seemed rather quiet. "You okay?"

He paused awhile before responding: "Yes, I'm good with all this, partly because it all makes sense, partly because anything to do with boats and harbours is fun stuff for me, and largely because it's doing this together with all you folks. I'm a little nervous about being the public face of Awan Lake Marina Part 2 because I am really more shy than I may seem. However, I guess I can kick myself when I need to – Coast Guard command training taught me some of that stuff. I just hope I can live up to your – and everyone else's – expectations."

He pushed back from the table and stood up: "Anyway, gotta go. I promised old man Beckman that we'd go out this afternoon and bring in his Beneteau 29 for the winter. He usually does that with his wife, but she's back in the city at their daughter's place, recovering from surgery."

"Is that the boat that uses the one cradle that survived but needs some repair after the fire?" asked Arnold.

"Yup. I think maybe some of the pads that got scorched and the covers melted. We probably should skid the cradle away from all the junk, fix it, and put it in my yard for the winter so it's not in the way when we go to clean up."

"Can we leave his boat tied up to the dock for a few days, until we're ready?"

"Oh sure. Normally they would have left it out at the cottage until the October long weekend but the old guy really wanted to get everything wrapped up and put away now so he can go back to join his wife."

"Okay, we'll see you two later."

"Cheers. See you all soon," and he and Marjorie left the Spirit River Inn lounge by the side door to go to his truck and return to the dock.

SEPTEMBER 2

Spirit River, ON, 0730: "So what's the weather like this morning?" Anderson yawned and rolled over on his back. He had stayed up late the night before, sketching preliminary plans for docking arrangements at a re-built marina.

"Typical autumn weekend weather: dawning dismal and dreary with a dank drizzle," was Marjorie's reply. "Coffee's fresh and hot, though, and don't forget we have Sergeant John and probably Tony coming over just after eight."

"Geez, yeah. That did it... now I'm up. Say, can you remember the Latin name of that international group Tony was talking about yesterday?"

"*Acta Non Verba.*"

"Right... Actions not Words. And there was something about the Masons in there too, but not exactly like the Masonic Temple thing in Maple Falls I wouldn't think. Tony told me he is *officially* a Mason but he never goes near them. He says Jean would kill him because they don't allow women to join. Anyway, he said she never join them anyway and he had never been a joiner of anything much, but had been invited to be a member when he was in his last year at college. It was apparently *the thing to do* for men who wanted to get ahead in their profession, but he told me the meetings were boring, and anyway he soon learned that the simplest way to get ahead in your profession is to work hard, learn everything you can, and provide good service."

"He's 'way too gracious to have added *be smarter than everyone else* but he probably should have. D'you think Tony will even show up this morning? There's a pretty brisk wind out there along with the drizzle."

"Oh yeah, Tony's a tough old bird and a good boatman. And that lovely old antique launch of his is a pretty good bad-weather boat, at least as long as you're wearing a good raincoat. I know this is important to him, so he'll be here."

"Should we maybe have breakfast before they get here or are we gonna eat all John's donuts?"

"Actually, Sergeant John said he was going to bring out several of those egg-and-sausage-and-cheese-on-a-biscuit things for us all. That'll be a change."

"Last one of those I tried was awful. The bacon was tough as leather and full of fat."

"Yeah, I told him something like that and he said the sausage option is away better."

Tony was the first to arrive, having tied his elegant launch with the brass fittings and varnished wood decks alongside Anderson's dark grey workboat and walked down the dock and up the roadway to the house. He had only just pulled off his slicker and sat down with a fresh coffee when Sergeant John pulled his OPS cruiser into the yard and stumbled in out of the rain wearing blue jeans and carrying his portable radio, a briefcase and a large take-out box from Tim Hortons.

"Breakfast." he announced. "Drove as fast as the law allows – maybe even more – but we'd best get at these breakfast sandwiches right away while they're still at least warm."

"Hope you brought one for me. Breakfast was a long time ago and I love those things."

"You bet, Tony. Frank told me you were coming in. There should be a couple for each of us, and some donuts for dessert. Didn't bring coffee though... much as I like Timmy's coffee it doesn't compare with what Marjorie and Frank serve, especially knowing they'd have a fresh pot on the go when I got here."

After he had joined the others at the table, passed around the breakfast sandwiches and unwrapped one for himself, the Sergeant asked, "So, I am itching to know what you folks can tell me about that McKinney Island and whatever the hell it is that they are planning out there. I had never even heard of the name or the island until Thursday when Super George called me from Toronto and asked me to poke around. He said it all seemed innocent enough on the surface, but there are some heavy-hitters involved, including federal big-wigs I guess."

"Well John, I've known about them for quite a long time – my company was engaged as auditors for old Sam McKinney in the late 1990s, then later for his estate after he died, in about 2008 I believe. Jean and I had bought our place out here in 1995, so of course I was always interested in the McKinney story. Oddly, I never met old Sam out here at his island until just before he died. The first time I met him was in Ottawa, when we took a trip on the canal downtown on what was then the Queen of Ottawa. He told me that although he was fond of Awan Lake and his family's island out here, he had always fancied having a place on the Rideau Lakes, near Smiths Falls. He said it was less isolated and being closer to Ottawa had a better class of social life. He was definitely a snob, the old bugger."

"How'd he make his money?" asked the Sergeant.

"Mrs. Sam. His rather elegant wife was born into money, with roots in industrial England – coal I believe – and in Canadian finance. Sam was just a fighting man who looked great in his uniform and who had a very strong sense of how to play his cards politically. They made a good pair."

"Tony," Anderson asked, "didn't you tell me there was a similar story at Big Rideau Lake, an island where an old Admiral and his wife had retired? Kinda the same thing, with a well-off wife and a military man with serious connections?"

"Yeah, the old Kingsmill estate on Grindstone Island. Different forces, different wars. McKinsey was an army man who rose up the ranks in the Second World War and retired as a General, but while Kingsmill had been born in Canada, he served with the British navy and then was appointed by the Canadian Prime Minister to build a navy in Canada during the First World War. He was knighted for his troubles, and retired as an Admiral. He lived out his days mostly on an island near Portland on Big Rideau Lake."

The Sergeant had finished his sandwich and taken a fresh A4 notebook from his briefcase. "So, the way I understand McKinney Island so far, the general is dead, the family has been bought out, and some weird bunch of pacifist Masons from California – where everything is weird even on a normal day – have taken over the island so they can hold lectures and training camps. Check?"

Three people at the table giggled, so the Sergeant shrugged and continued, "I guess it's not that simple, then. Fill in the blanks, please."

Anderson smiled across the table at his friend: "John, I doubt I have ever seen you with so much paper. Maybe with a notebook, but never with a full-sized notebook. And a briefcase? Super George must have put the fear of God into you."

The Sergeant laughed: "Not really, but he did say to me last week that I was getting another Sergeant on my staff so that I would be freed up to take on special assignments. I figure this must be one of them."

Marjorie had just finished pouring a second round of coffees. She settled in her chair and began: "As you know, John, Frank and Tony were out at the island yesterday afternoon, taking a look around and learning, I think, quite a lot. While they were at the island, Jean and I did a lot of talking while we polished off a bottle of wine. We also played around on the internet. Then Frank and I talked a lot before we went to bed and finally, at four o'clock this morning, I couldn't sleep anymore so I went back to the internet. And yes, Tony, I've been steadily emailing back and forth with Jean."

"Yipe." said Anderson. "I thought you said you always sleep like a log."

"Not last night. And I've learned lots: frankly, I am pretty sure that what we have learned makes the bosses at Robertson Group International look like angels and all the world's crazy conspiracy theorists look like prophetic geniuses. For starters, this *Acta Non Verba* thing is – at the moment anyway – just a concept without shape or function. It may have its roots in the Bilderberg Group, an older international society which still meets annually, and, probably more likely, in a variety of *New World Order* and *Illuminati* movements. In short, they see themselves as a new elite: highly educated and super-smart with deep international connections. Believe me, I've been calling them *A.N.V.* for short but mostly I call them seriously scary."

Marjorie paused, took a sip of coffee and continued: "As Frank commented last night, they sound on the surface like a bunch of bored old greybeards teamed up with ambitious young dreamers, planning to recreate the world in their own image. Actually, Frank may have a point: these folks may soon get bored and go after the next shiny idea that comes along, but they do worry me. You see, the one driving principle linking all these ANV folks is the frustration that if the world waits for democracy to actually work properly (or for a truly enlightened dictator to descend from the clouds) it will be too late and life as we know it will revert to the Dark Ages or worse. They are in fact positioning themselves to be those truly enlightened dictators. As Jean suggested last night, the battle cry of this self-proclaimed new elite could be *We know exactly what the world needs, but you common folk are either too scared, slow or stupid to do it, so we're going to do it for you. Stand back.*"

"Delightful." The Sergeant was passing around his package of cigarettes. "We are always on the watch for that in the service. Cops tend to grow a kind of *Git 'er Dun* cowboy mindset anyway and sometimes, if a cop puts that mindset together with the IQ of a groundhog in January, they get themselves – and us – in trouble. When poorly-trained members go down that rabbit hole, everything screws up and innocent people die. I find that infuriating when it's just bad cops, but Marjorie, I find what you describe as terrifying."

Tony waved away the cigarette the police officer offered him. "No thanks, John, I gave up smoking a couple of years ago. Some days, I wish I hadn't and this may indeed be one of those days." He continued: "So when Frank and I were out there yesterday afternoon, we were given a tour by Christopher Karlsen, who is the overall boss out there – I guess more correctly called the executive director. Nice young guy, and without going into any detail he's a believer in what he says are the larger goals of the *Acta Non Verba* bunch. He sees *ANV* as clever dedicated people trying to find ways to fix a severely challenged world. It's almost a spiritual thing for him, and he enjoys being part of something international in scope under which – like the Masons – there is local autonomy under a quasi-religious umbrella. It all sounds wonderful, at least until you start digging a little deeper like Marjorie and Jean have been doing."

"It all scares the crap out of me," Anderson said from the kitchen area where he was preparing to make a new pot of coffee. "And even Christopher was nervous about this training session being planned for two weeks from now. On the one hand, he thinks it will run smoothly but on the other hand, he doesn't want the police involved. He's afraid they'll barge in and arrest some of their trainers, and by the way, these so-called *trainers* all belong to a motorcycle club in Toronto. I can't think why the police might be a wee touch concerned."

"Geesh. Does anyone know what club, and who is their leader?"

"Christopher said he didn't have that information, and he's so cheerful and naïve that I believe him. He did give us the name and contact information of the man who is putting the event together. His name is Marcusson – Dr. Frederik Marcusson, I believe – and he lectures on psychology at the University of Toronto."

"Forgive me for sounding cynical, but the U of T is a pretty big place, and psychology is a pretty broad topic area. What does he do – or at least study – that would give him a reason to think that using a bunch of Harley riders to provide training for world leadership is a particularly intelligent thing to do?"

"Frank," Marjorie laughed, "you define the word "cynic" but in truth, I found myself asking the same question, as did Jean when we talked about it early this morning. I think somebody had better chase this guy down and have a little chat. Obviously, in our little world that falls to our new *Special Assignments* friend with all the stripes on his sleeve, but Jean did suggest we ask a certain high-profile academic guy she knows if he would start the conversation..."

"Mmm, I figured Jean might say that," Tony chuckled. "And I guess she's right: academic courtesy dictates that the good doctor Marcusson will at least have to listen to my questions, if not necessarily provide me with answers. And there's one more wrinkle that Jean mentioned this morning... something or someone named *Q*. It's a person or a thing connected to a chain of conspiracy theories that began back in the sixties, and apparently *Q* is devoted to the takeover of international power under the leadership of the current US President. I can run that name by Marcusson as well and see what kind of reaction I get."

"That would be perfect, Tony. I'm pretty sure the guy will shut off like a clam if I track him down as a cop. Can we move this along with some speed? That event is only two weeks away."

"Oh sure – I can start calling him right away – even today after I get home and dig through my desk – and computer – to see what information I have about him."

Anderson had moved over to the door and lit a cigarette. "I have a question that keeps slithering around in the back of my mind: am I the only person who wonders if the murders of our late Member of Parliament Garnet Cameron – and maybe even Leonard Hamilton-Dubois – have any connections to McKinney Island? Tony said the other day that he had seen Garnet out there on occasion, but of course he was killed at his home in Maple Falls. Leonard, whose tie to the island seems unlikely at first glance, was in fact murdered on his boat quite near the island. I have always assumed it was just Manville and his thugs in both cases, but I am beginning to be less certain. Or perhaps that's another part of the connection Of course, I have no evidence or insider information to go on, but somehow it gives me things to think about."

"Well, so far we have no leads at all on Garnet Cameron's murder, and actually the evidence connecting Hamilton-Dubois' death to Manville is also far from solid. In fact, as I recall, some of that was your idea, Frank."

"Yeah, yeah, I know. Maybe I got a bit carried away. Just wondering. Perhaps there's still hope that Manville will open up with some confessions as his trial approaches."

Marjorie grinned: "And, of course there's no evidence at all that Manville or RGI might – or might not – be connected somehow with McKinney Island and the Acta Non Verba crowd, or maybe this *Q* character. No evidence yet, that is."

"I'm going back to work before you folks drive me crazy," the Sergeant laughed. "Talk about conspiracy theories."

"Just because we're crazy doesn't mean we're stupid, y'know."

"I don't find that in the least bit comforting."

SEPTEMBER 3

Spirit River, ON, 1020: It had been barely three days since Wendy and Anita had learned about the brutal murder of their friend, journalist Priscilla Morgenstern. For Wendy, it felt as though Priscilla had reached out from beyond her charred and blood-drenched grave in Africa to tap on Wendy's shoulder and introduce her to her boss, Arthur Brighton.

Brighton, managing editor at the environmental newsletter Envirowire, had insisted during their heart-rending telephone conversation that Priscilla held Wendy's ethics and writing skills in very high regard. He told Wendy that Priscilla had said before she left for Africa that if she needed help with this – or any – story, it would be Wendy Webster whom she would call.

So, although it is a very long way – about 7500 miles in fact – from the city of Kolwezi in the DRC to the village of Spirit River in Ontario, Canada, and although it had been only three weeks since Wendy, her lover Anita and her sister Marjorie had waved Priscilla goodbye as she drove down Spirit River's main street on her way back to her home in Albany, New York, those distances in space and time had somehow compressed to zero as Wendy's sister and friends had waved her through security at Toronto's Lester B. Pearson Airport for a flight to New York City earlier this morning. In New York, she would meet with Brighton for the first time, attend Priscilla's memorial service, then travel to Paris, on to Kinshasa and finally to Kolwesi.

"Life surely has a way of crowding a person, don't it." said Anderson as he poured second cups of coffee for Marjorie and himself. "Who would have thought that Wendy-from-the-island in June would turn into Wendy-headed-to-Africa in September."

"Mmmm. And who would have thought that Wendy-Webster-public-relations-consultant would become Wendy-Webster-investigative-journalist, taking on her former client, all within three months. I am so happy for her, but that doesn't mean that I don't find myself worried sick about it."

"It's the *former client* bit that has me worried. Wendy was high enough in the pecking order at Robertson Mines' office in Toronto to have attracted attention, especially after she quit there and took on some of the investigative work she did earlier this summer."

"Well, that worried me too, but she assured me that – as an arm's-length contractor and not in the human resources network – she was sort of invisible except to her immediate supervisor. She never served as a spokesperson for Robertson Mines, just as a strategist and writer. And, that was only in the Canadian office anyway – apparently she never did any work at all for the international head office in Washington. And on top of all that, she never really quit them – she had turned over the Robertson contract to her only employee at the agency, to whom she sold the agency and who had been doing a lot of the work anyway."

"How do you think Anita is taking it?"

"Poor Anita. She was pretty hysterical at first..."

"I love Anita dearly, but she's pretty much always hysterical." Anderson quipped.

"Yeah, I know. But things calmed down once Wendy arranged for them to meet in Paris in a couple of weeks, on Wendy's way back. She also asked her to go a week early to do a little digging around corporate circles in Paris. Anita has enough French to be useful, and she's young enough to play the part of a college girl doing research for a master's thesis. Like all of us, Anita is worried about the risk Wendy is taking, but I'm sure that at least being a part of the research makes Anita feel better."

Anderson's phone was buzzing. He picked it up and looked at the screen... "geesh, it's Sergeant John. Wonder what's on his mind at this time on a Sunday morning?"

He swiped the call button: "Hey, Sir John, good morning. What's up? This morning? Sure, we're just wasting good coffee without ya... come on over. Twenty minutes? Good, see ya soon."

Anderson clicked off. Marjorie sighed, and asked, "Do you suppose by any chance that he'll bring donuts? Haven't had any since he was here yesterday."

"Oh I'm sure he will. He was telling me last week about teasing that RCMP sergeant Marianna. He said she's such an Ottawa city girl... she thinks we're all a bunch of crazy beer-drinking rednecks out here. Figures all we do is drink beer and coffee and eat hamburgers and donuts, and on top of all that, even the women smoke. And then, of course, John smoothes things over by telling her that all she and her colleagues think about is lattes and lettuce leaves, so that if they get killed on duty they'll still be looking just like they did on prom night."

"Well, maybe that works. She's got a pretty good figure... not like me who shouldn't ever have donuts or any of that stuff."

"Yeah, well, you've got a great figure and on top of that you've got boobs. Just stay healthy and eat them donuts."

Staff Sergeant John MacLeod drove into the yard fifteen minutes later. He found his giggly and somewhat sheepish-looking hosts slow to answer the door. He chuckled, put a Tim Hortons box on the small porch table, and sat down to wait. It was a beautiful day, if a little crisp, with a modest westerly breeze as a reminder that summer was coming to a close. It would be just a month until Canada's Thanksgiving holiday and there was already a chill in the air even if it was a nice day for coffee on the porch.

After the three of them got settled with their coffee and smokes on the old varnished wooden chairs, Sergeant John started to fill them in on the murder – assassination – of Thomas Manville: "We knew almost immediately, of course, that he had escaped from North Bay Jail a couple of days ago, but it was just this morning that his body turned up at a picnic area on the highway between North Bay and Mattawa. Body was a mess... he had been crudely buried under some scrub brush and dirt, then equally crudely unearthed by a bear, they figure. DNA isn't complete yet but everything else – including dental records – fit exactly. He had been shot execution-style by what appears to have been a single shot from at least a 9mm, but there was no casing to be found. The bullet had entered the back of his skull, exited behind the left eye and it wasn't found either."

"How did he get out of jail? It's supposed to be a maximum security facility, or so you guys said?"

"Yeah, Frank. I agree it's a bit frustrating. Manville was a smooth talker and had powerful friends. It hadn't taken him any time at all to get a prison job in the kitchen and storeroom. Someone apparently made arrangements for him to walk onto the grocery van during its regular delivery, but it seems that while his powerful friends were quick to get him out of jail, it was just because they wanted him dead, and silent. They evidently didn't share that last piece of the plan with him."

Marjorie was pensive: "I find myself wondering if Manville was a victim of his own ambition or merely of his manifest – and seemingly perpetual – incompetence."

"That's a really good question, Marj. Certainly, from many hours of questioning, we were leaning toward incompetence. Seems like even when the most obvious - and productive – course of action would be to interfere as little as possible, he consistently screwed things up by going over the top – or at least by failing to rein in his contractors."

"Were you able to get any information from him that would connect him or his minions to the murder of Sebastian Horowitz? If there was any one thing that seemed 'way beyond reasonable, that was it."

"Like with everything he talked about, he was always shifting the blame. He admitted that he knew a little about that, saying that RGI head office types contacted one of his former colleagues at Campbell River about some troublesome old guy at the University in Nanaimo. We think that's BS. He gave us a name – Danny someone – but we're pretty sure that was BS too, because a real name would lead back to Manville himself. Every person he blamed is dead."

"Like Bob Adamson, for example?"

"Absolutely. In fact, to hear Manville tell it, everything bad – including the drug smuggling fiasco three months ago – was Adamson's doing, with a little direction maybe from Maurice Bonner (whom we all know was fired over a month ago, before Manville came to Spirit River)."

"I wonder where Maurice is these days. I kind of liked him, and I find it hard to believe he's tied up with any of this. I would be surprised if he was more than just a low-key executive who was a better engineer than a boss and whose big mistake was not keeping a close enough eye on his staff."

"We'd really like to find him, of course, and believe me we've been looking, but so far all we've uncovered is tracks and they all end near Vancouver. We assume his wife is with him, because we can't locate her either. Their house here in the village is closed up but apparently not on the market. RCMP found their car parked at a marina in Richmond, where they keep their 35-foot sailing cruiser. I should say they had kept a cruiser there – it's been gone since the first week of August. Obviously, they didn't file a sailing plan."

Anderson chuckled: "Well, Marj, maybe we'll meet up with him on a foggy day out of Campbell River."

The Sergeant chuckled too: "Don't laugh. We'll make sure you have a photo and some details before you leave for your fun-in-the-sun holiday. Maybe I should say *fun-in-the-fog-and-rain* holiday. How's that coming along? Got any more definite plans yet?"

Anderson had gone into the house to make a fresh pot of coffee, so Marjorie responded. "We've been in touch with Keith's widow Suzy, and she is thrilled we'll be there for Christmas. She put the word out to all her marina contacts and within a few days she found two or three suitable little cruisers... she'd have more to choose from but many of them are sailing charter boats and Frank is less than keen on dealing with cramped quarters and wet sails. Says he's not much of a sailor anyway, although he admires the boats. Anyway, we're debating about flying out there, maybe even this week, to look at a couple of boats and make some arrangements."

"That's so cool. You two are going to have a ball out there. So, what do you think Wendy and Anita will do over the winter? Head to the city, or rent a place in the village?"

"Oh, I guess we haven't been keeping you up to date as much as we should have. Wendy left for Africa via New York yesterday afternoon, and Anita will follow her as far as Paris in a couple of weeks."

"Well, damn. That's a bit of a drive. New York, even Paris maybe, but Africa?"

"Yup. I am sure you will remember that young journalist who was at the Love Our Lake event in August? The one from New York – Priscilla? She was murdered a few weeks ago, in Africa, on a reporting assignment looking into a Robertson Group copper operation in the Congo. The whole thing came to a head after the mine fire and murders here, although Priscilla's (and now Wendy's) boss at Envirowire has had RGI and the US Government in his sights for longer than that."

Staff Sergeant John MacLeod's face froze. Although he had already realized, with regret, that a love affair with Wendy Webster would not be in the cards, she still held a warm place in his heart and he had a deep admiration for her willingness to stand up for her community. He knew her convictions had already cost her a good job and a promising future. "Shit. Don't tell me she's headed off to one of the most dangerous places in the world to try to take down a corporation that considers murder as a useful tool for growth."

"You pretty much nailed it," said Anderson as he sat back down. "But there was no talking her out of it. I guess it's sort of like the yin and yang of journalism... for her, exchanging the dark side of public relations for the bright light of investigative journalism is a no-brainer. I honour her for making that choice, even if it drives her friends and relatives nuts with fear for her safety."

"The one thing that makes it seem less terrifying to me is that

— as her sister — I have never seen her so excited and passionate."
Marjorie sighed: "Guess if it works so well for her, then I'll just
have to be as happy as she is."

• • • •

Douglas, SK, 1015 MDT: Jim and Pat Lucinski hadn't been out
of bed all that long. Pat had told their two young children to
have some cereal and watch *Ice Age* on TV and crawled back into bed for another hour's sleep. There was a light rain this Sunday morning, which put a stop to any thoughts of harvesting for
a day or so. In any case, the Lucinskis and their employees had
been in the field until well after midnight last night, and it felt
good to stretch out and get a bit of rest.

But not, apparently, without being disturbed. A white SUV
with RCMP markings pulled into the yard just as Jim was pouring coffee: it was their nephew Gerard, who was working out of
the Blaine Lake Detachment on his first assignment after gradu-
ating from Depot in Regina. Jim went immediately to the door:
"Hey Gerard, how are ya doin' this morning?"

"Morning Uncle, pretty good. Still got coffee on?"

"You bet. Late night last night and anyway it's raining a bit,
so we ain't goin' nowhere this morning and this is our first cup.
Here, take mine and sit down. I'll go tell Pat you're here.

A few minutes later, with coffee poured and some muffins on
the table, Jim pointed out that his nephew was in uniform, driving a police vehicle and it was early in the day, so perhaps this
was not just a social call.

"Actually, no, sort of an official call I guess. Probably no big
deal, but is that Daniel guy still working for you?"

"Duck-Duck? Yup. At least he was here yesterday. I told all

the guys to stay home and get some rest if it rained this morning, maybe come in after lunch and we'll do some maintenance. Duck-Duck asked for an advance last night – said he had to pick up some stuff in North Battleford and this morning would be a good time. Gave him a grand – probably owe him more than that but I held some back for deductions."

"Why Duck-Duck?"

"Well, his last name is *Millard* – kinda like *mallard* – and he was wearing a bright green shirt when he arrived, so you know this bunch, everyone gets a nickname. Started off as Danny Duck-Duck, got shortened to just Duck-Duck. Why?"

"Something to do with a missing person out in British Columbia. Does he ever mention anything about B.C.?"

"Well, he said he used to work as a logger out there, but he never said where. Doesn't say much about anything really."

"Keeps to himself?"

"Well, yeah, sort of. He gets into conversations with the guys about machinery, trucks and fishing but never anything more personal than that. At least, not that I know of... he's one of those guys that make me feel uneasy, a bit, like there's stuff he knows that you're not supposed to know."

Auntie Pat spoke up: "Yeah, I agree with Jim. I've met frozen fish who were more friendly than him. Not rude or anything, just cold. And then there's that fake American accent, like he's putting on that he's from Texas."

"Hadn't noticed that, but you're right, Pat. He does have a very non-British-Columbia twang there somewhere. Gerard, do you need to talk to him? He's staying in that old trailer on Guido's place, along with one of the other seasonal guys."

"Yeah, maybe I'll drive over and see if he's there." The Constable downed the rest of his coffee, gave his Auntie a kiss on the top of her head, and put his business card with the RCMP crest on the table. "I've probably missed him if he went to the city this morning, so if you learn anything, or hear something, please give me a call... calling this number will find me anywhere, anytime. And thanks for the coffee and muffin. Or two."

"Or three," his Uncle chuckled. "Take care of yourself..." and he watched his nephew as he walked to his SUV. The young officer turned as he opened the door and called back, "Did you give him cash or a cheque?"

"Cash. I always keep some on hand for these guys... they're always short of cash on the weekends and stuff."

"Good to know. Thanks." and he got in and shut the door.

Two hours later, when the crew arrived at the farmyard to start servicing equipment after lunch, there was no Duck-Duck. "He left nearly two hours ago," said Brandon Sykes. "He took off right away after he talked to some cop who showed up this morning. Told me his sister was in trouble near McBride and that he had to head out there right away. Said to tell you thanks and to say goodbye to the crew."

"Thanks Brandon. He didn't say anything else?"

"Nope. Just seemed kinda worried and in a hurry. Can't blame him I guess... I hope that old one-fifty of his makes it out to B.C."

"Yeah, hope so. You go ahead and help Zach with the air filters. I'll be back in a few minutes." Jim Lucinski headed to the house, where he retrieved his nephew's business card, dialed the number, waded through the answering systems, then left a message: "Gerard... this is Uncle Jim and it's about twelve-thirty. That guy you're looking for took off right after you talked to him.

He just told the guys goodbye, said he had a sister in trouble near McBride in B.C., and split. He's driving his old green Ford and if you didn't get his plate number, I did – I'll dig it out and text it to you. Talk later, 'bye."

SEPTEMBER 4

Nanaimo, BC, 0835 PDT: "Like Yogi Berra said, this truly is déjà vu all over again," said Anderson as the Airbus A319 banked into its final approach to the airport at Nanaimo. "It's been just over a month since I landed here on the same flight, in time for Keith's funeral. I have to say that landing here with you is a helluva lot nicer."

"Yes, you were not a happy camper going on that trip, and there I was, back in my own home in Toronto freaking out that you'd get stuck out here with some pretty lady and stay in sunny B.C. After all, we'd only known each other two weeks. Anyway, who in the world is Yoga Berry, or whatever?"

Anderson laughed: "Ha ha, yeah, I can tell you're not a baseball fan. Pretty young, though. It's not Yoga Berry, it's Yogi Berra, a catcher and sometime coach with the New York Yankees. Actually, I think he died a couple of years ago. Anyway, he's the guy who first said *déjà vu all over again.*"

"And here I thought it was a song by John Fogerty," Marjorie mused.

"Nah, he had to wait in line to use that old saying. I have to say, though, that was a really good song of Fogerty's: *Did that voice inside you say I've heard it all before... It's like déjà vu all over again.* Used to sing it sometimes."

Forty minutes later, they were turning out of the Nanaimo airport onto Highway 19, which would take them to Campbell River or – if they chose to drive further – all the way north and west to its end at Port Hardy near the western tip of Vancouver Island. It was Labour Day, September 4, and they had been able to grab a cheap overnight flight from Toronto to Vancouver late Sunday. After the early morning flight from Vancouver to Nanaimo and a quick drive north along the coast, they planned to meet Suzy for lunch at Dick's Fish and Chips in Campbell River, where today the weather was outdoing itself: warm and sunny with a slight breeze, an unexpected and very welcome surprise after Labour Day weekend at Awan Lake, which had been dreary, wet and cold. They chattered about working for the Coast Guard, about Anderson's late friend Keith, about Suzy, and about living by the ocean, with its sensation of connectedness to the big wide world and how different it was from living at Awan Lake, which felt somewhat insular – albeit more peaceful.

By eleven thirty, they had met up with Suzy, shared hugs and chatter, and now Anderson was busy with his fish and chips. They were, as promised, delicious and were, in fact, even better than the ones Florence and her team served at the Spirit River Inn. He put a knifeful of tartar sauce on a forkful of fish and grinned inwardly as he glanced around the table at his two favourite ladies: Suzy, the widow of his best friend, and Marjorie, his (very new) lover and soul mate. They, apparently, had only just found each other after a lifelong search and were chattering enthusiastically together, totally ignoring Anderson. He found that a huge relief.

At 12:45 when Suzy had to leave for her meeting, she took a ratty-looking notebook from her purse, tore off a page, and handed it to Anderson: "Frank, first-off I suggest you guys go down the road and look in at George's – George Samuels' – marina. You remember George?"

Anderson nodded.

"Good, he remembers you, very well, and he is looking forward to seeing you again after all these years. He's got a couple of 35-footers there – trawler conversions – that he thinks would be perfect for you, and are available this off-season. And, he's gonna want to talk deals – he wants help moving stuff around – he's got boats scattered up and down the island (including Port Alberni) as well as a couple across the creek in Vancouver somewhere, that he wants brought back here for haul-out and servicing."

"Hmm, that's a thought... might be fun. What time should we head over to your place?"

"I have an appointment after lunch but I can't imagine talking to this lady for more than two hours. To be on the safe side let's say 1600 at my place."

"I never asked – same place as before?"

"Yup, I'm still just a trailer-park gal. We bought the lot, so we've kept on doing improvements – addition, garage, siding and stuff, but it's still just the old mobile home."

"Perfect. See you at 1600."

After Suzy had left, Anderson and Marjorie finished off their coffees and got back into the rented Traverse to drive the quarter-mile to the marina. "Suzy's a delight." Marjorie said as she buckled into her seatbelt. "She's fun to talk to and has lots to say."

"Yeah, she was a perfect match for Keith... mostly he just grunted."

"So, you know this marina guy from years ago?"

"Yes. George wound up in the marina business literally by accident, but he is certainly good at it. He came in from one of the Indian Reserves up the coast – about thirty years ago I would think – and went to work for the marina owner at the time. A couple of years later, the old guy – I forget who it was – was killed in a car accident on his way into Nanaimo for parts.

The family had no interest in keeping the business and offered it to George, who was able to get a loan – I expect through one of the government programs that assist folks to get involved in businesses off the Rez – and the original owner's family helped too. He's still at it, and it sounds like he expanded into the charter business, so I guess it's worked out well. He was good friends with Keith and Suzy, who were good to him ever since the early days. Keith would help him out with some of the boat stuff, and George gave Keith a place to moor his little cruiser... and there he is, over there by the office."

They had pulled into the marina gate and crossed the parking lot to a rather faded sign that said "OFFICE". There was a lot of George, certainly over six feet tall and weighing well over 250 pounds. Anderson opened the door after he had nosed the SUV up to the building and turned it off: "Hey George, haven't seen you for awhile, and I see you didn't lose any weight while I was gone."

"Anderson. Yeah, well, you didn't get any damn younger either. Suzy told me you were coming by and bringing a lady with you, but she didn't tell me the lady would be so much prettier than you are handsome." He stuck out a large paw to shake hands with Marjorie, then grabbed Anderson around the shoulders: "It's good to see you, old friend. I missed seeing you at Keith's funeral... I made nice excuses of course but really, I don't do those things very well. Later I did hear people say you did a helluva good job talking about poor old Keith."

"Yes, tough times, sad times. Suzy seems to be doing okay, though."

"She's a tough woman. She and Keith had just made a deal to buy the trailer park where they live – about 20 lots I think –

when he was killed. She didn't walk away from the deal at all. She just buckled down and finished setting up the business loan and made it happen, about a week ago." He paused to divert an incoming call on his cell, then continued: "So, Suzy tells me that our friend Anderson and his lady want to spend some time honeymooning on a fancy yacht. Will that be the one with the teak-floored helicopter deck and a pair of mahogany mini-subs with platinum-plated propellers?"

"Well, possibly, but first let's check out the next size down."

"Cheap bugger. Well, if your lady – Marjorie, you said? – doesn't mind working, I can let you have one that takes two pair of oars and has a tent for overnight."

"Yes, it's Marjorie and no, I don't mind putting up the tent, but where's Frank going to sleep?"

"I like her. Let's go down to the dock and see if we can find her a boat."

• • • •

Campbell River Trailer Park 1600 PDT: Over the past twenty-five years, Suzy and Keith had created a rather spectacular mobile home. It was fully enclosed by a secondary shell with six-inch walls, varnished siding and a cedar shake roof. Since they had two vehicles and no children, they had built a detached two-car garage. The only thing they had added to the footprint of the old 72x14 trailer was a gigantic wooden deck with a brick and stone combination fireplace, including a wood stove and a propane barbecue.

It was just before six o'clock, the sun was starting to settle behind the mountains to the west, the fireplace was lit and Suzy, Marjorie and Anderson were lounging on deckchairs drinking their way through the second growler of locally-brewed Wheel-Bender Stout that Anderson had picked up on their way to Suzy's from George's marina.

Suzy had things to talk about: "Gotta tell you guys about my visit with Carole this afternoon. She's a sweet school-teachery kind of lady, probably a little older than we are, who lives with her old man in Powell River. They had retired and moved there from Alberta a few years ago. Seems they were having a picnic about twenty miles north along the shore a couple of weeks ago and found a body floating at the water's edge. Of course they called our Powell River office which responded immediately and all that, but the horror of it all sort of stuck with her. Carole has a bit of a fixation on the topic of human trafficking and has done some pretty serious academic-level research. She almost feels that the girl they found that Sunday is sort of reaching out to her for help. I mean, not in a crazy way, but in a sort of *we're all alone and we need help* kind of way." Suzy looked somewhat quizzically across at her guests.

"Actually, I think I get that," Marjorie replied. "I expect it's sort of a girl thing, at least in my experience. Kind of a *collective spirituality,* perhaps."

"That's exactly what I was thinking as I listened to her. And then her tale got even more interesting, at least from an RCMP perspective. She told me they had dinner with a couple of retired folks who had landed their sailing cruiser in Powell River a few nights ago – long story about her husband running out of gas, but that's not important. These folks had been at anchor at Whaletown on Cortes Island the night before and had watched what appeared to be a hand-off of six young Asian women from a good-sized fishing boat to a blacked-out van which then drove onto the Quadra ferry, then presumably to here and then south toward Victoria or another ferry to Vancouver."

Anderson had been listening intently. "I had read somewhere that human trafficking of women for the sex trade in Canada was more connected to women and men from Indigenous communities and from eastern Europe, and Asian women not so much."

"It's everywhere and everyone," Suzy replied, "and it's heartbreaking, it really is. Certainly the body Carole and her husband found was Asian, and not long ago a couple of tourists turned in a small woman's shoe – including some human tissue wedged in the toe – along with the life-ring from a missing trawler. They had found these items along the shore on the Johnstone Strait, maybe thirty miles northwest of here, and we're still wondering how to follow through on that one... it's pretty creepy. But there was another reason I wanted to tell you all this. What's the name of your lake in Ontario? I forget."

"Awan Lake."

"Thought so. Carole said these folks she was talking to had named their cruiser *Awan Lady*, which she thought was a pretty name. They had told her the word *Awan* was an Indigenous word for foggy, in the Ojibwe language she figured."

Anderson was now sitting straight up on his deckchair: "Did you catch the name of the folks who have the boat?"

Suzy gave him a funny look: "I'm not supposed to..."

"Yeah yeah I know you're not supposed to. What was the name?"

"Bonner – Morris, or Maurice maybe – and Vivienne."

"It's Maurice. And we need to talk."

"Really? Okay, I guess we do, then. You sound pretty serious..."

"Yes," said Marjorie. "It's serious. Frank, this poor lady has no idea what you – we – have been up to."

"I was going to make salads and burgers and stuff, but if we need to talk seriously, forgive me but I'm going to order two really good pizzas to be delivered and ask you to pour me another glass from that growler."

"Absolutely. No pineapple on mine."

SEPTEMBER 5

Campbell River Trailer Park, 0730: Pizza had been a good idea, because it had turned into a very long night. Anderson and Marjorie did most of the talking, bringing Suzy up to speed on the Robertson Group, the fire at the mine, the earlier drug-smuggling fiasco, the murders (solved and unsolved), the African connection, and – of course – the significance of Maurice Bonner. As Anderson had pointed out, it was entirely possible that Bonner was unaware of any of the criminal activities his bosses were involved with, either locally or internationally. They decided that – before Suzy said anything to her RCMP colleagues at the local detachment – Anderson would telephone Sergeant John to get some idea of what interest the OPS had in Bonner's whereabouts.

So, at 0730 Pacific Daylight Time at Suzy Kirkpatrick's house in Campbell River it was 1030 Eastern Daylight Time at Tim Hortons in Maple Falls, Ontario, where Anderson caught up with Staff Sergeant John MacLeod on his cellphone: "Hey John, Frank here. No, we're still in Campbell River at Suzy's. Where? Timmy's? Guess I should have known that. We've found Maurice Bonner and his wife Vivienne. Well, no, they're not exactly where I'm standing, they're out on their live-aboard yacht drifting around the Strait of Georgia. No, let's talk privately a bit more before you take this upstairs. It might be a bit more complicated than it seems. Okay, call me back when you're in a quiet place."

Anderson rejoined the two ladies, who were industriously slurping coffee and talking about the possibility of breakfast –

sometime. "So I reached Sergeant John, and of course he was at Timmy's and he's gonna call me back from somewhere more private. Suzy, not sure if I pointed this out last night, but just in case, *Sergeant John*, as we call him, or simply *The Sergeant* is actually Staff Sergeant John MacLeod of the Ontario Police Service and he heads up the detachment at Maple Falls, near our village and Awan Lake.

"Yes, I got most of it last night, but maybe not the staff sergeant bit. Interesting that his boss is George Daniels, though. I remember them talking about him leaving the Coast Guard and becoming a cop. That was a couple of years after you left to become a... what did you become, anyway?"

"A floating carpenter with a passion for sexy women and jelly-filled donuts..." and his phone started to ring.

"I can see that the wise-ass never left the building."

"No, Suzy, seems like he never really did," chuckled Marjorie.

"Hi again, John. You okay to talk now? Good. I'd like to put you in the middle of the kitchen table so we can include Marjorie and Suzy, okay?"

Anderson tapped the speaker button on his iPhone and put it on the table. "John, meet Suzy Kirkpatrick, speaking privately but in fact engaged as senior dispatcher at the Campbell River RCMP detachment. Suzy, this is Staff Sergeant John MacLeod of the Ontario Police Service, stationed at Maple Falls. I'm sure I've told enough lies about both of you to each other, so I won't do any further introductions. From where we are sitting, we can see the Georgia Strait two or three blocks to the east with the mountains of the Coast Range beyond. Somewhere on the waters of the strait, Maurice Bonner and his wife Vivienne are happily floating around in a sailboat named *Awan Lady*, totally unaware that Marjorie and I are here or that Sergeant MacLeod or anyone else is looking for them. They are, however, potential witnesses in a case that the RCMP is working on about human trafficking and the sex trade. The Bonners' involvement is not an issue, but they did witness the transfer of some young Asian women between a fishing trawler and a handler in a vehicle at a dock near where they were anchored. John, am I making sense so far, and do I have it right, Suzy?"

The iPhone said, "Yup," and Suzy answered, "Good on my end."

Anderson continued: "Okay, then my question of the day for you, John, is how badly do you want to make contact with Maurice Bonner? I guess I have a sense that the Bonners may be far more useful to the trafficking case out here in B.C. than to your investigations into the RGI arson and murders in Ontario."

The iPhone was silent.

"John? You still there?"

"I'm thinking, I'm thinking already. Could you make contact with the Bonners, and maybe get a bit of a feeling for what they may know about the stuff that went on out here?"

Anderson looked across the table: "Suzy, do you suppose we could find their boat? Would that Carole lady have a clue where they were headed?"

"I'm pretty sure they told Carole they were headed down to Nanaimo for a couple of weeks – something to do with the University. But they did trade phone numbers with her, and I have the number in my notes. Hang on a few secs... I'll get my notebook from my backpack and take a look."

The Sergeant on the iPhone broke in: "If you guys get to talk to them, Suzy could engage them in the discussion about trafficking but Marjorie – or Frank – you could also get a feeling about what they might know – or not know – about all the stuff that went down at Robertson Mines at Awan Lake. Hell, they might even know something about Sebastian Horowitz and his murder."

"Geez, is the Sebastian Horowitz murder part of the Awan Lake story too?"

"Yes, it sure is Suzy. What do you know about it?"

"Not a lot, really, but one of our gang is working on that case. She's now looking for an American citizen who used to work at one of the mining companies in this area, but he's been gone for about a month."

"Ah, Suzy, hello. Would he have been working at the Robertson Group International facility northwest of here?"

"Damn. Of course. Yes, of course he was. Some kind of IT security guy I think."

The iPhone on the table spoke again: "Susan, can I get your direct phone line, or cellphone number? I have a feeling we will need to talk again soon."

"It ain't Susan, it's Suzy, and I'll text you my cell number (I see your number in the middle of the table.) Call me any time."

"Thanks Suzy. My RCMP contact here is in Ottawa – Sergeant Marianna Mankowski. Seems like the RCMP is freaked out by the physical distance between B.C. and Ontario... Marianna's great, but there are a lot of long pauses in our discussions. Day and days."

"Yes John, I know exactly what you mean. Emails and texts travel across the country literally at the speed of light, but the bureaucratic mindset seems like it's always light-years behind."

• • • •

Marjorie had been able to reach Maurice Bonner almost immediately. She talked briefly about her interest in the human trafficking story that her sister was apparently researching in Africa, gave Bonner a heads-up about her relationship with Frank Anderson, and then asked if they could meet in the next day or so.

"I'd be happy to get together, Bonner replied without hesitation. "I always had a lot of respect for Frank. We're moored at the yacht club marina docks near the university for a few days. Can we touch base?"

"How about later this afternoon? We're staying out here with a friend in Campbell River – she and Frank used to work together in the Coast Guard."

"So we just bought a tiny little electric car here in Nanaimo and we have some running around to do after lunch. Why don't we split the drive and meet at the White Whale in Courtenay at, say five o'clock? We can have a drink and they have great food; nothing fancy but really good."

"Looking at my Google Map, it looks like we get the best deal on driving distances, but if it works for you, that'd be perfect. Five o'clock?"

"Indeed. We'll see you there... by all means bring your Campbell River friend, and it'll be nice to catch up on things at Awan Lake. Nicest place I was ever posted and in fact, we still wonder about spending our summers there, and winters living onboard on one of the coasts. Haven't sold our house there yet, and Vivienne loves the garden in the summer."

Marjorie put the phone down and turned to Anderson and Suzy: "I don't think they even have a whiff about all the stuff that's been going on at Spirit River, almost in their back yard. They must live in an oyster shell and the oyster is on holiday. Anyway, dinner tonight, all three of us. How long does it take to get to Courtenay, Suzy?"

"Forty-five minutes. Not a big deal. The White Whale, you said? Food's great, service too."

"Marj," Anderson chimed in, "we're going to get really spoiled for food this morning. Suzy's been putting together her famous Campbell River eggs benedict for breakfast."

"Been a long time since I made it. I'm just delighted to have a chance to share it with folks. It was a favourite of Keith's – and Frank's."

"Sounds marvellous. Hollandaise sauce is so fiddly, and where can you even get back bacon these days?"

"The sauce isn't as difficult as it seems, as long as you have the right stuff and a nice even stove – you notice my stove is gas, not electric. And back bacon? Nah, in Campbell River we make it with smoked salmon. Breakfast should be ready in ten minutes."

Anderson was standing at the front window looking along the street than ran through the mobile home park. "If you had some yellow tape around the trees, it'd look like a crime scene out there, with so many police and government vehicles."

"That's why we decided to buy it. Over the years, Keith and I sort of became the agents for landlord, because of our Coast Guard and RCMP connections. Since we had no intention at all of moving, retirement or not, it made sense. A bit of security of ownership, and a little extra income. For years, Keith had been doing a lot of the upkeep, so there was that, too. And, I'm pretty sure it's the safest neighbourhood in town."

"Did you and Keith keep on playing music? I see your old

D-18 is still on the wall."

"Well, that was sort of a sad story, really. After you moved away, the two of us played a bit, but not often... too many things got in the way. A few times we tried to get together with some other folks, but the last ones we spent any time with made us so mad we just quit."

"*Just quit* sounds kinda drastic... what happened?"

"Well, they didn't play guitars all that well but she thought she was a singer. I think they just wanted Keith and I to play for them so she could sing and be some kind of star. And worse, they kept saying they had 'education' and knew about proper music, telling us we didn't do the songs like they were on the record so we were doing all songs wrong. Even those two that Keith wrote, they said he shouldn't do them the way he did because they knew how to make them so much better. Keith was nicer about it than I was... I finally said screw it and quit, and that was it."

"That's sad. It was really good, back in those days. I still miss them."

"Yes, it is sad, and yes, I still miss it, even now that Keith is gone."

• • • •

Courtenay, BC, 16:20: Anderson, Marjorie and Suzy had arrived at the White Whale in Courtenay at least a half-hour early for their meeting with the Bonners, and selected a table on the patio overlooking the water. A plate of nachos and a round of local beer seemed a good way to pass the time, and they were deep in conversation about butterflies or boat anchors or anchovies or something when a deep voice behind them chuckled, "Frank Anderson, you're a long way from the dock at Spirit River."

Anderson looked up, grinned at the new arrivals and stood up to shake hands. "Maurice, Vivienne, this is Suzy Kirkpatrick from Campbell River and Marjorie Webster from Spirit River, whom I think you have likely met before."

"Certainly have," smiled Vivienne. "Marjorie, I remember you from a community cocktail party put on by Maurice's former company a couple of years ago. And Ms. Kirkpatrick – Susan – I believe you are the RCMP connection that Carole Byers from Powell River was telling me about a few days ago. It's nice to meet you."

As they were sitting down, Maurice looked across at Marjorie: "Yes, I remember you well. As I recall, you were at the cocktail thing with your sister – Wendy, I think? She had been doing some work for Robertson's head office in Toronto, public relations I think. In fact, I expect the whole cocktail party thing was her idea."

"Hi Maurice, and Vivienne, good to see you again. Yes, I remember that evening. Wendy dragged me there, of course, and I remember that while I wasn't thrilled with the idea, I quite enjoyed it once I got there. Frank, you weren't there, were you?"

"No I certainly wasn't. Cocktail parties just ain't my thing... instead of sipping and mingling with everybody I wind up in a corner guzzling and yapping with one or two people."

Maurice continued: "As you know, I am sure, I'm no longer with Robertson. After twenty years, they walked in, took my keys and showed me the door. It was kind of insulting, but that's the way things like that happen these days and we haven't lost any sleep over it... we didn't hang around more than about two days before we closed up the house like we do for a couple months every fall, booked our tickets and flew out to the marina in Vancouver where the *Awan Lady* was berthed. Time to begin our early retirement doing what we love – cruising around in the islands. Of course everything was kind of ready for that anyway... we have been taking August off for years to come out here and sail. Since we came out, I've picked up a very part-time position as a lecturer at the University of Nanaimo, which is why we're *in port* here for a few days. How are things in Spirit River? I had heard there was some kind of fuss connected with that protest event, but we hardly ever watch the news and of course local television gets almost nothing from east of the Rockies unless the Lions are in the Grey Cup and it's being played in Toronto."

Marjorie and Anderson looked across at each other and were momentarily silent. Vivienne leaned over to Suzy and muttered, "I think there's something going on that we don't know about?"

Suzy frowned, then smiled back and said, "Yeah, pretty sure there is." She turned to Anderson: "Out with it, Frank. Looks like I know more than they do and I've never even been there."

"Yeah, well, *some kind of fuss* doesn't quite catch the last couple of months at Spirit River." Anderson paused. "In all, ten people have been murdered, including your colleague Bob Adamson out at the mine, and the numbers continue to come in. Robertson's facility where you worked is now a mass of burned and crumbled concrete and twisted steel. The marina in the village is no more – just a few scattered wharves and some burned boats."

"That's impossible. That can't be..." Maurice and Vivienne Bonner were staring across the table at Anderson."

"It's not impossible. It's what happened." Marjorie looked across at Anderson, and continued: "And yes, in many ways it's still going on. You two are well to be safely and comfortably out of Robertson, because they – the international offices of RGI in

Washington anyway – are substantially the cause of all of that and much more. You mentioned my sister Wendy? As we speak, she is on assignment in Africa as an investigative journalist, looking into RGI's illegal operations there and trying to find information about the murder of a friend of ours – a journalist who had covered the Awan Lake story – while she was en route to an RGI facility south of Kinshasa. Yes, there's lots going on in the fog around Awan Lake."

Maurice Bonner stood up and slowly walked to the patio railing, where he lit a cigarette and stared across the water. His wife rose too, going briefly to his side and putting her hand gently on his arm before returning to the table, where she stood and turned toward her husband: "Maurice, you are simply an engineer. I know you as a kind man, and that none of this was your doing. The only thing I regret is those years when I kept pushing you to be more aggressive about rising up the corporate ladder. You refused, and you were right. You were not cut out for all that, and thank heaven. Come and sit down with our friends."

He did come and sit down, but he somehow seemed a lot older. "I should have paid more attention," he said. "Little things. Rumours. Stuff I shrugged off as harmless. I should have paid more attention."

Vivienne again spoke up quietly: "There's a book by Anthony Doerr that I often think about, particularly the title: *All The Light We Cannot See*. I wonder, if indeed we could see, if we could know, would the horrors that pass us by as merely shadows in the night, would they empower us to be better, or would they overwhelm us. Tonight, I fear the latter, but perhaps if we can help Suzy and our new friend Carole grapple with sex-trafficking and save even one girl, the light will shine a little. Suzy, what do you need?"

Suzy smiled at Vivienne, and put her head on one side: "I don't know how come, but all that stuff you just said, I somehow understand. Thank-you." She paused, took a hard swallow of beer, and continued: " First, you need to know the good news – I am not a cop. The bad news is – I am not a cop. So, while I am not bound to repeat everything that I hear, if I did talk about something important, there's no guarantee the real cops would listen anyway. But the best news is that I know lots of stuff and have many friends in the system who do listen, so when someone like Carole Byers comes to me with intelligence and passion about a topic that burns holes in my heart, you bet I listen. She has found some like-mindedness in the Bonners, who also have information, so let's share it all and see where it leads us. I'll wait to involve the guys and gals with the stripey trousers once things begin to make sense."

Anderson had just ordered a second round of beer. He got up and said to Maurice, "I have a couple of questions I need to ask you about Spirit River, and I need a smoke. Let's take our beer down along the dock to that bench over there. I'm sure the ladies will soon fill us in on what they are talking about."

"Sounds good." Maurice stood up, picked up his beer and followed Anderson off the patio onto the dock.

They left the White Whale at about eight o'clock. Anderson had learned that it had been Manville who had delivered Maurice Bonner's termination notice, and that no, they had not met each other previously. Maurice knew by corporate rumour that Manville had some strange ideas and had earned a tough-guy reputation when he worked with RGI facilities in South America. He also knew that Manville had used security contractors when he was stationed at the RGI facility west of Campbell River. Suzy knew that too – her RCMP colleagues had talked often about their discomfort with having highly-trained and armed private security personnel in the neighbourhood – although they hadn't connected that to Manville himself.

"I think it's like people owning assault rifles," Vivienne mused. "Nobody understands what could be wrong with that, until one day someone gets killed with one. That just proves how important it is to own one, and on it goes. So when bosses hire security guards, pretty soon it just becomes the new normal for people with power and money."

Maurice had been mildly surprised that Manville had been arrested and held in custody, but when Anderson told him he had been snatched out of prison and assassinated, he and Vivienne were deeply shocked: "That speaks to much heavier hitters upstream in that corporation than I even knew existed," Maurice admitted. "I'm sure glad to be gone."

Suzy also knew that her Ottawa colleagues were looking for one of the RGI security contractors in connection with a murder on the Departure Bay to Horseshoe Bay ferry a couple of months ago. The murder victim, of course, was a professor from the University at Nanaimo, and when they heard this, Maurice's and Vivienne's mood went instantly from shock to terror. "Who?" gasped Vivienne.

"Sebastien Horowitz," said Anderson.

"He's dead?"

"Very much so."

"That's the guy who was going to speak at that protest event at Spirit River?"

"The same. He never made it."

"Son of a bitch." This time it was Maurice: "That's the guy Vivienne was hoping to meet and learn from at the university here. I know he had studied to be a pediatrician, but he also has degrees in chemistry and molecular biology. When it came to industrial impacts on the chemistry of wetlands and rivers, there was no one who knew more."

"Geesh," said Anderson. "Vivienne, did Maurice's former bosses know that you were flirting with the dark side?"

"They sure as hell didn't, and I was trying – still am actually – to learn all I can before I go public with anything. The media – and the government and corporate types – never did catch on to why Horowitz – a pediatrician – appeared to jump careers into the science of water and the politics of conservation. The answer is simple: he saw what industrial chemicals were doing to children's brains, and how widespread was the threat. For him, children were the canaries in the coalmine of source water management: first in line and first to die."

"I am 'way beyond impressed," said Marjorie. "Just out of interest, did you and Maurice meet at some university where you both made a habit of terrorizing professors?"

"McGill. Maurice was finishing off a Masters degree in engineering while I was working on a PhD in chemistry."

"Frank was right: *Geesh*." Say, have you folks ever heard of a movement called *Acta Non Verba*?"

"I've read a little. Perhaps I've read too much: in fact they scare me a little. Lofty goals like making the world a better place do not justify tearing apart the very things that make it worthwhile in the first place. That whole *New World Order* movement, as old as it is and despite its own evolution over a century or more, is... well, not to put too fine an edge on it, it's creepy and scary all at once."

"Frank here thinks it's just a bunch of creepy old white men who are fascinated by the idea of playing God."

"Frank's not far off, I fear. As the decades pass, so too do the old white guys, but the scary thing is that this movement has kept tweaking its mission to make it seem more acceptable to younger people – mostly men of course but they are beginning to attract some female leaders as well. Some of them come across as scarier than the guys because they seem to be in more of a hurry."

Campbell River, BC, 0645: It rained gently but steadily most of the night. After they had returned to Suzy's, Anderson had gone to bed early. The last thing he remembered was Marjorie and Suzy sipping Southern Comfort with beer chasers, nibbling on peanuts and talking intently. This morning it was Marjorie – always the early riser – who was sleeping in, on top of Anderson's left arm which by now was also asleep. He retrieved his arm gently and sat up. He could hear Suzy rattling around in the mobile home's little kitchen, probably preparing sandwiches to take to work. She had managed an extra day off over the weekend but she was due back today and, in any case, Anderson and Marjorie were headed back to the airport later in the day to fly back to Toronto and home.

Anderson pulled on his jeans and a fresh shirt from their suitcase and shuffled down the narrow hallway to where the trailer had been expanded to accommodate a large living-room and main entrance. "Mornin', Suzy."

"Well, there he is. Thought if I thumped around enough you'd get up and have coffee with me."

"Looked like you two girls were never gonna go to bed last night, so I figured I'd better get some sleep. What time did you gals quit?"

"Something like one-thirty or two. I adore your lovely lady, Frank... she is away more than you deserve. She adores you, and she's a hoot, too... such fun to talk with."

"Mmm, yes. Marjorie is an unexpected and totally welcome addition to my little world and you're right, she is 'way more than

I deserve. What time do you have to get to work?"

"Zero eight hundred. I like to get there a little early to make sure I'm caught up with whatever might be new, so I'll have to leave here just after seven thirty. When do you guys fly out?"

"Eighteen hundred, to Vancouver, then we catch a flight that gets us into Toronto just before 0600 tomorrow. Seems like we both sleep well enough when we're flying so getting in that early is a bonus – we'll be at the lake by morning coffee."

Suzy poured a couple of mugs of coffee which she placed on the small kitchen table. They sat together gazing out at what looked like a return to wet weather, although it wasn't raining at that precise moment. She waved at a uniformed cop going by in a marked SUV who grinned and waved back: "That's Tony. He's been a huge friend since Keith died... either Tony or his wife Beth keep in touch daily. Been here almost four years now, so I guess he'll get his Corporal stripes and be moved pretty soon. Too bad. In the world of the RCMP, it's easy to make friends but you don't have them long before they're half way – or all the way – across the country."

"Coast Guard was a little better, as I recall. Two – well, three – coasts but nobody stationed in between, as long as you don't count Ottawa."

"Who counts Ottawa? Where is it anyway?"

"Now now, it's the nearest big city to where we live."

"Aren't you lucky. Anyway, before I forget, and while we're on the subject of Ottawa, there's a sergeant there who's been asking us about some guy who might have worked just west of here at the copper mine. We started talking about that when we had your friendly OPS sergeant on the phone but it slipped out of the conversation and I forgot."

Anderson laughed: "Oh yeah, that would be Sergeant Marianna. Marianna Mankowski... nice lady, and yes, our conversation with John kind of skated by that, although it did come up when I was talking to Bonner last night. Why?"

"Well, I called into the shop yesterday and asked some questions. They think we have a name – Millard, Dan Millard. He's a US citizen on a special work permit, apparently granted at the request of the federal ministry of natural resources. He has a ragged past... US Marine Corps in Afghanistan then later a contractor with Halliburton or one of those *flag of convenience* security firms the US government loves to hire. Most recently, though, he's been with RGI, first in South America and then here on the island. But... he hasn't been seen or heard of around here since late July."

"Timing is perfect. According to Frank Anderson, he is very likely responsible for breaking that science professor's neck and stuffing him under a boat tarp between here and Horseshoe Bay. Of course, not everyone is listening to Frank Anderson, but some are."

"You get around, don'tcha. So who was giving this Dan guy the orders?"

"Another dead guy who was being held in remand in North Bay, escaped and was assassinated, rather carelessly."

"You mean they didn't mean to kill him?"

"Yeah, they most certainly wanted him dead, but they made no real effort to cover up the crime – or the body for that matter. Perhaps someone wanted to send a message... did I tell you that someone also shot our member of parliament at the same time as all those other murders? And that he had been a former federal minister of natural resources?"

"No shit."

"No shit. Things aren't all that pretty around Awan Lake these days."

"I learned another word the other day – from that Carole lady perhaps – she was a teacher. The word is *ubiquitous*. So if I tell you bad shit is ubiquitous, it means even at Awan Lake. And, a minute ago I referred to the US government hiring recycled military guys as contractors. Well, that is now, apparently, ubiquitous: The Canadian government – several departments anyway – hires lots of 50-year-old retired military guys to do "special projects". Our cops hate them, because they are untouchables and are able to do things we can't do. We have to uphold the law... but these guys have free rein to bully people into compliance with whatever their supervisors order. Plus which their take-home pay – pension plus contract – is obscene.

"I've wondered about that. Hell, even I get paid a little bit for some of the stuff I do with the boat, for the OPS mostly. My Coast Guard background makes that possible, it seems. In any case, you're right. There is bad stuff everywhere... I have heard far too much about sex trafficking over the last few days... makes a little lake water pollution at Awan Lake seem kinda benign."

"It's all about greed." The speaker was Marjorie, who was paddling into the kitchen in bare feet, rubbing her eyes.

"And good morning to you too," laughed Suzy. "Sleeping Beauty has risen from her feather bed."

• • • •

Spirit River, ON, 1515: "So what time tomorrow do Frank and Marjorie get back?" Arnold and Marion Jamieson and Sergeant John were into their second refills of coffee at the Zoo, and

Marion was the one with the answer to the Sergeant's query: "I think they land at Pearson just around six, so they should be here sometime around eleven. Frank called earlier today to ask Arnold if there was anything he needed to have picked up in the city, but there wasn't anything so I would expect them for late coffee... maybe early lunch. Need to get in touch as soon as they're here?"

"Nope. Well, yeah, maybe. They tracked down Maurice and Vivienne Bonner. Sitting here in Spirit River, that's just weird somehow... the Bonners are out there floating around off the coast of B.C. like nothing ever happened here. It seems like all they know about Robertson Mines is that Maurice had been told he was taking early retirement. They had no clue about the fire, the staff murders, or anything else."

Marion was laughing: "I never did think they were the brightest bulbs in the box. Really nice, but really absent-minded. She was a sweetie, always happy, always polite."

"He was kinda the same," returned Arnold. "I got the impression he was more a scientist than an engineer, and he sure as hell was not a mechanic. Didn't know the difference between a carburetor and a sparkplug, but at least he never tried to say any different. Always a nice guy, very thankful when you helped him out. He also volunteered on the fire department and helped out at the rink during hockey games. Good neighbour."

The Sergeant's cellphone interrupted: "Staff Sergeant MacLeod... Tony? Hi Tony, how can I help? So you're at the Co-Op and I'm at the Zoo... you say we should talk? You bet, I'll wait here for you. See you in ten? Great." And he clicked off.

"Guess I'm meeting Tony Barker in a few minutes. Before I forget, I had a pretty long call yesterday with Frank and Marjorie and their friend Suzy, who works as a dispatcher at the RCMP detachment. The three of them met with the Bonners and were pretty convinced that the Bonners really had no clue about what was going on here after they left in early August. And it's not like they avoid us police folks either – they are currently potential witnesses to human trafficking activities on the coast, and are apparently eager to help."

"Human trafficking? What the hell... I thought that was always in Africa or Bangladesh or somewhere..."

"No, Marion, unfortunately not. It even goes on here, with pimps grabbing young chicks when they leave the Reserve and head to the city. Poor kids get moved around across Canada and even into the US, sold to the highest bidder and moved again. They don't even know where they are half the time, and they're groomed to perform sex acts right from the start. The RCMP usually gets more involved than we do, as human trafficking is largely under federal jurisdiction, but we do get involved at a community level as well as through our gangs unit."

The Sergeant paused for a moment: "Sort of on the same subject, have you folks heard from Wendy? Or Anita?"

Marion shook her head: "No, nothing. And I'm not surprised. Before she left for Paris yesterday, Anita told her mum not to expect texts or even news about Wendy until she was back from the DRC and in fact she shouldn't even mention Wendy in emails or text, at all, until they were both home. Important to remember and – considering what happened to Patricia – is probably necessary. Anita is going to Paris as a student, doing research for her Masters – a thesis on the influence of African percussion instruments on European music in the 15th century."

"Something she knows about, I assume?"

"Not a damn thing, her mother says. Actually, poor Georgina and Fred are terrified for her. Proud as hell, but terrified."

"I'm not surprised. I hope those two ladies haven't bitten off more than they can chew."

Arnold stood up and put his hand on Marion's shoulder. "Here comes Tony, John. We'll get back to the store and leave you with him."

"I expect Tony'd be happy to have you here, but who knows. I'll keep you informed."

Tony and the Jamiesons met at the restaurant door, exchanged greetings and the Jamiesons went on their way back to the garage. Tony came in and joined the Sergeant.

"They would have been welcome to stay but they said they had to get back to work."

"That's okay, we can track them down later. Tell me what's on your mind."

"Well, I talked to that so-called professor – Marcusson – and I don't know if he's bone stupid or a raving nut. Academics aren't supposed to talk about each other like I am right now, but this guy is dangerous."

"Jeepers. How so?"

"Well, for starters, he expects that next decade – beginning in 2020 – is when the Great Inversion takes place."

"*Inversion*? You mean *Invasion*?"

"Nope, I mean "Inversion". In 2020, there will be some sort of global trigger event, like a pandemic or a nuclear explosion. The New Elite, to become known officially as the Masters of the New World Mission, will turn the world upside down and establish a universal governance system. *The Apostles*, as they are being called, are already being selected from chosen elite around the world (I assume Marcusson is one from Canada) and are starting to train teams of *Disciples* to enforce the *Actions Not Words* doctrine. *Stand Up or Stand Down* will be their battle cry."

"Tony, that's just too weird. Sounds like the worst of end times Christianity mixed up with a bad sci-fi movie from Net-Flix. Margaret Atwood will be in her element."

"You're right on with that, John. It would be comic if it wasn't so real. I spent an hour with this guy, questioning everything very respectfully, and he went to great lengths to fill me in on everything he knows about the 2020 edition of the New World Mission and the shaping of a movement that has a very close resemblance to extreme evangelical Christianity – but isn't. To start with, according to them, there is no God in their universe: whether or not you believe in a God, there isn't one. There is no supreme being, there is no earthly king or queen, there are no prime ministers or presidents, there is just The New Elite: faceless, un-named and all powerful. People can still have names if they choose, but they will not be defined by their spoken or written name. No more secret handshakes like the Masons: they will be known officially by the code on a tiny chip implanted deep in the muscle above their right breast."

"Geesh, Tony, this is pretty scary and weird stuff. If it shows signs of coming true, I fear for my teenaged daughter and her friends in the future, for sure. But today, as a cop, I can't let my imagination get the better of me – which it is close to doing. I need to know what's gonna happen a week from now out at McKinney Island. Tell me what you know about that..."

Spirit River, ON, 1100: Anderson and Marjorie went straight home at the end of their three-hour drive back from Terminal 3 at Toronto's Pearson Airport. Multiple telephone conversations with Arnold, Tony, and Sergeant John had managed to empty the batteries on both Anderson's and Marjorie's cellphones yesterday afternoon, and despite being plugged in and fully charged on the red-eye from Vancouver, Anderson's phone was already back down to half-charge thanks to a lengthy couple of calls on the drive home.

It was a beautiful sunny day, but the sun had not warmed the house much, so Anderson's first order of business was to start a small fire in the big old Franklin-style stove in the centre of the living space near the main table. He had installed baseboard electric heaters in the house so he could come and go as he wished in cold weather without worrying about freezing the place, but this was early autumn so he hadn't bothered to turn them on. "Sorry it's a little chilly, Marj. Perhaps I should have turned the heaters on."

"It'll be nice and warm by the time the gang gets here – no worries. What time did they say they'd be here anyway?"

"Probably close to noon. Marion is bringing quiche from the Zoo for lunch and Tony's bringing wine. Sounds like a good reason to be home on time.

"Our friends certainly are in a big stir, aren't they."

"Yeah, I find some of this McKinney Island stuff kind of unbelievable. But, Sergeant John isn't the kind of guy who goes nuts over every rumour, and I really don't think Tony is very excitable either. Guess we'll just have to hear them out and figure what comes next... and, here they come. Well, here comes the Sergeant anyway. Good morning, Sir John of Maple Falls."

"Good morning, Lady Marjorie and Lord Anderson. I'm glad to see you have already chosen your proper titles under The New World Mission."

"Coffee, Sir John?"

"Yes please. Thank-you, Lady M. I don't know about you folks, but I find that whole World Order stuff somewhere between downright evil and absolutely unbelievable. I keep hoping it's like one of those Twitter and Facebook memes, and that nobody is really paying any attention anyway. It is a bit scary about this idiot professor out at McKinney Island, however. I really am worried about what craziness he could be up to, and how many people could get hurt. Nobody plays with that particular bike gang in Toronto that he's involved with. At least he shouldn't be playing with them unless he's wearing body armour and carrying a big illegal gun. This Marcusson guy probably thinks they're just a bunch of grey-haired weekend wannabes who have Harleys like him. Not. These guys are the real thing, with seriously bad connections."

"I don't suppose we even want them to know where Spirit River and Awan Lake can be found on a map, let alone have them come and visit."

"Trouble is, Frank, when I mentioned seriously bad connections, I didn't get around to explaining: one of those contractors from Manville's team out at the Robertson mine was finally arrested in Markham about two weeks ago – along with one of those same bikers, who was wanted for questioning about smuggled weapons."

Marjorie had just poured the coffee pot into a carafe and was busy making a second pot when she glanced out the window: "Here come Arnold and Marion, and I see Tony down at the dock tying up his boat. Gang's all here."

Fifteen minutes later, everyone had settled in with small kitchen glasses of red wine, hot cups of coffee and generous servings of quiche. Anderson pushed back from the table a little and gazed rather deliberately around the table: "Folks, we've been learning a lot of stuff over the last few days, some of which is kinda nasty-sounding. Over the long haul, there's stuff each of us probably should learn more about, but right now it's the short haul – like the next week or two – that we need to think about. I don't want to sound like a hellfire preacher or worse – a politician – but our poor little lake, and village, and community, may once again be under attack from something that really hasn't anything to do with us. So, John and Tony, the question really is... how much of a threat is a four-day social experiment with a bunch of bikers tormenting a bunch of aging hippies under the direction of a nutty professor?"

Jean Barker had accompanied Tony from their home and she burst into laughter. "Frank, you certainly have a talent for defining threats and focusing discussions. You're right, you know. We should probably focus on putting the fire out and stopping it from harming our neighbours before staying awake all night trying to figure out who brought the matches."

Sergeant John, too, was laughing. "You are, of course, right on, Frank – and Jean. This is hopefully – probably – just a cop thing. You all know how it goes: we tell the public this is merely a police matter then we just fly the flag, protect the citizens, let the crooks know we're watching, and be prepared to do some enforcement and make some arrests, even ones that are based on outstanding warrants – and there will be quite a few of those I expect."

"I don't get the impression that any of you are fully convinced about this New World Mission stuff," said Arnold, who had just settled into his second quadrant of quiche. "I get that. After all, I'm kind of a bread-and-butter guy, living by the Dwayne Johnson code: *If you can't fix it with duct tape, you're not using enough duct tape*, but as I look back over this summer, things have happened right here at Awan Lake that make me question pretty well everything I thought I knew. I don't even like to imagine living in a new world – under a New World Order or "Mission" or whatever – but you know... just maybe this stuff is real."

"I wouldn't let your customers hear that *duct tape* comment if you want any more cars to fix." chuckled Marion. "But yes, unfortunately I can see people falling for a New World Order when they look at the mess our governments are in. Especially in the US right now, but even in other countries. Everyone hates everyone else, and even in little Spirit River, just putting a stop-sign at a busy intersection has some local folks bitching about taking away their freedom."

"You're right, Marion. And I think the bad stuff that happens here is just a reflection of a much broader illness – a pandemic of evil, so to speak. Think about poor little Priscilla, here reporting an international story a month ago, and now dead in a ditch half a world away. Makes one wonder when blood will be flowing in the streets right here in Canada."

There was a short, uncomfortable silence in the room before Jean Barker answered: "Marjorie – and Marion and Arnold too

– from what I have read, you are echoing what thinkers around the world are saying. And Marjorie... blood in the streets of the USA, and even in Canada, is not an unreasonable prediction, horrible and crazy as it sounds. Where in Europe, or Asia, or South America, has there not been blood in the streets at some point in the last century? *Pandemic of Evil* is a great phrase, Marjorie, and we have felt immune to the illness for a long time. Now, maybe not so much: over a dozen dead in the last six weeks in our own neighbourhood, plus a reporter we know is murdered in Africa and a professor we invited here gets his neck broken on a ferry off North Vancouver, and every death is tied to that universal evil, greed."

Anderson stood up and retrieved the coffeepot, offering it around the table: "A furry little guy named Pogo once said, *We have met the enemy, and he is us.* I think he was referring to people who had littered the swamp that was his home with garbage, but it fits well right here: we have bigger problems than ourselves, but first we need to clean up and protect our little swamp. From what you have been saying, the biggest problem is that the idiots we have to step on may not be just mindless thugs on a weekend rampage – they may have an agenda and feel justified."

Until this point, the RCMP sergeant had remained silent, if very focussed on the discussion. His silence broke: "Heaven protect us from men with guns who feel justified. Frank, you nailed it: my job is to protect the swamp, and I'm going to need all your help because too many of my colleagues are currently more worried about things like Marion's stop sign."

"Where – and when – do we start?"

• • • •

Spirit River, ON, 1530: It had been four days since Daniel Millard had left his tractor-driving job in Saskatchewan. Back then he had a battered old green half-ton Ford truck, but now he had a newer model Chevrolet, born off the assembly line in 2013 and factory-painted white. The old green Ford had worked for him when he lived in the bush on Vancouver Island, but out here in what he called "civilization" he figured the best way to stay out of sight was to drive the same truck everyone else was driving. And apparently everyone west of the Rocky Mountains drives white crew-cab half-tons so he got himself one from a truck stop in Saskatoon, along with a new license plate for which he traded in a nearby Costco parking lot.

He was on his second burner phone since Winnipeg, and he had a couple more in the side pocket of the Eddie Bauer Cargo Pack he had picked up at Canadian Tire in Yorkton. He had saved one number into the phone's directory, and he called it now.

It rang twice: "Hello? Raimy? This is Daniel. I guess I'm here. I must be here because there's fuck-all else here. You said there are two marinas here, but one of them is hardly a marina – just one dock with a big old work boat tied up and a few little motorboats. Farther along the beach there's one hell of a mess where there must have been another marina. It's been burned to a crisp, and there's nobody around."

He stopped speaking long enough to light a cigarette while he listened to Raimy. "Yeah, Raimy, I ain't gonna screw around here in Spirit River. Small villages have big eyes, and I aim to stay out of sight, so I'm gonna go back to the next town – something-or-other Falls – and get a room and some supper. We can meet over supper or a beer after. Okay?... good. Call me around six and tell me where you are. We can set it up tonight, making a plan to get a boat and go to that island tomorrow. 'Bye."

• • • •

Spirit River, ON, 1830: Anderson and Marjorie settled into their chairs at the corner table in the Spirit River Inn and ordered a glass of house red each and a menu. "Geez, a menu already? No steak sandwich tonight?" teased Georgina.

"Can't let my new girl think her old man is stuck in a rut. How's things going... is Anita getting ready for her Paris trip?"

"She sure is. Her mother's not even close to ready, though. Frankly, I'm terrified for my little raven-haired baby. Every time I look at her she gets younger."

"Lots of people go to Paris and survive, y'know."

"Actually, Marj, not many know this but many years ago I went there myself. I was lots younger, and as dim-witted as only the young can be, but I did have a ball. Missed out on Woodstock, but I was into the music and all the New York and California hippies. But that's not what makes me nervous – Anita has been around the block on her own I guess. It's about that awful bunch Wendy is investigating in Africa. Those two kids could die so easily."

She paused for a moment, emotion clouding her face. "Sorry Marjorie, I didn't mean to scare you too. You must be worried sick about your sister. After all, she's the one that's actually in the heart of Africa where it's so easy to disappear."

"Yes, we do worry about her – both of them, really. Things really could go off the rails, but Wendy assured me she had everything cased. When does Anita leave?"

"Sooner than we had planned... Fred and I are driving her to the airport tomorrow. Hey, I'm forgetting why I'm here. I'm supposed to be taking your order..."

They laughed together, and ordered fish and chips.

"That's very brave and exotic of you." said Marjorie.

"Just to prove I'm not an old stick-in-the-mud," said Anderson.

"Anyway," Marjorie continued, "As I was saying earlier, I've been digging around on the internet to find out more about this New World Mission," Marjorie said between sips of wine. "There's some pretty wild stuff, so jumbled and full of conspiracy theories that it seems more amusing than scary. One of the most recent meetings of weird groups was the 65th Bilderberg Meeting back in June this year. There were over 130 participants gathered together just outside Washington in Chantilly, Virginia, representing 21 countries. The participants included people like an arch-conservative US Republican Senator, a former US Secretary of State, and... our very own made-in-Canada Minister of Finance."

"Now there's a group of characters I have no desire to spend an afternoon with. What the hell is the Bilderberg thingy?"

"It's simply called *The Bilderberg Meeting* or *The Bilderberg Group*. Every year since 1954 it has held a conference, somewhere in Europe or in the USA. According to their own admission – on their website – they have often been the target of anti-globalisation protests and conspiracy theorists. I guess, with their original purpose styled as ...*a three-day forum for informal discussions, designed to foster dialogue between Europe and North America,* it's not surprising that the tinfoil hat crowd could find something sinister in there, but no matter how hard I look, I see no references to overthrowing government, or social control."

She paused to light a cigarette and continued: "Actually, I've been finding out more about that *Q* thing. Seems like it's perhaps an umbrella organization for all the conspiracy theorists from the American alt.right, people who hate things like the United Nations' Agenda 21 or the Green New Deal – stuff that seems to be so fundamentally evil to the alt.righters in the US and the UK."

Anderson washed down some french-fries with his wine: "I can hardly figure the American alt.right idiots getting all bothered by a group of old white guys at Awan Lake Ontario, unless we have somehow attracted the attention of power brokers from Europe or the Middle East. So now I am really curious about the politics of a certain Professor Marcusson from the University of Toronto. And it makes me wonder about how people like our late MP Garnet Cameron and maybe even Leonard Hamilton-Dubois might have been involved, or what they might have known."

"So... let's ask Georgina if Florence is here, and we can ask her right now."

• • • •

Ten minutes later, Florence had joined them with a hug and a glass of wine: "So what are you two into today?

"McKinney Island. Know anything about it, or about the new people who have taken it over?"

"Oh my God. I had hoped for an earthquake and that the damn place had sunk forever to the bottom."

"So are we to understand it wasn't your favourite place on Awan Lake?"

"I could never talk about it in polite company. To start with, that old army general McKinney was a classic... how can I say... prick. I shouldn't say that, I know. When he died nothing much happened for awhile then suddenly that religious political group bought the place and Leonard got involved, I think because Garnet Cameron was all excited about the fancy people from the Washington and Europe who were hanging out there... politicians, industry people, academics, even some Hollywood stars and a bishop from Ukraine. And... senior bureaucrats like Leonard, who dragged me over there for cocktails with some movie stars and the bishop – what an arrogant bunch of creeps. I even think the Chairman of Robertson Group International from Washington was there at that time and he was a prick too."

"Did Leonard talk at all about their plans for the island, and maybe their politics?"

"Leonard didn't say a lot to me – he knew I hated the whole scene – but Garnet wouldn't shut up about it when he visited us here. Leonard would take him sailing and they would talk and talk, and if they were here at dinnertime, when Leonard was busy on the phone Garnet would talk to me instead. He's not very bright, that man... I shouldn't speak ill of the dead, but he wasn't..."

"No, he sure wasn't," Anderson laughed. "I heard he was even too dumb to be a good hockey player."

"And that's the other thing he talked about. I have no idea how he kept getting elected here... makes me a little ashamed of my neighbours. He was a loyal Tory, but even so I know there was a time the party tried to prevent him from getting nominated. He won that battle, which only made him more conceited. He was away too crazy right-wing even for the party, but he fit right in with that McKinney Island bunch and their talk about protecting the world from the United Nations and the environmentalists. I know that whenever he had visited us here, Leonard was always glad to see him leave. *Idiot* he used to mutter when the car went down the driveway. But of course Leonard had to follow him around like a puppy dog because, back in the day when Garnet had been Minister of Natural Resources, he had been Leonard's boss."

"That explains a lot, Florence. I was getting my conspiracy theories backwards, assuming that the McKinney Island bunch were pacifist socialist do-gooders. Wrong."

"And that probably explains why that Marcusson guy is engaging bad-news-bikers for some kind of exercise in a couple of weeks. And on top of that, Sergeant John thinks some of those bikers were associated with the Robertson Mines security team."

Florence finished her last sip of wine, stood up, and paused: "You two be very careful. I fear that our beautiful Awan Lake may be hiding evil things in its depths. Sorry, I have to go – I'm still tied up being an executor and my cellphone tells me I have a lawyer to call. Apparently they never sleep when they are working on my dime."

"Whee. Rather you than me." said Anderson.

After Florence had left their table, Anderson grinned at Marjorie: "I remember the first time Arnold introduced me to Garnet Campbell and I asked myself why people kept on re-electing this dumb-ass hockey player to represent them in Ottawa. I was too polite to mention that to Arnold at the time, but I soon learned that he felt the same way."

"I guess people like him are useful. Kris Kristopherson wrote a song I always liked: *...it's never getting better, who's to bless and who's to blame?* Political organizers love to have someone to bless at election time and blame afterword, so the true movers and shakers can do their thing with nobody paying attention."

"Ah, Kris. I used to love his songs. Suzy always used to push me to sing "Jody and the Kid" for her and Keith. He was a good ten years older than Suzy – maybe more – but they were always together as kids. They actually got together as a couple when she was sixteen, if that, which apparently caused a bit of a stir amongst the wrinklies in Campbell River."

"Aw, that's a sweet story. It explains Suzy, too: tough, wise, and gentle with a good sense of humour, all at the same time."

They ordered coffee, and Anderson had headed for the washroom when his cellphone, which he had left on the table, began sounding a loud alarm that Marjorie had never heard before. She picked up the cellphone, clicked on the phone icon and listened to a pre-recorded message saying that the intrusion alarm on the workshop had been activated. She waved at Georgina across at the bar and yelled "Got an alarm at the workshop – we'll come back and settle up later."

She grabbed their jackets and the truck keys and was waiting by door when Anderson returned. "Have to go home... the alarm's gone off."

"Fire, or intrusion?"

"Intrusion." They jumped into the battered little S-10 and sprayed gravel onto the motel flowerbed as Anderson took the corner off the driveway and headed down Lakeside Drive toward Main Street, the dock, and home.

As they slowed to make the turn down to the dock, Anderson had to jam on the brakes and swerve even harder to the left to keep from getting hit by a much larger white pickup which was going fast and still accelerating from the direction of Anderson's workshop and home, barely a hundred yards down the street. The Silverado cranked a left turn onto Lakeside and headed west, presumably toward the highway to Maple Falls, and Anderson skidded his little truck to a stop by the workshop door and handed Marjorie his cellphone: "Call Sergeant John, but stay here until I take a look."

The house door was untouched. Anderson walked quickly along to the workshop entrance and sure enough, one pane of the four-pane door-glass into the workshop had been broken. The door, however, was still locked... the break-in artist hadn't counted on there being a security system, which went off immediately it sensed the broken glass. The intruder had left without unlocking the door.

Anderson walked back to the truck, where Marjorie was standing outside talking to the police dispatcher. "Just a moment please," she said and clicked the mute button: "John has gone off-grid for the moment so I was forwarded back to the office. I told the nice lady who and where we were and told her it appeared that someone in a white pickup had tried to break into the house... you might as well continue the conversation." and she handed him the phone.

He grinned at her, took the phone and clicked off the mute: "Hi, this is Frank Anderson – you have been talking already with Marjorie. Huh? Webster, Marjorie Webster. Yeah, the door glass was broken which triggered the alarm and they must have spooked out and left immediately... they never unlocked the door or gained access. Yes, we passed a white truck leaving as we were getting here. Chevy Silverado, crewcab, fairly recent model. The driver appeared to be alone, probably male?" he looked quizzically across at Marjorie... "yup, male. Nah, it's only just after sundown but it was too dark to get any details like that. He was headed your way when he left, and he was in a big hurry. Okay, please have John call me as soon as he's free. Thanks, take care now. Bye."

Anderson turned back to Marjorie, who had been watching the waterfront. "Kind of a crappy way to finish the evening. I'll get a chunk of plywood to nail over the door for now and go and re-set the alarms."

"Frank, take a look down there by that temporary dock. Someone's down there in one of the ski-boats."

He moved across to where she was standing looking down into the bay. The sun was well-down, but there was enough light to see where she was looking. In a moment, there was a light puff of blue smoke and the soft light rumbling sound of a well-tuned marine engine exhaust.

"What the hell, there are no vehicles around here. How did this guy even get here?" Anderson summoned up his best coast guard boatswain's roar: "Hey, you on the dock... identify yourself please."

By way of an answer, the man on the dock dropped the mooring rope he had been untying, jumped into the motorboat and pushed it away from the dock in one motion, stabbed the gearshift and throttle control forward and shot out into the bay, glancing off the side of old man Beckman's Beneteau and barely missing another small sailing cruiser before reaching open water and heading southwest into the darkness that was now descending onto the lake.

"D'you suppose I should try to call Sergeant John again?"

"Yup."

• • • •

It didn't take long for them to get in touch with OPS Staff Sergeant John MacLeod. "I'm at the top end of Main Street, just turned in off the highway and am headed your way. You guys at home?"

"I gather your dispatcher hasn't reached you anytime in the last twenty minutes?"

"No, why? Something going on?"

"Oh yeah. It's a two-cupper. We'll put on the coffeepot."

The Sergeant arrived before Anderson even put water in the pot. He was driving a black unmarked Yukon Denali with blacked-out windows. "Looks like Super Dave is back in town. You steal his ride?" Anderson asked.

The Sergeant grinned. "You aren't gonna believe this, but apparently Staff Sergeants specializing in special assignments get to drive one of these beasts. I could hardly believe it myself when it showed up this morning. Brand new, right off the lot."

"So you rewarded your bosses by taking it out on the dirtiest roads you could find in Awan County? How could you, John?" laughed Marjorie. "It's a mess."

"Sure rides nice, though. So... you guys have been lighting up the Maple Falls dispatch screen. What's up?"

"We were just over at the Inn finishing off our supper when the house alarm chimed in on my cell. We got back here in just a couple – maybe three – minutes, almost hitting a pickup that was leaving from here and heading west on Lakeshore. Checked it out and found a broken window which triggered the alarm and scared them off before they even unlocked the door. Then we were just standing here collecting our thoughts when Marj noticed someone down at the docks, who quickly stole a boat and took off up the lake."

"You think the two incidents were related?"

"Absolutely." I'm guessing that whoever it was – two of them – came here to steal a boat and thought they'd spring the alarm as a distraction. Couldn't have known we were so close."

"Any idea where the boat guy might be headed?"

"Nope, not really. He went in the general direction of the river marshes and the islands."

"Any details on the boat?"

"Yeah, we've been taking photos of our client's boats as they come in, then again for storage. I haven't looked at the pix yet but I'm sure this one – a really well-kept inboard ski-boat with a tower – belongs to George Hanson who has a cottage out there, fairly close in. He's gone to the city but I'm sure he'll be back by the weekend."

"Did you get a look at they either the boat guy or the guy in the pickup?"

"I've been thinking about that," Marjorie said, "because something seemed unusual even in the bad light. Frank, did you notice the guy's face when he looked up at us? I think he was black. Not shiny black like Adumbi, but certainly not white either."

"You're the artist, and would notice colours. All I saw was someone stealing a boat."

The Sergeant went outside to the Yukon and returned with a very pretty young girl and a Tim Horton's box, which he opened and set on the table: "I think you met my daughter Taylor when we were down at the locks this summer looking for bodies. She's my ride-along today. And here's some leftovers for dessert. I picked them up along with our supper."

Marjorie grinned at the girl: "Good to see you again, Taylor. Nice to see that when your father takes you out for dinner he only takes you to the very best restaurants."

"Hi, Mrs. Anderson. Skipping school for the afternoon was well worth having a chicken salad sandwich and a jelly donut."

"Thank-you for the *Mrs. Anderson* compliment, but my last name is actually Webster. Please just call me Marjorie."

Anderson chuckled and kissed the top of Marjorie's head. He turned to the Sergeant: "So where did you go to collect all the mud?"

"Well, that's another interesting thing today. We drove about ten miles south along that rough old road that follows the power line along the west side of the lake and winds up another fifteen miles north at the Rez. And of course at the ten-mile mark you're across from McKinney Island, which is still quite a ways offshore. There's not much on the shore there, really – just a short dock and a small heavily-locked steel shed which I assume holds fuel drums for their generator. There's also a telephone pedestal which takes the telephone cable from the power pole and sends it underwater out to the island."

Anderson had fetched a pack of Export A cigarettes from his desk drawer and offered them to Marjorie and the Sergeant. He lit them with a barbeque lighter, and the Sergeant continued: "Thanks. So the interesting thing, aside from your new pocket-lighter, is that there were several – maybe five – small motorboats tied up at the dock. Outboard engines, maybe 14 or 16 feet long, aluminum, with numbers painted on the side, so pretty obviously from a boat rental yard. I didn't recognize them as being from the yard at Maple Falls, though. Taylor and I could see where they had been launched from trailers, with some difficulty because there were skid marks from spinning tires all over the place, but there were no trailers in sight."

Anderson was looking puzzled. "So, what made you drive up there in the first place?"

The Sergeant laughed. "That's exactly what Taylor asked me when I picked her up from the school after lunch. So two reasons – I wanted a chance to spend the afternoon with Taylor who's been away working as a camp counsellor all of August, but where we went was triggered by a report from one of our folks on highway duty that they had seen several boats on trailers turning south off the highway. The officer who called it in, who has lived around here since she was a toddler and spends most of her time off fishing with her husband, said the boats were new to the area and she noticed they weren't carrying registration numbers. So I've been stewing over this McKinney Island thing for over a week now and I thought I'd just drive around a little and check it out."

"Hmm, maybe those boats are for the bikers. Have you heard from Tony today? I haven't."

"No, but maybe we should talk to him and see if he's heard anything more from that German professor guy – Marcusson – or even from Christopher on the island."

"It's early enough. I'll give him a call. If there's anything we need to get together about, we can meet back here in the morning."

SEPTEMBER 8

THE AWAN LAKE EXPERIMENT

Spirit River, ON, 0630: Marjorie was on a roll this morning. She had gotten out of bed at 0530 and had a shower, then walked down to the docks to see if there was any more evidence of last night's adventure. As she looked around she noticed a three-foot-square piece of plywood in a pile of materials on Anderson's barge, so she retrieved it and took it back to the house, standing it up beside the workshop door with its broken window.

Now she was frying bacon, the surest way she knew of waking Anderson without early morning cuddles. Even though she loved those moments, they were expecting Tony and Jean Barker at 0700 and Sergeant John shortly thereafter. Scrambled eggs and bacon would have to do this morning.

Sure enough, she was just starting to break the eggs into the pan when Anderson came up behind and gave her a warm sleepy hug. "Hmm. People arriving soon. I'll be ready in a minute."

And he was, pretty much. Marjorie, who loved long luxurious showers, was always amazed at Anderson who could shower and dress in less than four minutes. Even though they took their time over breakfast, chattering about the attempted break-in and the theft of Hanson's motorboat, they were well into their second cup of coffee before Marjorie noticed Tony and Jean pulling in at the dock and tying alongside Anderson's workboat. In turn, they were just walking up from the dock to the house when the Sergeant arrived. Tony – ever the auditor – teased him immediately about the cost of his new Yukon and the size of the Ontario deficit, so Staff Sergeant John took a quarter out of his pocket and made a show of handing it to Jean: "Here, Jean, would you please give this Tony? This is more than his share of my new work truck, so now that he's got his money back he can quit complaining."

After the laughter died down and the coffee was poured, Tony and Jean were filled in on the highlights of yesterday evening, and the advent of the new motorboats on the southwest shore. Tony Barker was looking very serious: "Marcusson has been achingly polite but he hasn't been in the least bit helpful. I think he see's through me, and figures that the people I know may not be people he wants to be forced to deal with. To an extreme-right fanatic, there's nothing worse than an accountant with a conscience. Christopher Karlsen, on the other hand, has been great... naïve but very helpful. The way I understand it, there will be no role-playing. The bikers are the shock troops, and will be training this batch of weak and idealistic New World Mission leaders to toughen up and fight back against all those wimpy liberal left-wingers who keep claiming the high moral ground. Marcusson (along with people like him in the USA and Europe) is trying to preempt the otherwise rational goals of the folks involved with the Bilderberg Meetings. I challenged him in a telephone conversation to admit that the people in his group were merely *fascists-in-a-hurry* and just for fun I added *just like that bunch of conspiracy theorists at Q*. As I recall, it was at that point that he flew into a rage and slammed down his phone. His last epithet for me was *you fucking commie bastards are all the same*, so I don't expect to be talking to him any time soon."

Marjorie chuckled, and poured more coffee: "I didn't think there was any such thing as a fascist who wasn't in a hurry. I'm willing to bet that all the Qs are just the same."

"Good point, Marjorie. I just wanted to get under his skin and finish the conversation, which was getting worse and worse."

"I would say you succeeded. Which probably works in our favour."

Anderson squinted up at the OPS sergeant: "How so, John?

"Well, your old Coast Guard buddy, who doubles as my boss, thinks it may be time we reconsider our *Protect, Serve and Defend* motto and place a bit more emphasis on *Defend.*"

"Hmm. That's a fine distinction, but I get it. In a different conversation yesterday, Marjorie quoted the title of an old Kris Kristopherson song: *Who's to bless and who's to blame.* Seems we may be living in interesting times... are we all okay?"

Jean Barker stood up. The Barkers were not at all young... certainly the oldest in the room, probably closing in on their seventies in a couple of years. Tony was a well-set, energetic and dignified man who kept himself in excellent shape, and Jean was not to be outdone: a tall, statuesque woman with flowing silver hair, shining eyes and a figure that stopped much younger men in their tracks. At this moment, Jean's facial expression was infinitely sad, but the shining eyes looked unmistakably angry: "This finishes it, for me," she said in a quiet steady voice that nonetheless could have been clearly understood out the door and across the bay. "For weeks now I have been thinking of Priscilla, that poor young reporter from New York who died in a ditch in Africa, and of the cold fear that chills the blood of mothers like Georgina and sisters like Marjorie as their girls try to fight the battle for freedom they inherited from their dead friend. How about the injustice done to an elder truth-teller like Professor Horowitz, dead with his neck broken for the crime of speaking truth to power. Awan Lake is where these international terrors have come together, and now there are more people with power who want to use our home to grab what is not theirs and twist it into their own ugly vision of a devil's paradise. But this is OUR home, and if we can't put up a wall and scream NOT HERE, we will stay condemned to go on weeping in silence. Together (and with apologies to Marjorie) we are the old, but we have the vision and we have the skills. Yes, Frank, we're all okay. Let's fix this."

Marjorie stood up and went over to Jean, whose body was now shaking uncontrollably, and stood hugging her. Anderson looked across at Tony, then the Sergeant. "Okay, then. We have been told, and I for one am in full agreement. John, make sure you wink at Super Dave for me and tell him he owes us all a growler of Vancouver Island brewed pale ale. Together, John, we will make sure we do not embarrass him."

He stood up and looked around at everyone, then turned back to the Sergeant: "John, what's next?"

"So, moving forward means that instead of letting them set the stage, appoint the actors and bring the play to us, we reset the stage to our own liking, adjust the script and force the actors to play in the open where they will do illegal things and get caught. That's quite a hornet's nest over there at McKinney Island, and Tony, you just poked a big stick into the boss. I drove over yesterday and flew the flag on the west shore, so I suggest we use the navy to harass them even more, soon. We don't want to threaten them in such a way that we force them to cancel their party... we need to make them absolutely determined to go ahead with their plan. We might even do a fly-over every now and then. Frank?"

"I wonder when the baby bikers arrive. We can do one round of stick-poking before, and then again right after the bikers are onsite. The bikers – and Dr. Marcusson – need to be made really angry about talk of cancellation. We'll use their elevated testosterone levels to our advantage, getting their tempers flaring. Tony, did you get any idea from Marcusson when the gang arrives?"

"From what he said, apart from yelling at me, I think they get here this weekend."

"Okay. John, let's do the navy thing Saturday night, late. Unfortunately the moon is only a couple days past full, but the weather forecast is calling for overcast and maybe drizzle, so that would be about as good as a new moon if not as predictable for staying out of sight. We can leave here after sunset, sail by the island a couple of miles away with the boat dark, and then come in from the southeast. We'll get in fairly close and circle the island, making just enough fuss to let 'em know we're somewhere out there, then disappear to the western shore – almost. Then return, circle and flash a light or two and retrace our course to the southeast before going home. We'll be back home before they ever figure out where we came from."

"Sounds good, Frank. And I feel badly – I forgot that we need to touch base about all that stuff that happened last night, with the break-in alarm, the white truck and the stolen boat."

"Don't let me forget, I need to make an official statement to you guys about old man Hanson's boat. I also have to call him this morning to let him know that he won't have that boat to get to his cottage if he's planning to go there tonight. I can take him to the cottage, and I know he has a slightly smaller aluminum fishing boat out at the cottage that he can use, assuming it's running properly. I'll need to get the ski-boat serial numbers from him for our insurance, too."

"Sounds like last night was eventful, Frank?" It was Tony.

"Yeah, just after supper someone in a pickup tried to break into the workshop while another guy stole George's ski-boat. At least we assume the two guys were together. You guys help yourselves to coffee – it's almost nine o'clock and I'd better get on the phone," and he headed across the room to his desk, turned on the power-bar to his computer and took out his cellphone.

Jean stood up and gave Marjorie a hug, then turned to her husband: "Tony, I think these folks have a long couple of days ahead, so maybe we should stop up at the store for a few bits and pieces and get back home."

"Yes, we should. John, Marjorie, please keep us in the loop. If I hear from Karlsen or Marcussin I'll touch base immediately. I think you all need to be very careful. This whole thing may very well be just a tempest in a teapot... but then too it could just as easily blow up all over the place."

"You bet. Have a good day... I'll follow you out and head to my low-budget Chevrolet SUV ... I might as well use the radio so I can talk to everyone who's on duty at the same time. I'll be right back, Marj."

• • • •

An hour later, they were having coffee and cinnamon rolls at the Zoo with Arnold and Marion. They were close friends, and although they didn't always travel in the same orbits, there wasn't much that Frank Anderson would do without bouncing it off the Jamiesons, and of course now they were working together on the marina project. They were waiting for the Sergeant to finish his phone and radio calls and join them, but Anderson and Marjorie had time to describe the activities of the past couple of days and they had begun to outline their plans for the next night and beyond when the Sergeant joined them.

"So, have you been filling in the Jamiesons about all the fun we're having?"

"Really only just got started, but they have now heard about stolen boats, idiots and half-tons."

"Well, I got some stuff about that – well, the half-ton anyway. At about midnight last night – nobody knows exactly what time – a crew-cab Chevy was set on fire along the Seven Bridges Road about five miles north of the highway. It had been white and it was not wearing a license plate. It appeared there had been some gas in a plastic jerry can that they used to help start the fire, and then threw the can in the ditch but the fire didn't catch it. Our guys have the can and think there are some prints on it, and of course they've got the V.I.N. from the truck which they traced to some guy in Manitoba where it was stolen three days ago."

"Seven Bridges Road... wasn't there a song about that?"

"Yes Marj," replied Arnold. "Eagles, 1980."

"And many others before that," Anderson added, "including Joan Baez and Dolly Parton. Great song. But the road wasn't in Awan County, Ontario. It was somewhere in the deep south. Is there some connection?"

Arnold and Marion were sort of giggling. "Yeah, Frank, you'll never guess how that happened, so here goes: there used to be six bridges on that road, which crosses the Spirit River (over the canal) and crosses five little creeks on its way south to the county line. Gary Edwards, who used to be road foreman, loved that song so he replaced a small steel culvert over a mostly dry creek-bed with a little wooden bridge and then changed the sign at the highway to read *Seven Bridges Road*."

"And he wasn't fired?"

"Nah, everyone loved Gary, he loved the song, and there ya go."

"That's a cool story," said the Sergeant. "It's that kind of thing that makes me love this part of the world."

"John," Anderson asked, "did you send someone out the west side road to check out if maybe Hanson's ski-boat had joined those five aluminum fishing boats opposite McKinney Island?"

"Sure did. I suppose they're part way up there by now. Cell service will be non-existent, but we have satellite phones and I told them to take one, so we'll probably get some news within a half-hour."

"I assume they're in a marked car?"

"Half-ton, actually, but yes, marked. Crap, hang on..." The Sergeant's cellphone had begun its singular tone for an impending call from dispatch.

"That's quite the little sports car that our stripy friend is driving," laughed Marion.

"Poor John, we've been teasing him for two days now. Yeah, nice ride. I guess it sort of comes with his new duties – and title." Anderson paused, looked across at Marjorie and said, "I see it's ham quiche day at the Zoo... are we all in for an early lunch?"

The Sergeant was just ending his call and signalled a thumbs-up across the dining room, then returned to the table. "Quiche for lunch sounds great. That was the RCMP – Sergeant Mankowski. Marianna gave us lots more about that white truck. Her gang out west just phoned her to say that an old green Ford pickup was burned along the Yellowhead Highway near Portage La Prairie, west of Winnipeg and most importantly within a couple of miles of where they tell us our white pickup had been stolen. And apparently someone stole a Manitoba plate from another white truck in a mall parking lot in Portage.

"So why does someone from west of Winnipeg wind up near Awan Lake three days later?" asked Arnold.

"There's even more. The RCMP says that same old green

pickup had last been seen a couple of days before at a farm in Saskatchewan where it was being driven by a guy named Dan Millard. And Dan Millard used to work for the Robertson Group on Vancouver Island, where he is under suspicion in the murder of Professor Sebastian Horowitz. How's that for a day's news for ya?"

"Holy crap, the system really does work sometimes." Anderson stood up looking restless: "This is about away more than just stolen trucks. This is telling us – well, telling me anyway – that the late Thomas Manville's team of security mercenaries is still alive and well, and must not have been entirely controlled by Manville because by now he is too dead to lead or direct them. John, didn't you say that a couple of those guys you arrested – but then had to let go after the Robertson Mines fire last month – wound up involved with some bikers in Toronto?"

"Yes – there were two of them I think... there were six in all, and two were killed in the fire-fight that was part of the fire at the mine. We arrested three, as I remember, and a fourth made it across into the US the next day. We had nothing we could use to hold the other two, who both had valid landed immigrant status, so they were released after 24 hours. Seems they headed for the city and since then all we know is a couple of reports shared with us by undercover city cops who were wondering what we knew about them."

"I have to admit that I didn't think it was all that bad a thing when Manville was found murdered, because he was an evil little sucker. But now we're learning he wasn't the big dog in this fight... there's someone else. And that makes me more than a bit nervous because the guy who's at the top of this pyramid has to be a seriously mean bugger and really well-connected. I never thought Manville was a genius, but mostly I think he just over-played his hand all the time, trying to be big-time. So John, I ex-pect you are beating the bushes to find Dan Millard, since it's al-most certain he's around here somewhere. I expect the RCMP is part of that search as well?"

"Yes, Marianna and her bunch are actually taking the lead on the Dan Millard thing because the crimes for which he is want-ed were all committed in B.C. and in Manitoba so far, not in Ontario. And anyway, we have enough on our plate at the mo-ment. I'm just as worried about his colleagues and how they are involved with the bikers and now this McKinney Island thing... Millard is just one of that bunch and I don't think he is any kind of a boss. He's too blunt an instrument."

Marion had been quiet, obviously somewhat lost in thought. Marjorie leaned across the table and asked, "Is there something bothering you about all this, Marion? I am learning from expe-rience that when Frank and John and Arnold get together and start throwing around ideas, things can seem sort of crazy. I'm guilty of that too, I'm afraid."

Marion smiled: "Me too, actually. But often with you guys, you're all asking about *what* and *how* and *who* and *when*, so sometimes I sit back and wonder, simply, *why?* What's behind all this fuss? There's a run-down old estate on one of the most iso-lated islands on the lake, a nearly depleted – and now destroyed – copper mine, and a really rather quiet and boring little com-munity a good two-hour drive from anywhere on a bad highway. Why all the fuss?"

"Well, when you put it that way..." Marjorie laughed: "Maybe we are all a little touched. But I remember something Frank said in his speech to the community at that media announcement we hosted by the marina. He told us this: *Our communities are our ecosystem – which includes our people, our land and our water.* So I guess that's why we get all worked up when we are threatened."

It was Arnold's turn to laugh: "Yeah, you know how it goes, Marion. We talk a little, kill a few people, burn stuff down, drink some beer. Same old, same old."

"Arnold, you forgot the donuts. I always bring donuts. I need to go back to The Falls, folks. I've pretty much abandoned my new Sergeant and I should go back and fill her in on all this stuff. She's great, she's smart, and she's confused. The confusion part is my bad, so I'll go fix. We'll need her fully functional and up to speed if things get weird."

"And we need to go back and prep *The Beaver*... change fluids, fill her up with diesel, that kind of stuff. John, are you bringing one or two of those little C8s? We should never have to use guns out there tomorrow night, but I would rather be prepared with something that has a bit more range than my shotgun."

"Yup, two Colt C8-CQB carbines are on my to-do list."

• • • •

Robertson Mines at Awan Lake, ON:1330: "Hello Bonnie."

"Oh my God – Raimy. You're alive. I thought you had died in the fire. They told us that a couple of you guys had apparently made it out alive and headed back to the US, but you weren't one of them. You look great."

"I'm hangin' in there. Was going back south but thought I'd stick around Toronto for awhile. Bonnie, this is Danny, a guy I used to work with in B.C. He's another IT specialist, just like me only bigger."

"Hi Danny, it's nice to meet you. Are you both on the same security team as well as IT specialists?"

"Not normally, but the RGI development branch in the States has asked us to do some preliminary security assessment work out here. Simple stuff, like see how clean-up is going, help figure out how soon the company can start re-construction and what security planning we need to do, as well as check on our friends – and enemies if there are some. Are there any enemies?"

"As the only black chick in Spirit River I may have a warped idea of who are our enemies and who are not, but as far as Robertson Mines go, I think we had lots of enemies before the fire, but not so many now. Folks have woken up to the fact that when we lost the mine they lost one hundred and twenty-five jobs. Maybe now they are worrying less about dying birds and poisoned water and more about paycheques."

"I didn't get out into the community much when we were here earlier this summer, but I didn't think being black up here was any problem. In fact I used to hang out at the Inn with that young African student who worked with the environmental group, and he seemed okay."

"Adumbi? Hah. Good lookin' black men, no problem as long as you've got money. Overweight black chick with three little kids and no husband, not so good. And that arrogant prick with his fake limey accent was no help."

"Mmm. Who's your boss now?"

"Morrell... Charlie Morrell, like before. Adamson was killed, and that Manville dude wound up in jail. Never did like him very much."

"Tommy? Tommy Manville? I knew him out on Vancouver Island." Danny Millard paused thoughtfully: "Actually, I always thought he was okay as a boss, although perhaps not the brightest bulb in the pack. And I know the big bosses in the US maybe had second thoughts every now and then. Used to ask me a lot of questions."

"You guys going to be hanging around?"

"For awhile I guess. Staying at the West End Motel in The Falls... give me a call if you're ever in there. We need to see Charlie... is he in today?"

"This is a pretty small trailer... does it really look like he's in here, turkey? He's took the afternoon off and went home... but you know where he lives in the village anyway, don't you."

"Easy, chicky, be nice. Don't mean no harm..."

"It's okay. I get it, nothing ever really happens for me up here in the north woods. Talk to you another day, asshole."

• • • •

Spirit River, ON:1445: Two hours after their early lunch, Anderson and Marjorie had re-fueled the workboat, checked the engine and transmission fluids and run through the wiring, lights and electronics to make sure all the components were working properly. Adumbi had been working on outboard engines in the shop but had left for a weekend in Ottawa at about two o'clock. Anderson put plywood over the broken window on the workshop door and both he and Marjorie had turned their attention to the house, cleaning and tidying and gathering stuff for a laundry day.

At three o'clock, Marjorie had just opened them each a beer and suggested they sit out on the little porch in the sunshine when her cellphone rang, showing an unfamiliar number and country code. It was Wendy: "Hi Sis.... Is everything okay? ... You say you are in Kinshasa, in a park on a satphone? ... Two minutes? ... Okay, I get it. I'll grab some paper and a pen."

Within seconds Marjorie was back inside the house and sitting down at the desk, pen in hand. "What's up? ... Coltan? You say it's all about Coltan? ... Who the hell is Coltan? Oh, it's a thing, not a person ... Yeah, okay. I'll look it up. ... At Awan Lake? Robertson Mines? You're kidding. ... Okay, you're not kidding.

The conversation was over in just under two minutes. Marjorie clicked off and turned to Anderson, who was already on the computer Googling *coltan*. *In Canada, coltan is mined at Bernic Lake in Manitoba, northeast of Winnipeg,* he read aloud. *Coltan is a dull metallic ore found in major quantities in the eastern areas of Congo. When refined, coltan becomes metallic tantalum which is used to make capacitors that are found in almost all cell phones, laptops, pagers and many other electronics.* "And this article says that the recent technology boom caused the price of coltan to skyrocket to as much as $400 a kilogram. So, that's what it is. What about it?"

"It seems that she has found this out simply because coltan – or tantalum – is just one of Robertson Group's interests in Africa, which is likewise part of her research. But the reason she called so urgently today is to tell us that Robertson Group International has uncovered a massive deposit of the stuff right here at Awan Lake, maybe enough to eclipse production in the DRC and Brazil together. So if people are wondering if the Awan Lake mine will ever re-open, the answer is yes, and probably soon, but from the way she talked, we can expect there is already a lot of under-the-table stuff going on. Wendy limited her call to two minutes for her own personal security, but before she hung up she said, *don't try to call me, I'll call you in a day or so,* and that there was more – something to do with DRC and Canadian politicians being hosted by RGI at a special seminar at Awan Lake. And the last thing she said before she hung up was that we should call Anita immediately because she has uncovered some weird related stuff being filtered through the UNESCO office in Paris."

"UNESCO – really? The United Nations? That's kind of weird. Anyway, we should call. Do you have Anita's number?"

"I think it's the same as she had before, so I'll give that a try. I'm pretty sure there are no security issues for her in Paris."

"And I think we ought to call Tony again and see if he can reach out to Christopher on the island... one would think he would know if there were some VIPs due to show up out there. You call Anita, I'll call Tony."

That didn't happen right away. No sooner had he swiped the screen on his cellphone to call Tony when the phone rang and showed the Sergeant was on the other end. Anderson clicked and answered, "Hi John, what's up?"

"Feel like a chopper ride this afternoon? It's here on a training flight and I only have room for one, but I've asked if we can overfly McKinney Island."

"Cool. Where and when?"

There was a short pause: "Twenty-five minutes, at Spirit River's main air terminal."

"Right, wise-ass. I'll meet you out there. I'll see if I have money for parking."

Anderson took some paper from his desk and wrote a short note to Marjorie, taking it over to where she was sitting talking on her cell with Anita. He handed her the note, kissed her on her forehead, smiled at the puzzled look on her face and went out to his truck, closing the house door quietly behind him. He started the pickup's little 4-cylinder engine, waved at Marjorie who was now standing by the window, and drove off up Main Street to the highway and west to the bumpy little patch of grass the village referred to as its airport.

About ten minutes later, as Anderson sat on the truck tailgate waiting for the chopper, Marjorie must have finished her call to Anita and called him immediately: "Well, that was weird... you're off on a flight?"

"Yeah, but I won't be long. John has access to a chopper on a training flight so he's gonna fly us over McKinney Island. How's Anita?"

"She's in great form, enjoying Paris and having a blast investigating anything and everything. Yes, there is indeed a Congo-to-Awan-Lake thing, sort of mixed up with UNESCO's biosphere reserve presence in the DRC and a recent overture to UNESCO from the First Nation south of here. She's sending me a pile of stuff. And I guess there's a contact at Ryerson University – she thinks it's Dave Bradshaw but she's checking it out."

"Geesh. University Wars – Marcusson and Bradshaw. I so want to stay clear of that one. Crap, better go, here comes the whirley-bird. I'll be home soon."

The Eurocopter EC635 thumped its way down, settling near Anderson's pickup. He waved, ducked down and made his way across the grass to the open port-side door and climbed aboard. He was welcomed with a handshake and a set of earphones, and they were off, travelling low over the village, pausing momentarily over the docks (and a waving Marjorie) before it climbed rapidly and headed southwest toward McKinney Island.

What would have been about a fifteen-minute flight "by

crow" added about seven minutes to swing west to the shore then south along to the little dock where the rental boats were tied up. The Sergeant directed the pilot to drop to about 300 feet above the water and make the flight over McKinney Island, just over a mile offshore, heading east at about half-speed.

The island itself was long and narrow, positioned north and south with what was almost certainly the main house at the north end. As they got to the west side they passed over a long dock with the boathouse. "I see a couple of boats down there," said the Sergeant through the Eurocopter's ICS."

"Yeah, that bigger one has belonged to the McKinney estate for decades. It's quite elegant, and very slow... they use it to pick up stuff at the village and I think that sometimes, for VIPs, they take it down to The Falls."

"It would take me all summer just to varnish that thing."

"Yup. Pretty, but high maintenance."

The Sergeant motioned to the pilot to make a second slow turn over the island. "Sounds like my first wife. How about the other boat? It looks a lot newer... could that be the one that was stolen the other night?"

"I was thinking the same thing. However, it's a pretty common type of boat for cottage people. I'd have to get an awful lot closer to really know. That makes sense though."

The helicopter was beginning to attract some attention on the island. Half-way through the second turn-around, a man in shorts and a woman in a bathing suit had come out of the main house for a look, and Anderson was pretty sure he saw Christopher Karlsen standing with two equally tall men outside the boathouse on the dock. Karlsen was using binoculars.

"Time for us to go," said the Sergeant. "We don't need them

to figure out who we are."

"Won't they know from the markings?"

"Maybe, but they'll have to do some digging. This old gal is a new chopper to us – on loan from the Feds – so the record-keeping is a bit weird."

"I see. Alright then, Staff Sergeant with Special Projects, how's about we make this flight a little longer and swing over Robertson Mines... it's about fifteen miles from here. In light of what we're hearing, I'd like to see if there are any signs of exploration or new development over there."

A new voice came over the ICS: "I can give you two hours more flying time – inclusive of the usual fifteen minutes of post-flight – so one hour and forty-five minutes tops."

"I assume that was our captain speaking?"

"Yes. Thanks, Anne. Sorry everyone, I didn't do the introductions when Frank joined us. Frank, this is Lieutenant Anne Haroldson, our pilot, and in the co-pilot seat is Sergeant Peggy Dawson, who has just joined our Maple Falls detachment. She assures me she will not be touching the controls of this aircraft. Anne and Peggy, meet Frank Anderson who likes to be called pretty much anything but Mister Anderson: Frank, or just Anderson – take your choice. Frank is our on-call boat guy and strategist, and you've heard a bit about him already."

"Hi Admiral Frank," came the ICS reply from the front seats, almost in perfect unison. Then Sergeant Dawson spoke up alone: "Glad to meet you. As you can tell, your reputation precedes you, so no offense meant."

"None taken. Things always go better when there's more than one wise-ass on the ship."

"Yes, but so many?" said Sergeant John.

• • • •

Charles Morrell and his family of two girls and his wife Bernadette lived on an acreage that fronted on the lake, about a half-mile west of the Spirit River landing strip. This afternoon, Charlie and Bernadette were busy harvesting vegetables from their mammoth garden when they heard the unmistakable roar of a helicopter taking off from the airport. They looked skyward and watched as it thumped its way across the sky and over the lake heading southwest.

"The sound of those things makes me shudder," said Bernadette. "I can't get the memories of last month out of my mind, with helicopters overhead, fire on the horizon and it seemed like death all around."

"Me too. I think it was the glare from the fire shining through the window and reflecting on the wall of our bedroom that did it to me. That was a bad night."

They decided it was tea time, so Bernadette went into the house to prepare the tea and some cookies to snack on. Moments later, Charles looked up from his bean-picking to see a silver SUV turning in the driveway and up the short run into the yard. There were two men on board and he recognized the black one right away. He was less than thrilled by the visit, but nonetheless he greeted him politely: "Hello, Raimy. Haven't seen you since the early morning after the fire, when you told us you were headed back to the US"

"Well, I got as far as Toronto for a few days but they phoned me and told me they wanted me to do some more work."

"Who's your friend?" He motioned toward Millard who had remained in the front seat of the SUV."

"That's Danny Millard. He used to work for Robertson in B.C. but he has agreed to join us here."

"So what work does Toronto want you to do?"

"Not RGI Toronto. RGI Development in Washington. Setting up the logistics and security for the re-build and expansion."

"Re-build I get... we're working toward that every day, but expansion? Really? I've heard nothing about that."

Raimy Smith smiled and shook his head: "Yeah, that bunch in Washington is like that. They don't tell anybody anything they don't absolutely have to. Apparently they don't even tell the Canadian office in Toronto. None of them know what's going on up here. The geologists must have spent the last couple of years talking only to Washington, and even that's kept pretty quiet, at least until Monday."

"*At least until Monday*... what the hell does that mean?"

"On Monday morning RGI will announce in Washington that company geologists have found what is certain to be one of the biggest deposits of coltan in the world... here at Awan Lake."

"I surely do wish this company would let their employees know this stuff, especially the ones in full view of the public. I need to know this stuff... otherwise Robertson Mines at Spirit River is going to look like idiots if we can't answer media questions with anything better than *duh, I dunno.*"

"Well, sorry about that. It's just their style, I guess. I was told to give you the information, and I just did. Check your email – you shouldn't have taken the afternoon off, I guess. Now you gotta play catch-up."

• • • •

As the OPS helicopter made it's last sweeping circle low over the

Robertson Mines property and headed northwest toward the village of Spirit River, the light wind had dropped to nothing and the sun had ducked behind the clouds on the horizon. The late afternoon sky was darkening and the waters of Awan Lake were leaden. Despite the military-grade intercom, conversation in a helicopter is always a challenge and Anderson's thoughts drifted back to the conversation Marjorie had earlier in the afternoon with Wendy. Looking down at the silver-grey lake surface, he thought: *Maybe that's what coltan, or metallic tantalum, looks like. I wonder how much of that crap – at what price – is in my cellphone, and I wonder if toddlers dressed in rags are picking it out of piles of electronic waste in Bangladesh.*

The Staff Sergeant crackled in the intercom: "What time do you want to leave the dock tomorrow evening?"

Anderson jumped: "Sorry, my thoughts were elsewhere. Let's see, the sun sets at 1930 – seven thirty – and getting underway then makes sense. It'll be dark by the time we get anywhere near the island. How many crew are you bringing?"

"I've asked Peggy to come with us to get a feel for what we do out here, and normally I'd bring Cpl. Beauchemin – Marie – but I think I'll leave her in charge at the detachment and Andy Bathgate on call for the evening, in case there is any sort of trouble with bikers and their friends. Are you bringing Marjorie?"

"Yes, she wouldn't have it any other way. She loves that boat."

"Okay, so we'll bring just one of the other constables with us. Peggy, do you want to arrange all of that?"

"Yes sir, I'll get right at it before they start leaving the shop. Are you getting cell service out here?"

"Iffy. Here take my satphone and remind me to get you one too. Cells are fine in the town and village, but – as I have to remind the guys in Toronto seems like every day – we are basically a rural police service out here."

In fewer than ten minutes, the helicopter had left Anderson by his pickup at Spirit River International and risen into the sky to head back to Maple Falls. Anderson drove back into the village and stopped at the Co-op to pick up one carton of Export As, two bottles of Gravol, three Bic lighters, and one box of 12-guage #4 shells. "I'm not sure I wanna know where you're going with that assortment of stuff." laughed Betty at the cash register."

"Nope. Ignorance is bliss, my momma told me. Some things you just don't need to know. Have a good weekend Betty, and say hi to Larry for me."

As he drove down Main Street, Anderson called up Richard at The Lockmaster's House in The Falls: "Hi Richard, it's Frank Anderson from Spirit River... How's that?... Oh, we're doin' great... just wondering if you have room for Marjorie and I, maybe around seven thirty or eight?... perfect, eight it is. See you then."

He got home just in time to see Marjorie wheeling the barbeque out of the workshop where he kept it sheltered from the rain. As he got out of the pickup he called out, "Whoa... I just booked us at table at Richard's, at eight."

"Lovely idea, but not tonight," She called back, "or maybe anytime soon. You forget that we have enemies out there who seem very keen on breaking in and stealing or wrecking stuff these days..."

"Damn, you're right. I must have been off in a dream world... I'll call Richard back and cancel right away."

"As far as dinner, I picked up two nice little steaks which I will sizzle while you go and pick us up a pizza which we will have pre-ordered from the Zoo. I'm making a salad, and I even bought some wine."

"Perfect. I'll call Richard and cancel, then we'll open that wine and talk about stuff. Seems like there's lots going on and not all of it makes me feel totally comfortable.

The afternoon had turned chilly, so he lit a small fire in the old iron stove and they sat at the massive refectory table sipping wine from small kitchen tumblers. "I was sure glad we heard from Wendy – and Anita too – this afternoon. When does Wendy get clear of Africa and head for Paris?"

"Just a couple of days until her flight. I think that she thinks she's out of danger in Kinshasa, but I'm not so confident. She's currently staying at a 4-star Radisson hotel fairly close to both the Canadian and American embassies, but it's still Kinshasa in the Democratic Republic of the Congo, and that doesn't give me a warm fuzzy feeling, not after what happened to Patricia."

"Well, that was a long way from Kinshasa, wasn't it?"

"Yes, Kolwezi... roughly as far from Kinshasa as Winnipeg is from Ottawa. Still..."

"Yeah, I guess if the bosses in Washington can reach out to assassinate people they don't like on a ferry out of Vancouver, at a prison in North Bay, and a roadside in Kolwezi, Kinshasa doesn't look terribly safe. Come to think of it, nor does Awan Lake. Devil's choice..."

"Mmm. I gave up crossing my fingers years ago – it never worked and it hurt my fingers. Prayer usually works better, so I'll stick to that. About that UNESCO thing, I was able to reach Dave Bradshaw at Ryerson this afternoon, and yes, he has developed a network through the Canadian Commission for UN-

ESCO in Ottawa that reaches out to the Lufira biosphere reserve in the DRC, which is fairly close to some of Robertson Group International's mining operations in that country. According to Dave, in Canada, biosphere reserves – as of last year there are eighteen of them – have long been understood to have an environmental focus, whereas in many other countries including Africa there is more of a focus on Indigenous culture and sustainable development. He says that Canada is loathe to add to the number of biospheres, but the landscape is changing, so to speak, and consideration is still being given to potential areas with a fundamental indigenous focus. So Dave has begun to engage with that big reserve south of Awan Lake – Crazy Man Willy's home reserve – thinking he could build a linkage between our own indigenous people and the people in the DRC. The Robertson Group, of course, would be the common resource-extraction link."

"Bradshaw never sleeps, apparently. If there's a little hell to be raised, he'll be the first one out there cranking the winch. Do you remember the beginnings of our Protected Shoreline Project here? Back when he got us all together to pester our late Member of Parliament to get some funding? It was supposed to be just a simple little water monitoring thing with a bird-watcher's twist."

"Mmm... yet here we are. That Member of Parliament has been murdered and our neighbourhood has expanded to include Africa. Such a quaint little global village we have."

SEPTEMBER 9

Spirit River, ON: Saturday turned out to be a busy day, even if nobody went anywhere much except Staff Sergeant John, who had to take his daughter Taylor to a high school soccer tournament at Haliburton. That was also where she wanted to take courses in Integrated Design at Sir Sandford Fleming College after high school graduation, so they left early in hopes of having time to get a look at the campus.

George Hanson and his wife arrived mid-morning to talk about his missing-and-presumed-stolen ski boat. They stopped in for coffee with Anderson and Marjorie, who very carefully explained that they had a good idea where the boat was, and may even have seen it, but that it was currently at a much larger potential crime scene and the police really didn't want to go in and remove the boat.

George had things to say about that: "*Frankly, Frank,* to paraphrase Clark Gable in Gone With the Wind, *I don't give a damn.* This fall, our oldest child has finally fled the nest, so gone are those endless waterskiing weekends spent with strapping big teenage boys whose only goal in life, apparently, is to consume Alberta's total fuel production every day. I swear, that damn skiboat drank over two-hundred bucks worth of gas every day. Next year, Hanson Island will have an eighteen-foot aluminum Lund for fishing in comfort and for taxiing ourselves back and forth to the island, and maybe a small used sailboat for Jenny to play with if I can pick one up around here somewhere."

The four of them chuckled a lot and finished their coffee and some big gooey cookies that Jenny had brought from home.

Anderson then took them out to their island, where they had a rather ancient fourteen-footer tied up to their somewhat rickety dock. He left them there with thanks, a handshake and a verbal contract to put in a better dock for their new boat next spring.

Arnold came with the travel-lift to pick a couple of small cruisers out of the lake and take them to the old curling rink that temporarily served as boat storage, and he and Marion joined them for fish and chips at the Zoo for a late lunch. Charlie Morrell came into the restaurant to pick up some quiche for his and Bernadette's lunch, and when he saw Anderson he came over and asked quietly if he would mind stepping outside for a word.

"Frank, one of those security guys who were hanging around with Manville last month came by to see me at home – yesterday afternoon. Do you remember them? It was Raimy, the big black guy, and he had another big guy – blond – with him who stayed in the car. He said he had been instructed to tell me about a Robertson Group International media announcement to be delivered from a large island near the southwest corner of the lake – McKinley I think – on Monday morning. The event is being hosted by the New World Mission at that island, and principals from Robertson Group in Washington and Canadian government representatives will be there. The announcement concerns an expansion project for the RGI facility here to accommodate the large-scale production of tantalum from a new source of coltan here at Awan Lake. You're the Mayor of Spirit River, and I thought you should know before the phone lines begin to quiver. I think the media will go nuts – internationally too. This is a big and potentially controversial project because wherever it is mined, coltan is seen to be a source of conflict."

"I'm not the Mayor of Spirit River, Charlie, but thanks for

the info. What you say about that coltan stuff confirms what we have been hearing over the last couple of days."

"Yeah, I know you're not the mayor, but you should be. The guy we got now is such a useless twit and just embarrasses the village and our company whenever he gets in front of a TV camera. Having said that, go ahead and tell Klassen if you think that's best... I just don't want to deal with the prick and I won't be referring the media to him. Anyway, sorry to break into your lunch on an otherwise nice Saturday." and he left.

When Anderson got back to the table he repeated Morrell's information about the Monday media conference, leaving out the obvious comments about the Mayor but he did say he had been asked to contact Mayor Klassen and update him as well.

"Why would he bother you with that?" asked Marion.

"Well, let's just say that Charlie wasn't bashful about how he felt about His Majesty. He probably just thought I had thicker skin."

Arnold made a convincing clucking sound.

"Yeah, I know. I almost told him that general managers were supposed to be eagles, not chickens. But I didn't have the heart. He was looking pretty stressed out."

"Frank, can you put on some chest waders and sling some chains and ropes for me this afternoon? I want to start pulling out all those pieces of burned-out docks."

"You bet, Arnold. Let me go home, check my emails, call Klassen and grab the waders. You got the chains? Cool. Then I'm happy to get at it... just remember that Marj and I have to be underway with John and his boys and girls by about 1930, and I'd rather have dinner before we go. Incidentally, I am looking forward to seeing how his new Sergeant, Peggy Dawson, is working out. When I met her, she was just a lump of battledress with a headset, a helmet and a pleasant voice."

"Dawson? Peggy Dawson?" It was Marion.

"Yup... why?"

"Oh, you guys are going to like her. She's another one of Crazy Man Willy's grandaughters, so a cousin (of sorts – you know how that works out on the Res) to Anita."

"Peggy Dawson? Not exactly an Aboriginal name."

"Don't be a twit – nor is Anita, or Willy or Antoine for that matter. Yeah, Peggy's from Willy's reserve, obviously, and put in her time at some university, then a few years in the RCMP – mostly in Saskatchewan – then a long apprenticeship as an OPS corporal, serving out of Thunder Bay where it doesn't get much tougher for cops. I wasn't aware she had made it to Sergeant, but I expect she'll be a real asset to John."

"Geesh, I wonder if John even knows all this?"

"Well, it'll all be in her documentation, if he knows how to read."

" I'm pretty sure he does, but... does he ever take the time?"

"Good point."

"I'm outta here. See you at the docks in about half an hour."

• • • •

Arnold and Anderson spent most of the next four hours with Arnold's old farm tractor, and from time to time Anderson's miniature trackhoe, skidding pieces of burned dock and occasionally boat from the lake near what had been the marina boat launch. They would do what they could to clean up most of the wreckage from the fire, but they both knew they would have to hire a piece of much bigger machinery to finish removing all the scrap from the bottom of the lake along the shore so they could re-build the marina.

At one point, Arnold took a couple of cans of beer from under the tractor seat, offering one to a dripping-wet Anderson.

"Man, I'd love one of those, but Marjorie and I just can't. We go on duty with three or four cops tonight, I have an Auxiliary rank and Transport Canada doesn't want Captain Marjorie drinking either. I do have the rain check, though."

"Yeah, sorry about that. Actually, I knew that but didn't remember. But, you discarded the chest waders almost an hour or so ago so you must be frozen, so let's get you back to the house and changed, then we can do some drier stuff."

"You won't get much argument from me. It's getting bloody cold playing around in there."

• • • •

McKinney Is., Awan Lake, ON: 1630: Raimy Smith and Dan Millard were standing on the dock at McKinney Island, talking with Christopher Karlsen. It had been a long day for Dan Millard in particular... for the second day in a row he had to ride with Raimy Smith who had been given command over this operation by head office in the USA. He disliked and mistrusted Raimy but had little choice but to be cooperative: he needed the dollars and they were big dollars he and Raimy would be earning. Which was a good thing because not only did he resent the black man's control over him, he also didn't like McKinney Island, or Awan Lake, or Ontario or anything Canadian. He considered the USA.'s northern neighbour to be just another third-world country, though he had enjoyed his time on Vancouver Island where he took a special interest in pubescent Aboriginal women from broken homes. He found their gratitude especially touching, and other than that he had no Canadian friends because... he had no friends at all.

The bikers from Toronto had turned up about three hours later than expected, and there were seven of them instead of six as planned. The seventh was Gerry's new squeeze, and the others knew better than to argue with Gerry, or whomever was his squeeze at the time. Gerry wasn't the leader, but he was by many years the eldest of the group. He called his woman "Squeezy" and she was as noisy and mean as Gerry was quiet and patient. Squeezy did, however, drive the van and that was important.

The Magnificent Seven, as Raimy had nicknamed the bikers, had transported much of the contents of the van from the shore to the island and had settled themselves into a workers' cottage near the boathouse. Raimy had met each of them because he had hung out at their clubhouse north of the city, where they referred to him as "our designated nigger". For obvious reasons he had elected to house himself and Millard in the two bedrooms over the boathouse... as he had told Christopher Karlsen, "trained seals don't mix well with dumb animals."

"I was a little surprised that Larsen allowed that bunch of broomtails to come within a country mile of this," said Raimy. "He lives in Washington and wouldn't have any contact with a biker gang in Toronto, let alone a second-rate bunch like this one."

"I see what you mean," said Christopher, "but as I understand it, the lead guy in this adventure is Dr. Fred Marcusson, a university professor in Toronto and also a weekend biker. You know the type: old white guys livin' the dream.

"Yeah, I do get that. And yeah, I've heard of Marcusson from

Larsen, and I guess he's the one with the government contacts in Canada – Ottawa and Toronto anyway. Seems like he is also the academic face in Canada for a bunch of people planning to change the world. I think they are big-time followers of the current US President, although I have to say I have no idea why anybody with a half a brain follows that dumb bastard. Crapped out of the army – or maybe it was airforce – because he had itchy toes and daddy bought him a pass. Doesn't do anything for his reputation as a leader amongst us folks in the Marines and on top of that he is not only stupid: he lies."

"I have to say that – as executive director and therefore responsible for visitor safety out here, I am pleased that you and Dan are here, so at least we will have some adults in the room this coming week. Do you know what is the real reason to have all these VIPs headed out here, with this so-called "training session" on the side?"

"Yes, I do. And I'll tell you but keep it absolutely confidential until Monday. Dan and I work for Roger Larsen, who is the chief development officer for Robertson Group International. Robertson Group International – or RGI for short – has operations around the world, through national companies such as Robertson Mines here in Canada. RGI is the head office, based in Washington. So on Monday, Larsen's development group, along with the Canadian Minister of Natural Resources, is announcing an expansion of the Robertson Mines facility at Awan Lake. The expansion will extract and process a mineral known as coltan from what has been discovered to be one of the largest deposits of that mineral in the world, along the shores and under the lakebed."

"Well, that's pretty cool. What's the catch?"

"There is no catch, really, although if you thought the greenies were pissed off before, you ain't seen nothing yet."

"So why would the biker parade and the whole New World Mission thing be involved?"

"I really have no idea at all. This is Canada – ain't my country."

"Well, maybe it's something like this: We've hosted the resources minister and a bunch of other government and university types out here for one or two day meetings, and Marcusson has always been there with them. They always discuss fixing the world by fixing Canada and I have a sneaking hunch he may simply be showing off his influence through an internationally important event he can tap into. Make sense?"

Raimy didn't chuckle. He laughed: "Well, if he wants to impress Larsen he'd better have a better military presence up his sleeve than the bunch of weekend wannabees he's assembled in that cottage up the path. What's with you Canucks that you think international prestige, expertise and power are things you can accomplish with a pretty face, a college diploma and a bunch of Facebook posts?"

Christopher glanced across at Millard, who had burst out laughing, then back at Raimy: "Some day you'll have to tell us how you really feel."

"No offense, Chris. I can tell you're not the kind of folks I meant. But you get my drift?"

"Oh yeah, I do, and between us, you have pretty much defined Marcusson. He's an arrogant old fart so maybe this week he might get driven down a peg or two. Remind me to tell him about that chopper yesterday afternoon. He'll want to know that, but it'll keep him awake that night, I'm sure."

"Chopper? What chopper..."

"Yesterday at about three – maybe four – a big grey chopper came over from the shore over there, pretty low. It made a revolution of the island, circled again a little lower and then headed straight east to the far side of the lake and disappeared."

"Sounds military – how big?"

"Well, not huge... single rotor, maybe six or eight passengers and wide doors on either side. Looked like the ones they use for air ambulances, but not that colour."

"What time does your Mr. Marcusson get here, anyway?"

"He texted me this morning that he was going straight from Toronto to Maple Falls where he would be meeting some of the Ottawa VIPs who were coming in on a charter. I am to expect him around seven at the west side dock, where we will be picking them up with the launch."

• • • •

Spirit River, ON, 1915: The setting sun was not calling any attention to itself this evening. It hadn't been raining, but the sky had worn heavy clouds all day. *The Beaver* was laid alongside the dock in the calm bay, showing her full array of navigation lights. The slowly rotating radar antenna flashed under the masthead steaming light and the two diesel engines burbled quietly under the deck. The wheelhouse instrument panels were alive with the glow of small red or green LEDs, and the focsle light below decks was visible through the open hatch from the wheelhouse. Marjorie and Anderson were sitting outside on the engine hatch cover, smoking a cigarette, sipping black coffee and waiting for the police to arrive.

At 1922, a white SUV with OPS markings drove down the

road, across the yard to the dock, and along the dock to the converted lobster boat. The driver shut off the engine and all three OPS on board stepped out onto the dock, dressed in full tactical gear with holstered sidearms. "Good evening, you two," called Staff Sergeant MacLeod. "Sergeant Peggy Dawson and Constable Erin Watters, this is Marjorie Webster and Frank Anderson. We'll gather our gear and come aboard, if that's okay with the captain and crew."

"Fine with the crew," said Anderson, "but you'll have to check with Marjorie. She's the skipper tonight."

"Depends on if Staff Sergeant MacLeod brought donuts," said Marjorie.

"Yes he did." MacLeod turned to the others: "And so it starts. See what I mean? It's always like this."

Five minutes later with Marjorie at the wheel, Anderson used the forward line to spring *The Beaver* off the dock where she had been wedged between two small boats, and they were slowly underway out of the little bay and onto the lake. Ammunition, three C8 carbines, extra clothing and donuts were safely onboard and stored forward in the focsle – except the donuts and one of two boxes of coffee, which were safely placed on the port-side navigation table. When they were well clear of the harbour and Anderson had set a course on the GPS and autohelm that would take them to a point about three miles east of McKinney Island, Marjorie moved the throttle up to about two thirds and punched the autopilot before walking across the wheelhouse for a donut and a coffee refill before taking them out on deck to join Staff Sergeant MacLeod.

"Y'know, John, there are 'way too many Sergeants around here. We're just going to have to call you John for short and Staff

Sergeant when we have to be formal.

"Works for me."

"Other thing I've noticed... you have been attracting good looking young ladies to your detachment like honey draws bears. I'm glad I don't have daughters or you and I would have to have words. And Marion was telling us a bit about Peggy Dawson – we had no idea of her deep relationship to this community and to many of our friends. She was a real find."

"Super Dave was one of the best things to happen around here. Most superintendents take a lot of lunches to make sure their job is forever easy to do, as if the position is some kind of a reward for service excellence and a final posting before retirement for all those cops who will never become Commissioner. Or in some cases its a reward for having friends in high places. But not Dave. He is always looking for solutions to challenges and ways to keep his personnel alive and make them more effective. Peggy is a great example: he knows the writing is on the wall for changes to Indian Country here, changes that can make things very difficult for everybody, or changes that really could make our world a better place. So he went out looking for the right people, and guess what: he came across Peggy, an Indigenous female with an impeccable record in the RCMP, lots of personal drive and big-time star power – and as far as we could tell deliberately kept on a back shelf in Thunder Bay of all places, after she moved from the RCMP because she wanted to serve her home. And I'm the lucky guy who gets to work with her."

"Wow. I am impressed, at many levels. And... is it... Erin? The other girl?"

"Yup, lively, eager, sweet-natured and... green. Very green. Really green: she's a new hire, but I think she'll be a good fit."

Inside the wheelhouse, Anderson was enjoying himself with the ladies, neither of whom knew much about boats. Peggy, of course, had grown up near Awan Lake and had fished with her brothers on the Spirit River, but only from little rowboats and canoes. She had taken the usual basic boat stuff during RCMP training in Saskatchewan, and had spent the next four years or so basically doing non-stop highway patrol at various rural detachments on the prairies. And that's where she had to wear her red serge uniform at community events that weren't hers and where she was in demand only because she was female, good looking, Indigenous, and the lowest member in the pecking order.

Erin, on the other hand, had been born and raised in Sarnia and went waterskiing with her cousin once. But she was keen to learn.

Some forty minutes after leaving the village, it was dark. Marjorie had taken back the helm position and knocked the throttle back to about half, alternately watching the radar screen, GPS and forward through the windshield onto the lake ahead. Anderson and MacLeod were having a smoke on the afterdeck when Marjorie eased back the throttle, flipped off the autohelm and called out, "Gentlemen, we have reached that mark Frank set due east of McKinley Island. Where next?"

"According to the GPS chart, which is good enough for the moment, we are just over two miles away from the island." Anderson came into the wheelhouse, found the eastern tip of McKinley Island and punched in a waypoint directly south of there about a quarter mile. "Let's go there, at half throttle again," he said to Marjorie as he set the Autohelm and kissed her neck.

"So, we have about twenty minutes to go, if your speed is four knots?"

"Well, listen to you go, MacLeod. Knots already. Yes, pretty close. You figure it's time to roll out the cannons?"

"Might as well." Turning to his staff, he called for the carbines and ammunition to be brought back from the focsle (he called it the small cabin up front). They would check the guns, load them and line them up behind the forward bulkhead on the starboard side. "I want to leave the port side window easily accessible, so we'll keep our gear away from there. Also, this would be the right time to let you know that Frank is an official member of the Auxiliary with the rank of Sergeant and he has full weapons clearance. I know that's unusual for the Auxiliary, but then Frank is unusual."

He waited for the giggles to die down (mostly from Marjorie) and finished, "While that is true, the other reason is his dozen years with the Canadian Coast Guard, mostly as a deck officer with weapons training, and a letter on file from our Superintendent."

"McKinley Island coming on radar. Range seems to be about a mile northwest."

"Cool. John, do you want to keep on with lights blazing, or go dark?"

"How about we keep on with lights blazing until it's obvious they have seen us, and then go dark?"

"That'll be fun. We'll keep going straight for awhile, then come around the island clockwise. I'll take throttle back to one quarter for now."

The sonar indicated they had about 75 feet of water under the boat. They eased closer until they were perhaps 200 yards off the south side of the island when they could finally see what looked like porch and window lights through the trees. There was no indication they had been noticed. Four minutes later the sonar alarm started to screech and Anderson quickly acknowledged the alarm, throttled back to idle, and turned the boat to port. When the alarm had first sounded the screen showed 20 feet of water, which slowly became 16 feet, then 12, and Anderson was just about to go into reverse to get out of there when the reading went to 18, then 22, then 30. He took the speed back up to quarter throttle and turned the boat back to a westerly course, then northwest until again they could see lights off to starboard. These lights were much brighter... *that must be the boathouse lights in the bay*, Anderson thought. He had been there just over a week before and knew there was lots of water deep into the bay by the dock. He spun the wheel to starboard and aimed the boat straight for the boathouse light.

"You really want to poke that bear, don't you Frank."

"Might as well. If they don't know we came to visit, they won't be able to invite us back."

"Okay Sergeant Dawson. The records tell me you're our best shot, including me, so sling one of those carbines and get set to shoot out the lights – the high-up ones – if we are challenged. Frank, you will turn to port if we are challenged, I imagine? Dawson, take your position behind the wheelhouse wall, starboard side. Kneel, preparing to shoot as the boat swings. Wait for my order. Constable Watters, take your weapon to the port side. Keep your safety on until my order. Marjorie, please take the ship's binoculars – I've got mine here – and between us we'll watch for action on those docks. We'll watch from behind the wheelhouse, over the top."

"As soon as we start to turn to port," said Anderson, "I will douse all the lights onboard. I will also be pushing the throttle up to full speed immediately we are in that turn... this outfit isn't a race car, but keep your feet under you because she will react to the throttle and the turn. Is everyone in position?"

MacLeod looked around, and confirmed: "Yes everyone's set."

"Good. I'm going up to just under half throttle. I want that turn to be quick. Any sign of life in there yet?"

The Beaver had just come up to speed when they hear voices yelling on the dock. Suddenly the upper lights on the boathouse went out, and the yelling got louder. "I'm getting outta here." yelled Frank, switching off the master navigation and house light switches and jamming the throttle forward as he started his turn.

In thirty seconds he had completed a one-hundred-eighty degree turn and they were headed out of the bay at something like full speed. They could no longer hear the yelling over the sound of their own engine.

"Shots fired." It was Dawson. "And I saw the muzzle blast."

"Send back two shots, at the light of your choice."

It took her four seconds to return fire, two shots, one second apart. The third dock light from the left winked out. There was silence for almost ten seconds, except for the grinding roar of the diesel.

"Well, that's pretty cool." It was Constable Watters.

"Indeed it was, Sergeant. Well done. Well done everyone. Safeties on. We'll keep a close watch behind us... they may try to follow us with something, but I sort of doubt it."

"Shall I reload, sir?"

"Sure, good idea. As long as we are standing by we might as well be fully loaded."

"I'm pouring coffee," said Marjorie. "Who's in?... everyone?

... cool, but you're all getting it black until we get some lights around here."

"John, grab your binoculars, quick. Look back in the bay... looks like someone has a boat moving."

They all strained to see behind them in the dark. Suddenly, "What the... some clown has taken a boat off the dock, cranked the throttle and started to chase us... crap."

"What? What's going on?"

"What... geez... that's a riot. Frank, I'd never believe what happened if I hadn't seen it... oh, geez, now there are flames too. Some idiot jumped into one of their boats, hit the throttle forward, apparently lost control and drove the damn thing right into the rocks across the bay. Now there's nothing left but a medium-sized fireball."

"Never mix bikers with boats. It never ends well." That was Anderson.

"Was that a Coast Guard rule?"

"Yup."

• • • •

Spirit River, ON, 2315: *The Beaver* had returned to her dock by just after 1030. Marjorie had used the boat's GPS and the autohelm to retrace their course, taking them two miles east and then north to the village, running through the night with a lookout on the cabin top and a careful watch on the radar. They relaxed somewhat after they headed north a mile or so and turned on the navigation lights. They were not being followed.

Their discussions on the homeward trip were focused on what they might have accomplished and what might come next. Anderson started the discussion by saying, "I kind of feel like we're a bunch of dogs that went out and chased a car – and caught it. Now we're not too sure why we chased the car in the first place and worse yet, now that we've caught it we don't know what to do with it."

"Well, we wanted to let those people know that we understand they are up to something," said MacLeod, "and we wanted to force – or at least trick – them into making mistakes."

"Mission accomplished, I guess. I mean, if destroying a stolen motorboat on the rocks and probably killing the driver is a mistake, that worked out in our favour just fine."

"I think we had kinda hoped the results wouldn't be so dramatic. Like, that's why I asked sharp-shooter Dawson to hit the light-bulbs, not the dimwits. That truly is mission accomplished, thanks to her skill."

"Indeed. And don't forget that they fired first in any case. Whatever, let's just hope they don't cancel their plans. As long as they go ahead, they are almost certain to foul up badly enough that we can walk in and put bad people in jail. At the moment, this feels kind of like last month's Robertson Mines disaster in slow motion: one mistake leads to another leads to..."

SEPTEMBER 10

Washington, D.C. 0745: Roger Larsen slept in this Sunday morning, but already had been up for an hour doing his daily 10k on the treadmill in his home office overlooking the George Washington Memorial Parkway, a marina, and across the Potomac River. He planned to take his teenaged daughter out for a sail this afternoon but it would be a short one because he had to prepare for a flight to Canada, where he would be hosting a media release on behalf of the company that made it possible for the lifestyle he shared with his wife and two daughters.

He had cooled down to a brisk walk when his cellphone started ringing. "Who the hell at this time on a Sunday morning..." and he stabbed the telephone icon: "Larsen here, who's calling? Raimy?... oh yeah, Raimy Smith up in Canada. I'll be seeing you tomorrow morning, what's up? Got problems?"

He paused and listened, shutting off the treadmill and setting a pod of medium roast in the Keurig at the small table by his desk: "Why in the hell do they have a bunch of idiot bikers hired for security at an event that doesn't even really need security? Dr. Marcusson? Yeah, I know him a little. How come he's involved... after all he's just an old academic dreamer who missed his chance to change the world decades ago. He brought in these bikers to train VIPs how to do what? Ah, crap. Hold on..."

"Sorry sweetie, I was getting carried away on this call... it's a guy up in Canada. I'll be done in a few minutes and we'll have breakfast."

Larsen kissed his sleepy-looking wife on the cheek and went back to the phone as she shuffled off to the kitchen. "Sorry,

Raimy. You say they fired shots at someone in a boat and then ran their own boat into a rock and killed a guy...? Well, something like that?... Close enough I guess. Bottom line is that those bikers need to be removed from there immediately and be made to understand they are never coming back. Sink any bodies and that wrecked boat to the bottom of the lake – our geologists say the lake is very deep, but stay closer to the east side. Use lots of rocks, okay? And last thing, sit Marcusson down and explain that he's lucky the bikers are gone because otherwise he'd be in big trouble. Also tell him that you will be responsible for all security, you have reinforcements on the way, and that your bosses from RGI in Washington have been fully informed about what has just happened and are not at all pleased, okay?"

"Okay, keep me informed if there are changes. Thanks."

• • • •

After breakfast, Roger Larsen went back to his little office and closed the door. As he sat down and looked out onto the river, he reflected how fortunate he was to be able to do most of his work from home. He loathed office politics and in any case he had nothing to gain by playing that game. And he travelled a lot, so apart from a few business luncheons he was free to work from wherever he wanted – to do whatever he thought was necessary – to make the world's second-largest mining company even bigger than it already was. But this call was to Reverend Andrew Jackson in Montpelier, Vermont and had absolutely nothing to do with Robertson Mines International.

"Andy? It's Roger Larsen down in Washington. I'm doing fine... my favourite time of year down here, not too hot and muggy. Yeah, well, you can keep your winters. No wonder you're so interested in Canada... Not."

"Actually, this is about Canada. As you know, RGI has mines up there – and a new one – actually an expansion – is about to be announced Monday. What do you know about Awan Lake? Yes, that's the one. McKinney Island is where we're doing the media conference, which will be an international affair and I was sort of out of the loop on the arrangements. Now I understand they are having a New World Mission meeting there at roughly the same time... is that correct? Tuesday and Wednesday? Will you be attending? Cool. I know you don't have much use for Canada, but they too need some preaching of the Gospel according to Q. Yeah, they're a bunch of liberals but they'll have to join us some-day and it sounds like you've made some headway with some of the right-wing politicians...who is your contact there? The Min-ister of Natural Resources? Well, aim high, I guess... any fool can hit the ground. What do you know about a guy named Marcus-son?"

Larsen sat back with a grin as he listened to the Reverend say some very un-preacher-like things about Frederik Marcusson. "Yeah, Andy, I get it. I haven't talked to him myself but it seems like being a pain in the ass is standard practice for him. He was trying to make out like he was some kind of big cheese up there and hired a bunch of very miscellaneous bikers as his private army. They were idiots and I think they killed one of their own in a boating accident last night..."

"Absolutely, I will. I am having his bikers removed this morn-ing – permanently if necessary, and I've asked our guys to keep an eye on Marcusson, which I thought you should know. Tues-day? No, I expect to be out of there by late afternoon Monday. Well, I'll try... just thought you should be in the loop. Yep, you take care too."

Larsen clicked off the phone and shook his head: *I don't know about those guys. I like the politics but I sure have no faith in their collective IQ. Small wonder they resent "the elite".*

• • • •

Spirit River, ON, 1015: By the time Anderson and Marjorie had tied down and locked the boat, said goodbye to the police and walked home they were tired, cold and hungry. They fixed the hungry with scrambled eggs on toast and the tired and cold by crawling into bed, wrapping around each other like half an octopus convention, and falling asleep until 0915 Sunday morning. They were on their third cup of coffee when there was a tap on the door. It was Tony Barker.

"Hey. Good morning Tony. Come on in. Late night, so we're still sitting around drinking coffee. I'll pour you one."

"Yes please. Had a long call from Karlsen this morning so I already heard about your late night."

"Mmm. I bet that was an interesting call. He has some really interesting guests out there.

"One fewer this morning, apparently. One of Marcusson's bikers was killed when he ran a motorboat into a rock. I don't suppose you had anything to do with that?"

"Not really. Can't fix stupid and the rock has likely been there since the last ice age."

"Christopher is getting very nervous. I guess the bosses at RGI had sent up their own security detail – two guys – to make sure everything was in place for the event they're planning for Monday. He said they had seemed like reasonable guys at first but they have effectively taken over the island and let it be known that they are everything security. Judging from their accents they are both Americans, almost certainly ex-military, and are likely capable of being dangerous: already this morning they sent the bikers off the island and then they had a long and noisy conversation with Marcusson, who is now all upset and making a bunch of phone calls."

"I wonder which boat it was that got wrecked."

"Chris said it was an expensive looking water ski boat with an inboard engine that the security guys brought a couple of days ago. They were cleaning up the mess this morning and it's gone."

"Well, that at least settles the choices George Hanson has to make about whether to get a new boat or not. So Tony, what's this event they have planned for Monday? I'm assuming it has something to do with the proposed mine expansion."

"Exactly. We may already know more about the subject matter details than Chris – about this coltan stuff and so on. I gather the media and the rest of the VIPs are coming by helicopter on Monday morning. The whole thing is very controlled and hush-hush. However, he also said the Minister of Natural Resources was already there, along with his own special guests which include his parliamentary assistant and the deputy minister – the one who was appointed two weeks ago to replace the late Leonard Hamilton-Dubois."

"About now it would be sort of handy to have a Member of Parliament around here to replace the late Garnet Cameron. I guess now that will have to wait for a by-election."

"They won't bother with that. It's close enough to a general election so they don't need to fill the seat until then. Main reason I came by this morning, though, was to talk about Dr. Dave Bradshaw. It seems he's not as on the up and up as we have assumed he is, or at least let's say he has a hidden agenda: Marcusson is not the only person around here who is pushing the New World Mission thing... Bradshaw's into it too. Fred – Marcusson – is there for the political leadership part of it, while Dave is into crafting environment agendas, and that is why he is getting embroiled with UNESCO. They both seem to be pushing a "United-Nations-in-a-Hurry" agenda, which explains why the New World Mission they talk about reflects the New World Order of old – and the Illuminati of much older."

Marjorie had been listening intently: "They seem like unlikely friends."

"I know what you mean. However, I think that loyalty to the cause transcends personal style – the New World movement has to have a big tent to ensure there is room for all the egos, and that probably explains why it seems so secretive."

"Do they have a transparent organizational structure," asked Anderson, "or do they work in cells like many political groups – terrorist, criminal and otherwise – do?"

"I can only guess there must be cells – certainly at the working level. I don't think either Marcusson or Bradshaw are very high up the leadership ladder. I sense both of them are a bit squirrely to be very high up."

Marjorie giggled: "I would have thought being squirrely would be an asset to moving up the laddership."

"Frank, is she always like that?"

"Yes, always. Impossible, isn't she."

"On that note, let me buy you two Sunday brunch at the Zoo."

"That sounds great, Tony, thank-you. And, I think we will need to have another meeting with Sergeant John today, planning for tomorrow morning."

"There's more about Bradshaw, too, and John will want to know this: He let slip in our conversation last night that he has plans to be at the lake – and at McKenna Island specifically – for that media event tomorrow morning. It seems like there is a New World Mission thing going on in parallel with the Robertson event, and maybe some cross-over of personnel. And, Bradshaw was expecting he would have to house some of Marcusson's people at his island tonight... some sort of training exercise and Marcusson needed the space to house them."

"That would likely be the bikers who got kicked off McKinley Island last night. They took their three rented fishing boats and went somewhere, and Marcusson himself may have the McKinley Island launch. In any case, it certainly appears Marcusson is still in charge of the bikers. Definitely John needs to know all this... I'll call him now and he can meet us at the Zoo as soon as he's free."

Less than five minutes later, the three of them had just gotten out of Marjorie's Jeep in front of the restaurant when they noticed two shiny black Lincoln Expeditions turning off the highway and also pulling in at the restaurant. One man got out of the front passenger doors on each of the SUVs and the two men talked together for a moment before walking across to the main door of the Zoo. By now Marjorie and Tony were settling in at a table with a full view of the door and the street outside, but Anderson hung back.

"Forgot my smokes...I'll be right back," he called across from the door.

"He didn't... I've got them in my purse."

"I expect he knows that. Interesting looking couple of guys

from those trucks."

"I imagine Frank saw two big guys, shaved bald and wearing jeans and black leather vests and figured he should check out their SUVs and maybe the other passengers – I see another three or four of the guys are out of the vehicles having a smoke. Frank always worries about his village."

The two men in the restaurant ordered a dozen cans of Pepsi and a dozen donuts from Sam, paid the bill in cash, left Sam a Toonie for a tip and left. Anderson was just coming in the door as they left, and one of them held the door. "Thanks, man," he said, and rejoined Tony and Marjorie at the table.

"I think there's maybe eleven or twelve of them. All guys, kinda like those two who did the shopping. Those Lincolns are rental units – Enterprise, I think – couldn't see where from. I just wonder where they are headed..."

"Down Main Street, it seems. Let's hope not down the docks... we don't have very good luck this week with big military-looking men at our house."

"Not military types... these guys are bikers with haircuts. The others were more shaggy, so these guys may be the brains of the outfit, if such a thing is possible. You folks order... I'm driving down to the docks to see what's up."

"Be really careful, Frank."

"Don't worry Tony. The odds are not in my favour – brains or not – so I aim to stay pretty much out of sight."

• • • •

Anderson returned from his survey of the house, workshop and docks about fifteen minutes later, to find that another big black SUV had parked outside, Different brand, of course, and a worried-looking John MacLeod was standing by the table inside: "Glad you're back... I was going to chase you down but these two just said I should call you before I went. What did you discover?"

"I'm pretty sure those guys are reinforcements for Marcusson – and now Bradshaw too. When I got down there, there were three outboard fishing boats nosed up on the beach, with three guys standing having a smoke and waiting for the Lincoln gang to get parked off the road, unload and carry their duffles down to the shore and load them on the boats. It didn't take them long – in all, fourteen guys are now on their way southwest to the islands. Nothing to be gained by chasing them down... they haven't done anything wrong – yet. They will be headed out to join their buddies at Bradshaw's island."

"So tomorrow's the big day for this media announcement, and it wasn't until half an hour ago that we heard anything official about it."

"When you say *we* I assume you mean the OPS?"

"Yup. And we had to hear it from the RCMP, although even then I only found out because I have an unofficial open line with Marianna – RCMP Marianna."

"I wonder why all the secrecy. After all, we out here know there's weird stuff going down but to everyone else it's just another boring media announcement with politicians, wine and cheese – and quiche tarts because it's morning."

"Well, I don't think the minister of natural resources gets a weekend security detail, so unless there's some other reason we probably wouldn't worry out here. In the cities I expect things are different. Have you folks heard of a *Larsen* – spelled the Swedish way with an 'e' instead of an 'o'?"

Anderson glanced at his companions. "Nope, not us rabbits.

Why?"

"According to the very brief briefing note we got from Toronto, the name of the guy who issued the media invitation was Roger Larsen, who is apparently the chief development officer at Robertson Group International in Washington."

"I guess we could give Charlie Morrell a call. I expect he knows. He might be able to tell us what time tomorrow this thing is supposed to happen..."

"Oh, I know that," said MacLeod, "sorry, thought you knew already." He fished a piece of paper out of the breast pocket of his khaki shirt: "This letter issued by RGI is actually more a media release than a media invitation, but it does indicate that the event was held at 11:00 and the announcement was at 11:30. It also indicates that the Canadian Minister of Natural Resources and the Deputy Minister are both quoted, and that Larsen was joined by Charlie Morrell, Manager of Operations at Robertson Mines at Awan Lake and by Professor Frederik Marcusson, President of the Canadian Chapter of the New World Mission."

"Wow," said Tony. "I find it unbelievable that Marcusson has been able to con his way to such high prominence, not just in that New World stuff but also with our government and a massive international mining corporation. His academic credibility is almost non-existent and he seems to have the charisma of a slug."

Anderson grinned at Tony over the top of a forkful of waffle and maple syrup: "You obviously haven't met some of the slugs I have known, Tony. John, when do you think we should get to the island tomorrow? I know we were able to rattle their cage yesterday by surprising them, but my sense is that tomorrow we should take the highroad, getting there and holding position in plain view, flags flying, perhaps a quarter-mile off."

"Absolutely agree, Frank. I will have the document onboard (and a copy at the office) that authorizes *The Beaver* to be in OPS command so we don't get media blow-back. That chopper you were on the other day will begin to circle the island from a long way off, and Marianna has arranged for a really fast RHIB to launch here early in the morning, with two armoured officers on-board and instructions to defer to my command when deployed on scene."

"That'll help herd those bikers around if necessary. How many officers do you want onboard *The Beaver*?"

"Myself plus three. Peggy – Sergeant Dawson – again, plus Andy and Marie."

"What time tomorrow morning do you think we ought to arrive off McKinley Island?"

"Let's be there by 1000 hours. That'll mean boarding and getting underway no later than 0900?"

"Sounds about right. We have some work to do to get ready... check fluids, top-up fuel, that kind of stuff."

"You have one flag halyard for the maple leaf, which you usu-ally fly from the jackstaff at the stern. Do you have a place on the mast for an Ontario flag?"

"How about we put the provincial flag on the jackstaff and put the maple leaf on the masthead? I have a halyard for that."

"Good. That'll work fine. Might as well leave the dock to-morrow flying them both – I expect the RHIB will tag along with us."

"I hope they have a flag – actually I have a spare maple leaf for them in case. Regardless of what may be right and what may be wrong with all that's going on out there, our federal minister and his staff need to know the government he is supposed to be working for is watching over him, and the same goes for the American personnel and company reps. This is Canada, and Canadians are watching."

"That's nicely put," said Tony. "Thank-you."

MacLeod had stood up to leave but he turned back to the table: "One more thing, folks..."

"Are you having a Columbo moment, Sergeant?" asked Marjorie.

"Ha ha, Ms. Marjorie. No I am not. What I started to say was that Constable Watters – Erin, whom you will remember from last night – will be stationed here at the village in her marked cruiser, all day tomorrow watching the docks, the streets, and the immediate highway until we get back to the dock. She will have a uniformed auxiliary ride-along to keep her company – Adumbi Jakandi."

"We'll make sure to tell Arnold and Marion. Thanks for thinking of that, and I am absolutely amazed at Adumbi. Good for him... he sure seems to like our part of the world."

"Ask him about that during a snowstorm in January."

• • • •

McKinley Island, ON: 2322: Sunday had been a rather intense and tiring day of small workshops and one-on-one meetings, made especially exhausting after the excitement on Saturday night which unnerved all the guests of the New World Mission at McKinley Island. Dale – more officially referred to as The Honourable Dale Adams, Canada's Minister of Natural Resources – was a long way from home, having been elected a year ago from his Calgary constituency for a second term, and serving in his first Cabinet appointment which was a very senior portfolio at that. He was personable and intelligent, but he was still suffering from the ego-bruising reality of being from western Canada in a senior cabinet post usually reserved for members from Ontario or Quebec. His cabinet colleagues were just fine, of course, but the senior bureaucrats were somewhere between dismissive and downright cruel. His deputy minister, the late Leonard Hamilton-DuBois, had done his best to help bridge the gaps, but since he had been found murdered in his sailing yacht on Awan Lake a month ago, Dale was now faced with making some difficult choices with little support. In fact, his Assistant Deputy Minister, who would be joining him tomorrow morning for the RGI announcement, was very busy trying to line himself up for his late boss's position. Dale was looking for someone better, someone more capable of leadership and less "squishy" as he had shared with his wife during one of their long telephone calls.

He missed his wife, who always listened encouragingly to his rambling descriptions of life in Ottawa, but he often doubted that she was being any more than simply polite. She was left with two teenaged girls at home, and her life was always full enough of complications without trying to share his.

Monday's announcement, too, was fraught. The proponents, Robertson Group International, had been suffering some bad press recently, related largely but not exclusively to the massive fire which destroyed the Awan Lake facility. There had also been several homicides associated with the corporation, including the late deputy minister and the late member of parliament for the Awan Lake region who had also been found dead under suspicious circumstances. However, the announcement of the copper mine's expansion will certainly brighten the day for the region's workforce, devastated by the fire last month, and will propel his own portfolio forward. It was, of course, his job, with the support of the Prime Minister, to turn Monday's announcement into a huge boost for the government at national and international levels, both.

Dale was bright enough to realize that all this had been accomplished with no work at all on his part. He was the beneficiary of one courtesy telephone call from Roger Larsen at RGI in Washington, and the willingness on the part of the Prime Minister and his political advisors to quash some environmental regulations and invest several hundred million dollars in infrastructure. Born and raised as he had been in the rough-and-tumble of the oil and gas industry in Alberta, Dale was used to the politics of corporate investment and the art of regulatory manipulation, but still, part of him longed to experience some sort of moral growth instead of the perpetual feeling of unease that accompanies endless ethical lapses.

"Why so glum?" came the gentle voice of Giselle Matthews, a foot-soldier for the development office of the Robertson Group who had leaned over the back of the sofa where he had been sitting alone with his laptop.

"Does it show that much?" Dale said as he looked up over his shoulder.

"Well, a little... you okay?

"I am, really. Just going through my short address for tomorrow."

"If I get us a drink, would you like me to read it?"

"Sure. There's still wine in that decanter over there on the sideboard. I'll get the wine while you read."

"Deal."

She came around the end of the sofa and sat down, taking the laptop from him as he stood up. "I hope it's not too long... tell me the truth." he said before going down the short hall to the men's toilet. When he returned to the common room, he picked two large wineglasses from the sideboard shelf along with the decanter before returning to the sofa where Giselle was now sitting cross-legged while she read. He hadn't had a chance to really look at her before, but now he was quite taken with the long brown hair which flowed gently over her shoulders. It also seemed to him that she had loosened a couple of buttons on her blouse while he had been out of the room. *Surely not. I know she's sending off some interesting vibes but it's getting late and that does seem a bit fast.*

He poured two glasses of wine and handed her one. She looked up and smiled as she took the glass, and noticed his glance at the way her blouse opened a tiny bit more as her arm reached for the glass. She went back to reading but with a little smile on her lips. In a couple of minutes she closed the laptop, leaned across and replaced it on the coffee table, and said, "It's good. Not too long, feels genuine. One small spelling mistake in the first paragraph. Would you be angry if I undid the third button?"

"I thought I had noticed the first two. Unbuttoning the third – and even the fourth – would be very pleasant from where I am sitting."

So she did, and he was able to see that her left breast did not need a bra to stand out the way it did. She had been holding her wineglass in her left hand, so she brought her right hand across and into the almost- open blouse, cupping her left breast gently and moving it into full view. She took a swallow of wine and teased her nipple with her thumb, looking up at him invitingly. He paused for a moment, then set his glass on the table and leaned down to catch her nipple momentarily between his lips and tongue before sitting back up: "It's late, but if we are going to continue this we should do so in a more private space – your place or mine?"

"Mine is just down the hall. Bring your laptop... you don't want it lying around out here with your speech in it."

SEPTEMBER 11

THE AWAN LAKE EXPERIMENT

Spirit River, ON, 0700: Last night's occasional but cold rain had been vanquished by a light westerly breeze and the promise of better temperatures. Staff Sergeant MacLeod had returned to Maple Falls in the early afternoon, and Anderson and Marjorie dropped Tony back at his boat at the dock so he could return to the small island he shared with his wife Jean. She was going to be particularly glad to hear from him because he had left early in the morning, taking the only functioning cellphone between them since hers crashed last week.

Marjorie and Anderson had driven back up from the docks without stopping at their home, wanting to spend a little time updating Arnold and Marion. As soon as they arrived at the Jamieson residence they could see they were not the only people visiting. Willy Antoine, who lived alone four or five miles up the Spirit River from where it emptied into Awan Lake, had come for a visit with his son Fred and daughter-in-law Georgina. Anderson had only just met Willy earlier this summer and had shared some tragic moments and acres of mutual respect and affection with the charismatic Indigenous elder. And in that family, no visit to the village would be complete without spending a few hours with Marion – a family aunt – and Arnold Jamieson. There was strong coffee, Southern Comfort and smokes to be shared, along with the latest of Marion's dessert creations from the oven.

Willy was happy to hear glowing praise of his oldest granddaughter Peggy, who had just joined the Maple Falls OPS detachment after years out west, and he was worried sick about his youngest granddaughter Anita, on a high-risk fact-finding mission in Paris. He had not heard that Marion and Arnold, along with Anderson and Marjorie, had formally taken on the re-building of the burned-out marina, and he was hesitant about telling them that every six or eight years he completely re-finished his elegant antique cedar-strip guide boat with its make-and-break one-cylinder engine and the gleaming varnish overcoat. But Fred, who was not always wise but always kind and knew his neighbours, took charge.

"Did you folks know that once every few years Dad would strip and re-finish that old boat in one of the boat houses at the marina? He would stay with us in the attic – we have a spare bedroom but he always chose the attic – until he had the job finished. And it seems to me that this is the year he would do that, isn't that right, Dad?"

"Well, yes but I can't do that this year... you kids have 'way too much going on to worry about that."

"Oh yes we can, can't we Arnold? That boat is long and narrow and I can fit it in the shop and still have room for the other boats we're working on. Anyway, as I recall your telling me, that boat was born there, right Willy?"

"Yes, she was, Frank. Yes she was, in 1932. When I bought her at an auction in Portland in 1973 she was pretty beat up, so I brought her back here and spent a winter with the old man who used to own your place and we fixed her like new, so she was kind of re-born. I've spent a month or two on her every seven or eight years since. Are you sure there's room in there, Frank?"

"Sure I'm sure, Willy. Marjorie and I will be on the coast for Christmas and maybe a few weeks more, and anyway we should be done with servicing all those cottagers' boats by then, don't you think Arnold?"

"I sincerely hope so," Arnold replied. "We'll need to begin with some dock construction by then, so we should be out of the way."

Anderson and Marjorie had spent an hour or so at the Jamieson's house before returning to their home and the docks, where they made sure the workboat was equipped and ready to go in the morning before heading in to the Spirit River Inn for an early supper. Florence saw them through the window when they parked Anderson's battered quarter-ton and already had two draft beer on their favourite table. After two beers each, two orders of fish and chips, and a nice visit updating Florence about the goings-on at McKinley Island, they had headed back home for an early night.

This morning, it had dawned chilly but clear with a light breeze blowing offshore from the northwest. The house was cool, but Anderson skipped lighting the stove and turned up the electric baseboard heaters when they got out of bed. They both showered quickly: "You're starting to shower like a sailor, Marj," he told her when she was in and out in less that three minutes.

"I'll do the lingering shower thing when all this is done. Then you can join me with a bar of soap and a loofah."

Anderson had started breakfast, opting this morning for instant rolled oats and a gallon or two of maple syrup. "It could be a long day out there."

"Yes, and this is a great way to get ready. Our mum used to do this every morning we had school. No instant back then: she used to start it in a double boiler the night before and finish in the morning. No *instant oats* in those days, and no maple syrup either."

"No maple syrup... where did you live, anyway?"

"Toronto. Maple syrup was a Quebec thing and 'way too decadent for Toronto Brits."

"I'm definitely into decadence. Bring on the syrup."

"Yeah, me too.

• • • •

GOEA, ON, 0920: Roger Larsen had arrived at the Gatineau–Ottawa Executive Airport northeast of the Capital on an RGI-owned Bombardier Challenger 350 which had left Washington, DC at 0730. The sleek Quebec-made jet was full: Larsen, along with his slim and well-coiffed executive assistant and eight representatives of the top USA television and print media outlets, had all cleared Canadian Customs and Immigration before boarding. Their early start to the day had been rewarded with a champagne and orange juice breakfast during the hour-long flight to Canada's capital city.

After the Challenger landed at GOEA it taxied back in from the runway to a parking area in front of the small terminal building, where two Bell 525 choppers stood waiting. Larsen went to the still-closed door of the jet, turned and welcomed the passengers to Canada and the next leg of their journey to Awan Lake: "We will be meeting some RGI personnel from Toronto as well as a couple of members of parliament and four Canadian media representatives from CBC, CTV, Global and Canadian Press. Together we will board those two choppers sitting beside us for the last leg of our travels this morning. My assistant Madison, whom I am sure you have all met during the first leg of our trip this morning, has already made passenger lists for the helicopters so we can file those lists before take-off. So, don't run away when you see her coming in your direction."

"I might indeed run away, but I'd be running very damn slowly." quipped an older man who had been seated up front."

"You print-media guys can get away with comments like that," said a fresh-faced young man who had been fussing with his TV camera for much of the flight. "If I said something like that I'd be all over social media and out of a job by morning."

Madison was putting in double duty. Now she became a steward: she unlatched the Challenger's door, dropped and secured the steps, and invited the passengers to disembark. As they passed her at the bottom of the steps, each was directed to one or other of the two helicopters.

Both 525s would be loaded short of capacity by one or two passengers, and nobody noticed that Madison had changed the list to place herself on the flight with the gently wisecracking journalist.

• • • •

Awan Lake, ON:1040: By now, *The Beaver* was rolling gently in the light chop on Awan Lake, well past the main cluster of islands with their picturesque cottages and boathouses. The workboat and her crew were standing off about three miles to the east of McKinley Island, barely making headway, keeping a close radio watch on the new iCom A210 that Anderson had installed a week ago, as well as watching the radar screen set on a range of about five miles and taking turns on the binoculars. The team on board – Marjorie at the wheel, Anderson, Staff Sergeant MacLeod and three of his OPS staff – had checked their weapons and strapped on body armour and lifejackets.

It was a little later in the morning than they had planned, but until now there had been no sign that anyone had arrived at the island. At 1042, however, the A210 started squawking as two heavy helicopters cleared the west shore of the lake and made a bee-line for McKinley Island. There was a brief verbal exchange over the radio to establish a *follow me down* protocol for landing and the radio went silent.

"Take her in, Marj," said Anderson. "Full speed." The little ship put her nose up a little and swung to starboard as she picked up speed, her 300-horsepower Volvo D4 blowing a bit of smoke saved up from hours and hours of operating at slower, more civilized, speeds.

Of course, speed is a relative thing when it comes to boats. The fourteen knots that *The Beaver* could accomplish on a good day was standing still compared to the boat approaching the same island from the northeast. "Holy crap, look at that guy go." said Sergeant Peggy Crowley, pointing off to starboard.

Anderson swung his binoculars up and followed the direction she indicated. "Geez, ya don't see many of those up here. It's one of those go-fast cigarette boats. They go like hell... one hundred clicks is nothing for them."

"Are those the things they use around Florida to smuggle stuff – nasty stuff like drugs, guns and girls?"

"Those are the ones, John. I don't know what the hell you'd use one here for, except to show off. He can go around this lake in twenty-five minutes then roll over and die from boredom on his way home, wherever that is."

"It's pretty big," said Peggy.

"Yup – around fifty feet long. Basically a long pointy thing with, like, six or seven three-hundred horse outboards on the back."

"Seems like there are a lot of heads sticking up... maybe six or eight people onboard, maybe more?"

"Yeah, and I don't think there is any doubt that they mean

trouble. I think they've just seen the choppers, and maybe us, and they've turned west, away from us and slowed 'way down. I bet they lay low and wait for the choppers to land."

"Do you suppose that's Marcusson's bunch??

"Well, who else really? Came from the direction of Bradshaw's island so I bet there's a small herd of bikers on board."

"Frank?" It was Marjorie calling from the wheel.

Anderson let his field glasses drop onto the neck strap and stepped quickly into the wheelhouse. "What's up? Everything okay?"

"Yes, everything's fine. But I'm just thinking..."

"Isn't that a mite dangerous?"

"Smartass. Y'know, I really don't think that Marcusson and his biker crew had the know-how to find, transport and operate a boat like that, getting it all done in less than 24 hours. I'm much more inclined to think that's something those American so-called security contractors could do."

"Good point. And yeah, they likely have the budget – from RGI. That's a million dollar boat that takes a lot of skill to handle, so that silly bunch from Saturday night would almost certainly have smashed it on the rocks by now."

MacLeod had joined them in the wheelhouse: "Maybe take some of the pressure off, Marjorie... half throttle or so? We don't really want to jump into their laps. So, do you two think maybe the baby bikers have yet to come? If you're right, then we may have a really bizarre kind of gang war shaping up here... hold on, Maple Falls is trying to reach me."

By this time the helicopters were landing, one at a time, on a cleared landing pad at the west end of the island. The cigarette boat now moved quickly around the west end and headed in to land in the bay by the boathouse.

The Beaver was now less than a quarter-mile offshore. Marjorie had her stopped and was holding position as best as she could in the freshening wind. MacLeod clicked off his satphone and joined her and Anderson in the wheelhouse: "First, Frank would you give Richard at the Lockmaster's restaurant a call. He got a message to me through our office but I guess he wants to speak only to you."

MacLeod found a number on the satphone, pushed the button and handed it to Anderson before turning back to talk with Marjorie: "Have you heard from that RCMP boat yet?"

"Maybe twenty minutes ago. They had launched at the village and were heading our way, more or less. Said they'd radio when they got closer."

"Those older RCMP RHIB's are horrible things to radio from unless you're wearing full headgear... you're basically straddling an engine and drive train that's been bolted to an old inner-tube. Can't hear a thing."

"So what's a "rib" or whatever you call it?"

"MacLeod chuckled: "Ah, it's pronounced "rib" but it's spelled "r-h-i-b", which stands for "rigid hull inflatable boat". And they're called that because there is a hard fibreglass bottom and short sides under the inner-tube. They're tough and pretty fast... great police boats unless you plan to sleep or cook onboard."

"Okay, now I know. I've seen lots of them... just didn't know what they were called. Thanks."

Anderson rejoined them, offering MacLeod a cigarette and lighting a couple for Marjorie and himself. "Need a break from swimming around out here? You're doing a hell of a good job keeping us pretty much in one place."

"I'm okay, as long as give-or-take-a-hundred-yards is okay. I set a waypoint on the GPS against which I check our position every few minutes. What did you learn from Richard? It's been a couple of weeks since I used my credit card there..."

"Nothing like that. He saw that cigarette boat come through the locks yesterday afternoon, late, and they stopped long enough to pick up some unsavoury-looking characters... at least he thought they were unsavoury... he's probably a bit fussy that way. He said he figured there were eight or nine big guys with camouflage duffle bags on the boat when it left and headed up the river toward the lake. He said, *that's your lake Mr. Anderson so I thought you should know*. I thanked him very much, of course, and suggested to him that one of MacLeod's team might come by and interview him briefly, and have him point out their vehicle."

The marine radio chirped a call from the RHIB, saying they were in view and planned to come alongside in a few minutes. They also reported seeing a old inboard launch accompanied by three aluminum fishing boats headed up the lake about a half a mile to starboard, on the same course, and did command want them to be intercepted?

MacLeod shrugged, saying, "Why not?" before he took the microphone from Anderson and said yes, that would be a help and to get as much information as they could without making a big fuss. Some photos would maybe be useful along with a name or two.

They could see the RHIB bank into a thirty degree starboard turn and pick up speed as it headed toward the four boats. "That will cause a little consternation in biker country, methinks." said Anderson with a chuckle.

"So much for their vision of a weekend of yachting with politicians on Awan Lake, drinking martinis, eating lobster and getting massages from naked ladies," added Marjorie.

• • • •

McKinley Island, ON: 1057 The front hall of the main house on McKinley Island was a busy place this morning. Passengers had just finished disembarking from the two helicopters that had landed noisily a scant two hundred yards away and they were making their way as directed to the building's front door. The reporters and camera operators were provided with a small room for their equipment and by now they were busy setting up tripods and stringing wires in the main hall, which had been set up with a podium and chairs. It would be half an hour before the media event began, so most guests headed out the big French doors onto a wide verandah overlooking the bay and the lake beyond. Tables had been set with coffee and several varieties of juice along with plates of finger-foods. The silverware was solid and the flatware was elegant, probably not antique but certainly reflecting an earlier and more opulent time. The service staff were universally young and tastefully dressed in clothes that were not uniform but carefully chosen. There was a sense that putting in a summer working at McKinley Island on Awan Lake was a must-do for upwardly mobile first-year students in political science or business management. The summer was, in fact, over and university classes were back in, but arrangements could be made to free up elite students for a few days when the needs of Ministers of the Crown, international corporations and foreign dignitaries had to be addressed.

"Mr. Karlsen," asked a young reporter from one of the USA

networks, "looking out across the water I see two boats that surprise me. The boat that's a few hundred yards away over there," she pointed to the northeast, "looks for all the world like a lobster boat from the coast of Maine, and that cigarette-boat that just docked in the bay right down here is something I would expect to see on the Florida keys, but not on a remote lake in northern Canada. Tell me more."

"Hi, and welcome to McKinley Island and the New World Mission. I'm Christopher Karlsen, the executive director out here, but please, Christopher will do fine. You must be a reporter because your eyes miss nothing and you ask great questions... and I only really know half the answers unfortunately. That lobster boat was brought here years ago from Nova Scotia, I believe, so north of Maine – but close. It's owned by a local contractor who fixes stuff out on these islands, and it is sometimes commandeered by the provincial police to assist with their work." He picked up a set of birding binoculars from a small table by the railing, looked through them and handed them to the reporter: "Judging from the flags she's flying, I have to assume today is a police day. As for that noisy thing in the bay, I've never seen it before. You called it a cigarette boat? I recognize one of the men down there as a security specialist employed by the Robertson group... perhaps those are some of his colleagues who came up from the American office on holiday."

"Or maybe," said the reporter, "there's a little more going on here than meets the eye. Did I hear someone say there was an international water security specialist who was found murdered here last summer, as well as a deputy minister? And if you look out across the water towards that lobster boat, I believe you'll see what I recognize as a typical standard-issue police patrol boat. It too is flying the Canadian flag, so that would be the RCMP, I assume?"

Christopher shot a disarming smile at the reporter: "I no longer harbour any doubt that you get up well before breakfast, every morning. Unfortunately for both of us, I really have no idea why the police presence today, so I can't help you there, but I do know that the water specialist you mentioned was actually killed in British Columbia, although he had been on his way here to speak at a public protest in the village."

"So, putting two and two together, I get five, which I find odd. Are Robertson Group International's activities here the subject of many public protests? And by extension, is that the reason why the elaborate choice of location and travel arrangements for this media announcement that – frankly – nobody knew about until a couple of days ago? It almost feels as though it was planned like a military operation."

"You're asking me to transition from knowledge to speculation. We could have fun guessing back and forth for the rest of the morning, but I really think you need to talk with RGI's Roger Larsen – the tall guy over there – or his assistant Madisson who is talking to some folks over there in the corner. If anyone knows the answers, they should."

"Thank-you, Christopher. You have been most helpful. Here is my card in case you want to reach me about anything."

"It has been my pleasure. And now, I really need to do the final preparations for the media conference... I've been told that I am the master of ceremonies, albeit with a very minimal role."

"Good luck, and thanks again."

• • • •

Fewer than twenty minutes later, the invited guests and the media were crowded into the main hall. Most had chairs, but a few leaned against the tongue and groove pine walls that had stood the test of time for almost ninety years. Christopher Karlsen welcomed Dale Adams, Minister of Natural Resources, and Roger Larsen, Chief International Development Officer at Robertson Group International, as well as Dr. Frederik Marcusson, Master and President of the Canadian Chapter of the New World Mission, who has made it possible to host this media event in the same week as a major international conference of the New World Mission, which gets underway tomorrow morning.

Karlsen had just introduced the Minister of Natural Resources who was now heading to the podium when there was a loud explosion outside, a lot of shouting and the unmistakable chatter of a rapid-fire weapon, firing off two bursts.. Giselle Matthews had either received some emergency training or had extraordinary presence of mind, hollering for everyone to get down flat on the floor until they could find out what the danger was. Karlsen nodded to Giselle, motioning her to keep people down and went out on the verandah, keeping low. Immediately he could see fire over where the choppers had landed less than an hour before. He moved carefully past a couple of garden sheds to get a closer look and could see that one chopper was fully engulfed in flame and that the other had apparently just caught. He could see what looked like two bodies on the ground between the choppers and was headed there to see if he could help when the flames reached the fuel tank on the second chopper and explosion number two knocked him off his feet and wrapped him around a small maple tree, where he lay unconscious.

• • • •

Anderson had just poured coffee for his crew and was lighting a smoke when the first explosion went off. "Crap, light her up and let's move in, Marj. John, what do you want us to do? Looks like that chopper just blew up... they may need firefighting help in there."

"I thought I heard gunfire... Marie – you did? Okay, prepare your weapons everyone. Frank, let's not charge into the middle of something we don't yet understand. There's a lot of firepower in there between the two groups of special idiots and I don't want us to be in the middle if they get into a pissing match. Let's get the RCMP boat over here and put a couple of our team on-board to help, and get them to go around the other side of that point and closer to the fire. Then we can move deeper into the bay with our eyes wide open... I don't want any of the boats on this island to leave."

"Where's our friendly helicopter when we need her? I assume that was Anne who called us earlier."

"Anne Haroldson? I expect so, Frank. Half an hour ago things were pretty peaceful so I sent her over the village and back."

The A210 squawked and indeed, it was Lieutenant Haroldson: "What the hell are you guys doing over there... we can see thick black smoke almost from the village."

"Yeah, no kidding Anne. Both of those 525's just went up. We don't think it was an accident... Marie – Corporal Beauchemin – is pretty sure she heard a couple of short bursts of gunfire. But we have no established communication yet with people on the island."

"I wish I could reach Christopher. He has a satphone but he's not picking up, and his cell is no good out here."

"Keep trying that satphone – we need some intelligence in there before we land. If there are people badly hurt we'll need Anne to take them to Maple Falls."

Marjorie was holding *The Beaver* at the mouth of the bay, near where they had stopped several nights ago when the bikers stole George Hanson's ski boat and wrecked it on the rocks. Anderson tried Karlsen's satphone again, and this time he answered, barely: "Hello? Hello? Who is this? Frank? Do I know you? Okay, this is Christopher. I think I've been in an explosion. There's fire everywhere."

"Christopher, is there fire at the main building?"

"No, that looks okay. I'm standing up now... I'll try to walk over there. Call me back in five maybe."

It didn't take five. In about three minutes Anderson's satphone rang: "Hello? Mr. Anderson? Yes, he just gave me his phone... he needs to rest for a few minutes, he looks like hell. This is Giselle Matthews. I work for the Robertson Group. When the explosions started I was able to get everyone down on the floor. There was no way I could get the reporters and camera folks to stay put, so now they're out walking around taking footage, but I have convinced the VIPs and staff to stay inside, at least for now. What can I tell them?"

"Tell them you have been able to reach OPS Staff Sergeant John MacLeod who is the scene commander. Tell them we are working to ensure the island is secure before we land a police helicopter and personnel. You should be able to see that helicopter in a few minutes. Ask your people to stay in the main building for a short while longer, for their own safety. And thank-you,

Giselle... my name is Frank Anderson. One more thing, can you get a head-count? Ask staff members if there are others who may be off-shift and sleeping."

"I will do all those things. I am going to hand the phone back to Mr. Karlsen now, who is looking surprisingly healthy."

"Hey Christopher, it's Frank Anderson – you know, the guy with the big boat. Yeah, that's me. I know you were outside earli-er... did you see anyone who was hurt, or anyone with a weapon?"

"Okay, he thinks there's maybe two down, probably the chopper pilots. I don't want anyone to go look in case the bad guys are watching them too. This next step has to be a police job... can the chopper crew handle it or should they pick up a couple from us?"

"Yeah, good thinking. Frank. I'll ask Anne."

While he was calling the chopper, it was the marine radio's turn to squawk. The RCMP boat was just rounding the corner from the west and announced it would come alongside. Once tied up, the Corporal in charge said they had made a circuit of the island and had realized that there were two groups of armed men engaged in a low-speed stand-off along the west side of the island. One group she recognized as belonging to the aluminum boats and an old wooden launch they had intercepted and were now tied up along the shore. The other group appeared better organized, and the Corporal was wondering if they had arrived with the choppers or maybe on that Go-Fast boat docked in the bay. Interestingly, nobody tried to engage the RCMP boat, which had remained several hundred yards offshore.

"Frank, Peggy... let's talk in the wheelhouse so Marjorie can join us. I told Anne to make wide circles when she gets here, ob-serving and avoiding fire from the ground. I am seriously worried about next steps. We have perhaps thirty uninvolved people in that big house, and two groups of eight or ten each trying to kill each other on the beach and in the bushes. That's a recipe for chaos. And those ain't just ordinary people out there with the guns. The security contractors are deadly combatants with lots of experience who really don't want to die in a fight with a low-grade bunch of bikers on a lake in northern Canada, but they don't want to go to jail in Canada either. The bikers, on the other hand, basically have nothing to lose and would probably consider the glory of having a song written about them being worth dying for. If we try to land that chopper we risk it being shot down with no hesitation: they've already destroyed two other, bigger machines today. We don't need to protect either of those groups but we do need to protect the staff and guests at this place... any thoughts?"

"Yup. Let's take them off onto *The Beaver*, right here at the dock. We can take them all in one load, as long as you don't ask for permission from Transport Canada. While we're loading we can put a couple of armed personnel on the dock and up the path, and the OPS chopper can just hang there, armed, similarly protecting the route. The chopper can use its PA system to broadcast our intent. Once we're loaded we can retreat offshore. I recommend we take them to Barker's island – it's about a twenty-five minute trip and they'll be safe there. We could take them to the west shore where there is a small dock, but then we'd need a bus or something and we lose control of the situation."

MacLeod was silent for a long moment: "I like it. I mean, I don't really like it but it is a workable option. First things first, we secure public safety, then we shut down the gang war."

The Staff Sergeant paused, looking thoughtfully at the island ahead. "But y'know, Frank, the people over there are relatively safe at the moment. They are holed up in that big house, television cameras and all. Before we potentially stir up a hornets' nest, how about we start by putting our finger on the scale and tip the balance in favour of the Yanks who are, after all, here to protect the same people we are. We can direct the RCMP team – which still includes a couple of our folks – to go over on the west side and remove the four boats they have over there – just tow them away from the island and anchor them or bring 'em here or whatever. I guess we could just blow them up or sink 'em, but let's try to keep this civilized, it's not a movie set. Our chopper can lurk overhead during that exercise, and hopefully everyone gets the right message: bikers are suddenly out of options and the Yanks remain on the right side of the law. Sort of."

"You're right, y'know. Without the bikers and that Marcusson jerk, the security contractors would have been nothing but background noise, providing a higher level of apparent security than we Canucks are used to seeing in our own country. All very American, but all very – *civilized* – as you called it."

"*Guarding the wall*, to paraphrase Jack Nicolson?" Marjorie chimed in.

"Yes, I guess that's where it's at: *A Few Good Men* – and many good women," said MacLeod. Let's get this happening. Frank, get that RCMP lady and her boat over here and tell 'em what's up and what to do. I'll talk to Anne in the chopper, and Marjorie, maybe move a little deeper into the bay, toward the dock. Sergeant Peggy, keep a very close watch on the shoreline and trees to our right. I guess that's off our starboard side – I don't want Frank to beat me with a marlin spike."

"While I'm waiting for the RHIB to get here I'll call the

folks at the main house. I want to talk to that Giselle lady rather than Christopher if I can... I think she is brighter and has a better relationship with the other folks. She's less likely to pretend she's a boss or something. Pretend bosses are a pain in the ass... they keep getting themselves and everyone else into trouble."

"So you're saying she really *is* a boss..."

"Exactly."

Anderson had just taken out his satphone and started to hit re-call when he noticed that the RHIB was just coming along side. He put away the phone, left the wheelhouse and went over to the starboard side to take a line and secure the cumbersome-looking boat alongside. He couldn't resist singing the first couple of lines from Sesame Street's Rubber Duckie song, and laughed when the RCMP Corporal at the wheel grinned at him and yelled, "Oh shut up, Ernie."

He outlined the plan to the Corporal – Corporal Samantha Bolton – and her crew, which now included the two OPS officers as well as Ken Stephens, the rookie constable she had started the day with. Bolton immediately chose the rookie to be "the wet guy", not because – or so she told him – he was a rookie but because he actually did know his way around boats and probably knew more than she did. Once on location and preparing to tie onto the boats, the two OPS hands would focus on watching the shore for anyone trying to protect the boats and provide cover for their operation. Anderson asked about the boat's gear, and found there was only one short tow-rope that doubled as an anchor line and two very short mooring lines, so he fished out a couple of coils of half-inch rope and threw them in the bottom near the bow.

The RHIB cast off and headed out of the bay and around

the corner to the south. MacLeod was still on the radio with the Eurocopter EC135 so Anderson put in the satphone call to Christopher Karlsen's number on the island.

Karlsen picked up immediately: "Christopher Karlsen here, can I help you?"

"Hi Christopher – it's Frank Anderson here calling from the boat. How are you folks doing in there?"

"Wishing to hell we weren't here at all. We don't dare move because your cop told us to shelter in place, and every now and then we see one or two guys with assault weapons walking around on the shore. What's going on?"

"We're working on solutions, but you are correct to continue sheltering in the house. Could I speak to the lady who I talked to when you were still unconscious? I think her name was Giselle?"

"She's here. Why do you need to talk with her – she's a guest of ours."

"It's okay Chris. I think I may have a message here from her company."

"Okay. I'll find her."

Marjorie had been listening from her place at the wheel. She looked quizzically across at Anderson, who was perched on the edge of the seat at the navigation table. He looked back and rolled his eyes. "Somebody's nose is out of joint?" she asked.

He pointed to the phone and put his forefinger to his lips: "Shhh..." before he made a less polite gesture at the satphone with his middle finger and grinned.

"Hello? Giselle? Giselle Matthews? Thanks for taking this call. It's Auxiliary Sergeant Frank Anderson out here with the big grey boat and Staff Sergeant John MacLeod who is in charge of this whole operation. Are you able to talk privately?... okay,

I'll hold while you step outside. Stay under cover as much as you can."

He lit a smoke while he waited, but she was on the line right away: "You okay now? Good. Are you with the Robertson group?... so your boss is there too? How is he doing?... yes, I bet he's worried, as are you all. Have you talked with the Canadian government minister? Yup, Dale Adams... Oh, good... he has been helpful has he?

Anderson paused for a moment, as if to make up his mind about something, then went on: "Okay Giselle, I kinda hate to put all this on you but I think you are in a position to keep things together in there. Are there about thirty folks at the house, staff included?... Thirty eight?... okay, that's a good-sized bunch. Your having made friends with the Minister as well as having a good relationship with your boss is very important to us because I fear that Mr. Karlsen may be on the edge and possibly unreliable. How's that?... Yes, a massive concussion may well be a contributing factor, indeed. You are very perceptive, and a kind person as well. Can you make a team out of you, the Minister and your boss, and explain to them that you need to bring Karlsen (as host and boss of the staff) into the team as well to manage things over the next hour or so? We will be trying to shut down a bunch of out-of-control bikers armed with heavy weapons – that's the bad news. The good news is we are pretty sure they are not interested in you folks in the slightest bit... it's all ego stuff. What?... Professor Marcusson?... yes he will be of interest to them but without loyalty. He's using them, not the other way up. If he gives you any trouble just try to grab him and put him in a room somewhere to keep him safe. Tell him I said so... I think by now he's all bluster and shaking like a leaf inside."

He paused long enough to wink at MacLeod and Sergeant Peggy, who were listening in and laughing. "Okay, Giselle, thanks very much. Try to stay close to that satellite phone in case we need to talk. Bye."

He snapped the phone off: "If this all winds down the way we need it to, we will want to buy that lady a ham quiche from the Zoo and a martini from Florence at the Inn. How is it with the Lieutenant and her expensive flying machine?"

"She's on her way. She'll stay up reasonably high to avoid being shot at, and her crew will be at the side doors with their C8s in hand watching the ground."

"Marjorie, you just have to be getting tired of keeping this outfit steady. Need a break? It's been four hours."

"I'm okay, Frank. Certainly okay for another hour or until this next phase is over. I assume if the next phase is successful we'll be able to move in to the dock and tie up. Meantime, if you could take the wheel for a minute or two, my bladder would be gladder."

"It's that Tim Hortons coffee," said Sergeant Peggy. "Goes through you like bacon through a duck. Mind you, the amount of coffee you guys all drink would go through a whole flock of ducks in thirty seconds or less, never mind the brand."

"Never drink it?"

"One cup at breakfast, boss. Rest of the time I sip on my water jug."

"But you do eat donuts, though..."

"I'm a cop, ain't I?"

· · · ·

Fifteen minutes later, the RHIB called on the radio to say they were offshore and had all four boats in tow. "That can't be pretty," said Anderson.

Ten minutes after that the RHIB and its tow came into view around the west corner of the island. "You were right, Frank. That's not very pretty."

"Well, it's worked fine so far I guess. I'm a bit mystified that there has been no reaction from the bikers. I would have expected at least a token resistance, maybe a wild shot at the chopper or the RHIB."

"Okay, take a look ahead guys. There's guys with guns near the boathouse."

"How many, Marj?"

"Two is all I saw a moment ago. They'll be wanting that cigarette boat, won't they. Should I move up and squeeze it in a bit?"

"Not until we're better set." MacLeod was on the radio to the chopper: "Get overhead here at the dock. We have armed suspects on the shore at the boathouse. Stay high."

Anderson called the RHIB: "Hi folks, drop your tow and get in here to help squeeze these guys. Just tie your anchor securely to the towing line and let the boats hang out on it. It'll probably drag a bit but no worries. Just get here asap."

The EC 135 was just setting up overhead when Anderson's satellite phone signalled an incoming call. "Hello? Yes Giselle...yes, okay. Thanks..." He motioned to MacLeod, waving him into the wheelhouse. "Hello? Yes, this is Frank Anderson. "Raimy? Yes, perhaps we've met... RGI Security? Yup, you're one of the survivors from last month? ...The black one?... yup, now I remember. A good lookin' black guy mixed up with a bunch of testosterone-filled Norwegians, right?... Yeah, I'm pretty sure we get this: you guys were brought in to provide security at a remote location for government dignitaries and RGI's senior personnel, and some idiot brought in a bunch of baby bikers for their own purposes. Is that about right? ... Okay, your team is calm and under control, I assume? ... Good. It seems to me that the bikers would love to steal your million dollar boat and start importing drugs from Toronto or something 'cause they saw that in a movie. If you can have your team stand down out of the way, we have the tools and personnel to take down the bikers and your boys avoid having to be directly involved. After all, you reached out to us, which is the proper thing to do, right?" Anderson was watching MacLeod out of the corner of his eye, and was relieved to see his friend nodding, albeit with a kind of lopsided grin.

He continued: "Maybe have your team move a bit to the east of the main house and hold there. If you want to stay with the folks in the house you can help that lady – Giselle – keep them calm. She's really good, she's on the RGI team anyway and she has the government Minister's confidence I think... Who?... oh, yeah, maybe just politely ignore Christopher until this is over, then we can all apologize to him if needed. He can be a good guy when his world hasn't exploded, which it did.... Okay, we'll try to give you ten. Thanks, take care. Bye Raimy."

MacLeod looked over to Marjorie, then Sergeant Dawson, and said, "Smooth-talking bugger, ain't he."

"Old saying... something about catching flies with honey..."

"Okay. I'm going to ask the chopper to lift up a couple of hundred feet to take the pressure off, then, in say eight minutes they can drop to just above the trees. When that starts, Marj, take us right up behind that that cigarette boat – maybe fifty feet away – and hold us there unless things get strange. At the same time we'll get the RHIB to actually charge in and land on the opposite side of the dock from the cigarette boat. All safeties off at my command – Marjorie can signal that with a ten second blast on the horn. Remember that we are police, not military. These people are civilians, and we are not at war. Having said that, we must bear in mind that the only fully neutralized combatant is unarmed, lying face down with their hands clasped behind their heads... or they are dead."

Staff Sergeant MacLeod tended to the radio calls to the chopper and the RHIB, and they all checked their uniform and armour straps and weapons as they counted down the minutes.

At three minutes to go, their focus was shattered by the sight of a helicopter flying fast above the treetops from west to east. Not the bright-red chopper that they assumed was still above them, but a smaller, brilliant coloured yellow-and-purple Robinson 44 with call-sign of a Toronto-based news-talk radio station emblazoned on the side. MacLeod dove across the wheelhouse to the navigation table where he had put the hand-held radio he used to talk to the OPS chopper, pushed the talk button and almost shouted, "Get that red thing the hell out of here and tell them to stand down. We will proceed with the plan in two minutes, catch up to us as soon as you can. Mostly keep that news chopper out of the way."

While the MacLeod was doing that, Anderson got on the marine radio to the RHIB and confirmed that the plan was still on track despite the yellow-and-purple thing.

Time suddenly seemed to go by very quickly. Thirty seconds to go and MacLeod called it out. Fifteen seconds. Five... then Marjorie pulled the horn cable and pushed the throttle ahead.

Everything actually happened at once, just like Staff Sergeant John MacLeod had intended. *The Beaver*, of course, moved into place, complete with Sergeants MacLeod and Dawson on the deck with C8s trained on the shore. The RCMP patrol vessel made a fast and rather rough landing and disgorged four armed officers with side arms and carbines onto the dock. The OPS' EC135 helicopter was overhead and dropped fast to the tree tops, both side doors open and carbine-equipped police officers tied off at each door.

There was just one more – somewhat unexpected – detail, which happened before anyone could fire a round or get their hands in the air: a yellow-and-purple blob with blades on top whizzed from left to right across the tree-tops... about seven feet too low. The news-talk chopper's blades clipped the top of a tall pine, the helicopter heeled to the right and then flipped, landing upside down almost exactly on top of one of the previously-burned choppers already on the ground.

For the next fifty seconds, Marjorie was the only person out of the thirteen people onboard who had anything much to do, and she hadn't actually seen what had just happened. She calmly chose her moment to cut back the throttle, pause for five seconds and throw the transmission into reverse to reduce forward speed to almost zero. She really did not want to plant the big bluff steel-reinforced stem of an eighteen-ton lobster boat into that rack of expensive outboard engines, so she stopped about fifty feet away. She looked up to her left and saw the RHIB trailing off the dock on a short rope and two or three armed officers walking quickly down the dock toward the shore. She could hear the chopper overhead, then several short bursts of gunfire interspersed with shouts of "drop your weapon" repeated, then "hands in the air – on the ground". There was a tinkle of glass ahead of her, several more bursts of gunfire, apparently from the chopper, and a scream of pain from the shoreline to her right. She could hear MacLeod yelling an order to go through and clear out the boathouse, at about the same time she noticed that the boat was creeping sideways and backward in the wind. Leaving the throttle alone, she idled the boat ahead with just the transmission.

Then the voice of her beloved Frank Anderson, sounding like nothing had happened and suggesting she could edge *The Beaver* over to the dock and he'd tie her up. Then he said something odd: "Did you see that yellow chopper plough through trees and crash?"

"What yellow helicopter? I didn't even see our red helicopter, although I can still hear it."

"Really? It was kind like a cross between a kids cartoon and a war movie. Those crazy hyped up so-called media wizards in a city traffic helicopter just told the police chopper over the radio to go fuck themselves 'cause they weren't gonna let any provincial damn cops get in the way of their story, after which they promptly hit a tree and crashed."

"Right here, on this island?"

"Yup. Right in front of you. That's where the smoke is coming from. I guess it happened exactly when you were focused on getting in here and stopped."

"Well, you understand, officer, I may have been asleep at the time. Or maybe just busy not running into a tree, or a boat or something. And I had to blow my own horn, too."

She was giggling, but she paused: "A helicopter crashed? Really?"

"Yup." Anderson walked over and kissed her before leaving the wheelhouse and stepping off onto the dock with the bow mooring line. She went to the stern and handed him a second line to tie the boat securely, for the moment anyway.

"So I wonder where is everybody? I think I just heard our proper chopper land the other side of that big house and I hear lots of voices. Some of them don't sound very happy..."

• • • •

McKinley Island, ON:1645: The Beaver was on her way home to Spirit River with a rather unusual passenger list. It was the return trip this afternoon for MacLeod, Dawson, Beauchemin, Bathgate and, of course, Anderson and Marjorie. Added to the list was RGI development assistant Giselle Matthews, who had asked Marjorie, "Are you headed back to the village this afternoon?"

"Yes, we are. Want a ride? You came by helicopter, I expect?"

"Mmm. Well, I was brought in on a small float plane a couple of days ago and I was to go back by helicopter, but now there isn't one. There will be, I expect, but I really just need to get out of here."

"Let's do that, then. I'll tell Frank you're coming."

There were others onboard as well, arranged neatly across the afterdeck in body-bags: three bikers, two commercial chopper pilots, two radio news reporters (one of whom was supposed to have a rotary-wing pilot licence but there was no record of anything beyond a private fixed-wing license) and one former US Marine who had been working illegally in Canada as a security contractor. Apparently his name was Daniel Millard so as Anderson helped lifted the body onboard the boat, he nicknamed him "Danny Duck-Duck". MacLeod said Anderson had a macabre sense of humour, and Anderson responded, "You think

I'm macabre – have you taken a look at the cargo you've just put onboard? This ain't a ferry, y'know, and Awan Lake sure ain't the River Styx."

It had taken over two hours for things to get sorted out at McKinley Island after the nine surviving bikers were arrested and secured for transport by helicopter to Maple falls in two flights, while their three dead compatriots were now headed for Spirit River on the afterdeck of Anderson's workboat. As soon as the danger was over and MacLeod had given the order to stand down, the Staff Sergeant went to the house and gave the thirty or so people there permission to go outside. There was an instant media garden, of course, and it seemed that television cameras and tripods blossomed all over the island. Giselle Matthews had left her boss Roger Larsen and his administrative assistant Madison to handle the media interviews while she went in search for the guy named Frank who had kept in satphone contact and helped her manage and reassure the people trapped in the main house.

She had found Frank and Marjorie at the dock, tidying up the big grey workboat and preparing it for the trip back to the village. Marjorie had immediately opened the third jug of now-lukewarm Tim Hortons coffee and poured a cup for her using her best enameled tin tea-ware. Giselle had begun to thank Anderson but he had been called away by Staff Sergeant MacLeod, so she settled in to visit with Marjorie instead.

Eventually they were underway back to the village. Marjorie took the workboat off the dock, backed into the bay, turned her around and aimed for home. Then she set the autohelm on course and resumed her conversation with Giselle. While they chatted, Marjorie peeled off her lifejacket revealing the body armour she had worn underneath. As she started unbuckling the unfamiliar straps for the body armour, Giselle asked, "Which police force are you with? Seems like we have both the state police and the RCMP here, as well as some of our guys from the US."

"You're American, aren't you?" chuckled Marjorie. "So, you see, we have the Ontario Police Service – our provincial equivalent of your state cops, and the RCMP, which is our national police force. You'll know them from the movies where they always wear bright red jackets. And the Americans on the island apparently have something to do with security for the Robertson corporation, but I guess you'd know more about that."

"And you?"

"I'm none of the above. Frank is a local guy here who fixes stuff on boats and islands. He is ex-coast guard and an Auxiliary Sergeant with the Ontario cops, but mostly just a stand-up guy in the community and we are friends of Staff Sergeant Macleod. My sister and I own a tiny island on the lake – much smaller than McKinley – and Frank and I got together a couple of months ago. Turns out that I like driving old lobster boats and I'm getting good at it, I guess, so that's what I do. And, they give me body armour to wear so I can keep driving if someone shoots me. What about you?"

"Well, until this morning – actually until late last night – I was a healthy self-assured millennial blond chick who'd scored a good job with The Man, in this case Robertson Group International."

"It's been a long and difficult day, and you sound like a millennial blond chick who could use another friendly blond chick to talk to."

"That would be wonderful. I had a task to accomplish while we were here on the island and I met my employer's expectations, but now I am scared and ashamed, in equal measure."

"Your way of speaking is elegant, not average millennial chick."

"I like to write."

"Ah, I understand. I have a sister like that. She is in Africa."

"Africa. That's more than just the other side of Toronto. Why Africa?"

"Because of Robertson Group International."

"Why because of RGI?"

"She was a public relations consultant in Toronto but she has been tapped for a position as an investigative journalist." Marjorie watched Giselle closely for a reaction.

She was not disappointed, but Giselle recovered from her astonishment quickly: "So last night, I teased your Minister of Resources into bed, and got it on film. That was my job. The corporation needs his absolute complicity."

It was Marjorie's turn to look shocked. She looked Giselle up and down slowly, with growing admiration but rapidly failing respect: "I expect that was not too difficult for you to accomplish."

"It was what I hope was the worst night I will ever have. Not the sex. Your senior politician is a sweet gentleman and a lover like many of us can only dream of. Our time together made him sad."

"Remorse?"

"Maybe later, he has a family. But last night – just sad. I won't easily forget what he said, while we should have been experiencing the sweet satisfaction of a shared cigarette. He said, "As sure as I know that I should not be here with you, I know that I am also being disloyal to my country. Larsen now owns everything. It's all on my laptop, isn't it?"

"It was? How so?

"I pretended to check the news while he was in the shower. You can guess the rest. I had bumped the file to my office email address."

"Why are you telling me this? The company you work for has already killed a dear friend and a very talented young woman – a writer like yourself – and threatens by extension my own sister who is also investigating RGI copper and coltan mining in the DRC."

"Priscilla?"

"Yes, Priscilla. You knew her?

"She's dead?"

"Yes."

The tears hadn't started to fall, but the sobs that shook her shoulders almost shook the boat. Anderson came into the wheelhouse, took one look and pointed to the focsle, motioning that he had the wheel. He took out a cigarette for himself and flipped the pack to Marjorie as she was helping Giselle down the companionway steps. MacLeod came into the wheelhouse, looked forward and then quizzically at Anderson. "Everything okay, Frank?"

"I think so. Giselle apparently has stuff on her mind. Marjorie always winds up being the fixer."

"I know, I've watched her. I have no more to say than that she is a blessing. To you and to us all, I think."

"Mmm. She is. John, we're just a half-hour from the village. Do you have a coroner set up to meet us?"

"Yes, along with the large ambulance and a couple of police

vans. And, seems like they couldn't find a second big chopper so the US media and that Larsen guy all went back on one chopper and the rest of the guests are being put up overnight on the island. We have left an officer there as well and one is coming here with Corporal Samantha and her RHIB. She asked me if there was a way she could avoid having to take the RHIB out of the water overnight and I said I was sure you could find a place to tie it up. She left that green constable – Ken – out there as well. She'll stay here for the night, my officer will come back to The Falls with me and Samantha will probably stay at the Inn then go back to the island in the morning with some of the forensics team. We can expect Transport Safety Board inspectors to arrive in the morning as well – they may come by chopper but can you take them out if they request?"

"Sure, no problem. Maybe I'll get to collect back some of the fees I pay to Transport Canada so they can pester me every spring. Actually, kidding aside, it will be interesting to watch what goes on. Did Samantha and Ken grab that rope full of boats and tow them back into the bay after we left, I wonder? I forgot about that."

"Yes, she told me on her phone they had just tied them to the little boathouse wharf and she had taken her anchor and line back on the RHIB."

"Good thinking."

He turned to look forward just in time to see Marjorie appear at the focsle door, which she stepped through and closed behind her. "Asleep. She hasn't slept since before breakfast yesterday. Now I'm going to have four or five of those cigarettes. There's stuff we need to talk about – you too John."

"We're ten minutes off the dock. Should we wait until we've

docked and unloaded? It's gonna get pretty busy around here in a few minutes."

"That'd be fine. Maybe I'll wake her up, put her in the Jeep and get her settled in at the Inn and back asleep. Then the three of us could have a burger and talk. Maybe beer too. Definitely beer too."

· · · ·

Spirit River, ON:1925: It had taken awhile to get the bodies unloaded into the vans and to brief the coroner on what he would be looking at. The RHIB tied up on the lake side of *The Beaver* and Sergeant Bolton – Samantha – gave Anderson the keys to the ignition and padlocks in case he had to move the boat before early morning. She caught a ride to Maple Falls with Sergeant Dawson, where she would spend the night. Marjorie was sipping on a beer in the lounge while she waited – Giselle had eaten a chicken sandwich and was already tucked in bed for the night.

"Well, that was September eleven, twenty-seventeen." said Staff Sergeant Macleod as he and Anderson sat down at Marjorie's table. He pointed at her beer glass, glanced across at Anderson and signalled the server for the same, all around.

"So, tell us more about The Lady Giselle," said Anderson. "All I know is that she is smart and level-headed."

"She's also very pretty," said John MacLeod.

"That too. And if it wasn't for Marjorie she'd be a pretty wreck as well. What's her story?"

"Robertson Group International. They are even more evil than I thought, and Giselle, like Wendy used to, works for them. Well, also like Wendy, not now, but until today she was. Yesterday her job description included seducing the Canadian Minister of Natural Resources and gathering evidence on video. Her melt-down today began with that, but as she was telling me the story I got a little snarky and mentioned that sex means nothing but other people do and mentioned we had a friend who was murdered last month looking into RGI and its mining operations. She stopped talking, looked at me with eyes like saucers and blurted out *Priscilla?* So, that was the beginning of a flood of pretty disturbing information."

"Has she officially resigned?"

"No, John, she was going to email on her laptop as soon as we got to the dock this afternoon, but then she crashed. Not the laptop, she did."

"Good thing. Her laptop will be traceable to wherever she is. Let's get her into the detachment where she can use an OPS laptop that also won't show an ISP in Spirit River. Those RGI folks are as bad as the KGB or the CIA when it comes to intelligence."

"Never even thought of that. Maybe I should go and tell her."

"Maybe just take it out of her backpack and let her sleep. You can always blame me later."

"Maybe better that I take some tape and paper and tape her laptop shut with a sign saying to talk to me first. The last thing she – and even the rest of us – needs is for her to wake up in a panic and send any communications at all to RGI. I worry about her, of course, and I worry about us at Spirit River too but mostly right now I'm worrying about Wendy."

"I'll have my usual burger and fries," she said over her shoulder as she left to get some tape and a marker from the office and then go up to the room.

Anderson downed the rest of his draft beer and said to MacLeod, "John, I'm sure that RGI outfit can connect the dots quicker than a squirrel up a pine tree," said Anderson. "I worry about that."

"The squirrel, or the pine tree?"

"The squirrels. If RGI finds a squirrel at Awan Lake, they'll run that against all the information hanging on the branches of their pine tree database and they'll find Envirowire, then Priscilla, then Wendy, in less time than it takes me to say it."

"My God, yes. Wendy's got to get out of there," said MacLeod, "and Anita's got to get out of Paris. Can Marjorie reach them?"

"I think so. We'll get her on it as soon as she comes back down. Meantime, I'm putting in for two cheeseburgers and fries, and more beer. Whatcha having?"

"Same. Here comes Marjorie."

"Got it done. We could have a dance up there...Cinderella is still curled up like a ball and dead to the world." She sat down and polished off the last swallows of her first beer and started on her second.

"Drink up. We've got stuff to do... I'll wait for Frank to get back."

A moment later, Anderson returned after giving their orders to the bartender and a quick visit to the washroom. "Marj, we have to get the girls home. Now, or sooner."

Marjorie sat absolutely silent for fifteen seconds. "Yes, you're right. Of course we do." She picked up the cellphone which she had left on the table and began paging through the contacts. "I'll text her just two words: *Call Sis*. Then I'll telephone Anita, who may be able to reach her more quickly. They both need to come home."

Twenty minutes later she had finished her burger and was

nibbling fries and ketchup when her phone rang. It was Wendy. "Where are you...? Kinshasa? ... I can't talk. Get out of there and get home. Nothing is wrong here but we can't talk. Just trust us and get out of there... What? ... I have a call into Anita already... Paris is better but take the earliest possible flight back to Canada. Both of you... You can't talk to me from there but I guess you can call Anita when you get to Paris. Keep it short. I am not even sure if we will be able to talk from here... Buy a burner phone and text us your flight details so we can pick you up... Love you. Don't be slow.

"Well, that should rattle her a little."

"I hope so. For such a smart chick she was sure sounding dozy."

"So, Marj, how did she even know Priscilla Mogenstern?"

"Seems that Giselle is kind of a multi-tasking workhorse for that Roger Larsen's development office in Washington, and she gets to travel to RGI's developing properties around the world, charming people and generally snooping for information. She thought it would be a good idea to make all the friends she could with the media, even across the fence, so to speak, with outfits like Envirowire. She tended to seek out the print media folks – said they had bigger brains and smaller egos – so that's where she met Priscilla, at some media event right there in Washington. They were drawn to each other despite their vastly different job descriptions and they used to go out to concerts and even just furniture-hunting. Giselle was devastated when Priscilla was murdered... she had even been the person who dropped her off at the airport for her flight to Paris."

"Do you suppose there was a sort of Wendy-and-Anita thing there?"

"I didn't get that impression, John. I think they just had fun being girls."

"So the melt-down was more about her friend, or more about the penny dropping, stripping the cover off the horrible things her employer is up to?"

"I think a bit – a lot – of both, Frank. She had only hours ago realized she had the ability to take a really nice man and strip his body, his soul and his psyche bare to benefit the crooked corporation that paid her salary and the infinitely horrid man who told her to do it. That was such a dreadful perversion in her eyes that mere prostitution looked like a spiritual calling. On the subject of spiritual calling, she already saw herself on the way to some sort of purgatory when Priscilla's name surfaced – dead under the worst possible circumstances – and Giselle realized that her friend was a victim of the same corporation, murdering her to avoid being exposed for a battery of criminal activities. So tonight, I hopes she sleeps soundly and wakes up prepared to strike back at the devil, so to speak. And let's hope we can get our girls back safely, too."

"You going to stay here at the Inn with her?"

"Well, it would seem somehow cruel to wake her up from a comfortable sleep just to take her back to our place so she can sleep on a sofa."

"That's a good point. I can forgive you for being nice to stray ladies. John, you can drive me back to the house."

Marjorie looked over at Anderson: "I can drive you back. Would you stay with me long enough to have coffee and maybe dessert? I see a glass thing over there with cherry cheesecake under it."

He leaned over and kissed her cheek. "Of course I will. I

love cheesecake. John, what time do you think new disasters will break out in the morning?"

"I'll call you around 0900, okay?"

"Good. I'll at the very least have to refuel *The Beaver* before we go anywhere much. They have a cardlock at the Co-op but I may have to get some oil. Whatever, I'll have my phone with me."

With cheesecake and coffee ordered, they began to unwind some of the events of the day, particularly the subject of Wendy, Anita and now Giselle. "I've heard nothing from Anita, Frank. I'm worried."

Anderson punched some buttons on his cellphone and looked up: "Well, it's just before 2100 here, so in Paris it's about 0300, well before dawn and I don't suppose Anita is a particularly early riser. How many text messages did you leave?"

"Yes, you have a point. Just one. I guess maybe I should try a voice call, which will ring a few times before going to the message. I'll do that now."

That call went to voicemail after the third ring, but Anita called back almost immediately. Marjorie picked up: "Anita? It's Marjorie... No, nobody's hurt or sick, but you and Wendy are in danger. I reached her earlier and told her to get out of Kinshasa and get to Paris, pick you up and get home immediately if not sooner... I can't talk about it on the phone but you should know it is related to the Joan Baez thing... Okay, big hugs from Frank and I... 'Bye."

"Okay, now we wait."

"So, *the Joan Baez thing*. Is that a thing, I mean... what?"

Marjorie laughed. "Yes, you might indeed wonder. Priscilla thought that Anita looked and sounded like that American folk singer Joan Baez. She had her guitar in the room when they all stayed here, and she does have a lovely voice, long jet-black hair and a rather Spanish-American complexion. So Priscilla nicknamed her *Little Joanie.*"

It was good to hear her laugh, Anderson thought: "Okay, now I got it. Didn't know about that, and yes, Priscilla was right. And of course that Spanish-American complexion was directly inherited from her grandmother."

Anderson took the last forkful of cheesecake and sat back. "So, not only the Giselle thing, but I wonder where all this goes."

"It's like there's evil in the air, everywhere," Marjorie replied. "I almost expect there to be a black dawn tomorrow."

"Yipe... that's kind of poetic. But yeah, I get it. So many things seem to be going sideways. We had thirteen dead people laid out on the boat today, breaking last month's record of eleven – actually thirteen as well if you count the spin-off murders. I don't know if anybody else notices that twenty-six violent deaths is a big number for a community of not even six hundred if you count the summer residents. I always thought we were kind of ordinary people around here."

"Hmm. I'm gonna get Wendy to write a book: *Where Ordinary People Go to Die.* Actually, I was reading the other day about Asphodel, a town near Peterborough but also a flower. According to Greek mythology, the Asphodel Meadows is the place in hell where ordinary people go to die. That's what made me think of it."

"We're getting' weird around here. Cue the creepy music. Seriously, though, looking back over the summer it's easy to sort out the events but harder to identify the links. First, one nasty individual is smuggling drugs and getting a few local idiots to help him. He dies. Then we had an over-zealous manager order a few more-or-less prominent people to be killed, and then he lit a copper mine on fire. Now, as I see it anyway, we have an over-ambitious university professor trying to start an international political movement based on a social experiment in the middle of Awan Lake. Am I making sense so far?"

Again Marjorie chuckled: "It doesn't make the slightest bit of sense at all. But here we are."

"I think we can assume that Professor Fred – Marcusson – and his schemes are over. I understand there was meant to be a meeting of that New World Mission starting out there tomorrow morning, but I'm willing to bet that is cancelled and the place is basically locked down as a crime scene as well as a crash scene..."

"Are you sure that John remembers that info we got from Tony? If not, better call him right away and remind him."

"Absolutely. Now." Anderson took out his cellphone and hit the Sergeant button on speed dial. "John? Me again... Chaos around there? ...Yeah, sorry to bother, but did you remember that Marcusson and Christopher had another big meeting planned to start in the morning, with more so-called international dignitaries? ...Ah, good. They're going to The Falls? ...Perfect. I hate to be selfish but I don't want them here tomorrow either... Yeah, one nightmare at a time. Take care."

"So he got them to move?"

"I don't think he had much argument, from Christopher anyway. The place is a wreck and that young staff is a quivering mess after today. John said he told Chris that the place was a designated crime-scene for the foreseeable future, so whatever they had planned for tomorrow wasn't going to happen. It wasn't more than ten or a dozen people anyway so they were able to get a meeting room at the motor lodge."

"So what's next? I guess the clean-up starts in the morning, but I'm worried that I shouldn't get out of reach with my cell-phone until those two are safely home – or at least on an airplane headed back. Reception out on the lake is spotty or non-existent."

"I will miss you. A lot. And I'm going to miss you tonight too. Keep in touch as things unfold, and if you can't reach me tomorrow on my cell you can call the satphone John gave me last month. Do you have the number on your cell? Good. I do love you, you know... it's not just because you are a very fine helmsman."

"Helmslady?"

"Helmsman. I know the difference and will miss it, and that's all that counts. G'night."

SEPTEMBER 12

Spirit River, ON:0715: Marjorie called him just to say good morning. She and Giselle were having breakfast and would be seeing him soon. Anderson said he was wide awake and drinking coffee (he wasn't). He stumbled out of bed wondering why he felt so tired and reflected that he was a middle-aged man receiving a short lesson on the physical side-effects of extended stress: he had done almost nothing strenuous yesterday but he ached all over like he'd done a full game on the O-line for the Ottawa Redblacks.

He didn't bother with the bacon but he fried up a couple of local farm-raised eggs, put them on toast and gobbled them down while the coffee dripped. He put on a jacket, took his cup out on the porch and lit a cigarette. The rising sun was still only just over the horizon and so far had added no warmth to a day that was starting off chilly. He walked over to his quarter-ton, checked the tires, drove up to the Co-Op cardlock and filled the slip-tank with diesel. The store was struggling to life as staff arrived for work, so he picked up a case of DMO 15-40 motor oil and a case of grease tubes and returned home, parking on the dock to re-fuel *The Beaver*.

He emptied the fifty-gallon slip-tank and went back to the Co-op for another fill. By the time he returned to the dock a second time, RCMP Sergeant Bolton and Cst. Stephens were there, checking out the fuel and engine fluids on the RHIB. "Morning Samantha and Ken... were you able to get a decent sleep? Yesterday was a long day."

"Yup. We cut the partying last night pretty short though. Pizza and Pepsi at Ken's place and I went back to my room and crawled into bed."

"Yeah, after our banquet I watched half a hockey game and

fell asleep."

"Are you guys sailing today, or are you leaving us?

"We are waiting here for two guys from the Transportation Safety Board to make up their minds if they want a ride out to the island. They like to travel first class for the cameras so they got all the way to Maple Falls by car before they realized that Maple Falls might just be a little short of choppers this morning. There's the big OPS one, of course, but apparently it's not federal enough and wouldn't be for their exclusive use. They're phoning around for one of ours but I guess if they don't have any luck, nor do we because we'll have to spend the day with them. Pompous bastards. The only people they like less than cops are lady cops who outrank them."

While they talked, there was a scrunch of gravel on the driveway behind them as Arnold arrived in his pickup: "Morning, folks. You been watching the news this morning? You're all over it."

"Really? " I wonder how that happened. Wasn't like all the TV news reporters in Toronto and Washington were out at McKinley Island or anything like that. It must have been colourful."

"Oh, it was. Your boat looked very official and even serene, parked beside that long thin racing boat... what the hell was that?"

"Belonged to some security contractors from the US."

"Fast?"

"Should be. Probably 1800 horses strapped on the back. Who did they interview?"

"Just that Christopher guy you mentioned the other day, and MacLeod of course. Both of them were very good at not saying anything. But a few minutes ago, just before I drove down here, the Minister of Natural Resources resigned from Cabinet. He also announced he would not run in the next election. Said he had been at an important event on the weekend and had reflected that politics had been exacting too big a sacrifice from his wife and children. What the hell were they doing out there, anyway?"

"Maybe seeing the helicopter he had just been on get blown up and scattered far and wide made him question some choices, I dunno. Must've been scary." Anderson turned sideways and winked at Arnold. "We can talk about stuff later... I have to get ready to take John and his folks out there. Samantha, Ken, this is Arnold, who always finds interesting news. Samantha, does your RHIB need diesel? You can have what I have on the truck and I'll go up and get more."

"Thanks, I'm okay for the moment. If those TSB guys need me to go out, then yes, I'll need to fuel up. Otherwise, we'll just pull her onto the trailer and get out of here."

Arnold helped Anderson re-fuel and while out of earshot of the RCMP officers, listened while Anderson quickly filled him in on some of the details about Giselle and the connections with Anita and Wendy.

"I'd better not tell Georgina or anyone else about this until we know the girls are on that plane crossing the Atlantic."

"No, please. Just Marion."

"Do you and Marjorie really feel that RGI would really bother with this?"

"Of course. And RGI will be double mad because it has lost the Natural Resources Minister. By resigning at this stage, he has flipped their control over him. And they have lost two of their star public relations stars – slaves, but no longer – Giselle and

Wendy. On top of all that, they are now being investigated at two of their biggest mining plays, not just one. September is not turning out to be a great month for Roger Larsen, it seems."

By now, MacLeod had joined them on the boat, having arrived in his black SUV with an unmarked cruiser following. "Hi Arnold... sounds like Frank has been filling you in."

"Yeah. Crap, just when we thought it might be getting peaceful around here. What about those security guys of RGI's that keep turning up... I really find them pretty scary, but for what advantage to RGI except to scare local people and probably piss off our government."

"If I had a moment to spend with Larsen, I'd try to convince him that this is Canada, not the USA, and we're not part of Africa or South America. If they want to manipulate people here, they need to consider what they really want, plan their actions and choose their human weapons more carefully. Their attempt to trap Dale Adams was at least more subtle than an assault rifle even if it failed. Ten blond-haired ex-marine heroes on a racing boat with big guns just looks and feels stupid, let alone offensive, in our part of the world. And threatening and murdering intelligent young women is a crime, not a sport."

Anderson paused, almost out of breath. Then: "Hi John – sorry to have gone crazy. Do we have Transport Safety Board folks or are they going with the RCMP boat?"

"They want you to prove you have undergone a valid inspection before they get onboard to go to the crash site. They feel like it wouldn't look good in the press if someone found out that you hadn't been inspected."

"And I feel like telling them to take their inspection and shove... never mind. Samantha's right... pompous bastards. Anyway, I have the papers right here in the wheelhouse, as required under the regulations. Tell 'em to come onboard and look. I'm the ship's master, not their slave."

"Touchy, my friend."

"Damn right. Too many useless idiots combing their hair in the mirror while too many good people suffer or die."

• • • •

Awan Lake, ON:0920: As it turned out, the RCMP RHIB and the two RCMP officers were not needed because the TSB inspectors realized they would be much more comfortable on the workboat, especially since it was a properly inspected vessel after all. There was a slight chop running out of the west today so there might be spray, too. *The Beaver* had a cabin.

Frank Anderson had taken his workboat and its passengers on a slightly more circuitous route to McKinley Island than normal, slightly northwest to go by Tony and Jean Barker's Island, where he set off a blast of the air-horn to say good morning, then a little further east to go by Dave Bradshaw's island, where he didn't send a signal but he did sail one full turn around the small island, fairly close in. One of the TSB passengers came into the wheelhouse, followed by MacLeod who had been taking photos, to ask him why.

"Some people involved with the event at McKinley Island may have spent a night here. We know the owner, who is away, so we are just checking. Kind of a neighbour thing." MacLeod winked.

They continued to McKinley Island and pulled in behind the cigarette boat on the main dock at about 0955. Anderson asked Sergeants Dawson and MacLeod to tend the bow and stern lines to moor *The Beaver* at the dock. The TSB inspectors thanked Anderson politely and walked with Sergeant Dawson along the dock and over the path that led to the open ground where the two big choppers had been sabotaged by fire, and where the small helicopter with the news team had crashed. These inspectors were air transportation specialists, not water or land specialists and apart from confirming that the big helicopters had been on the ground when they burned, the only thing they were here to see was the little Robinson 44 that had hit the trees and crashed, killing the two people onboard.

After they had gone out of sight, MacLeod and Anderson poured a coffee, took a donut each and a pack of smokes MacLeod had brought and sat outside in the morning sun for a few minutes. Anderson had started the little diesel generator, flipped off the main engine, and flipped a few switches to keep house and instrument power. Oddly, the two men thought, nobody had yet come down from the house to greet them, or even find out who had just landed at the dock. They were talking about the Minister's resignation and the potential impact on RGI's expansion project at Awan Lake when a big man in his forties walked down to the dock from somewhere behind the main building. He was wearing jeans and a sweatshirt and carrying a large duffel bag, which he placed in the cockpit behind the operator's station on the cigarette boat. He turned and headed back up the path, but not before he said "hello sir" and gave a quick wave.

"That's one," said MacLeod.

"Mmm," said Anderson.

Several more times, in singles and pairs, the process was repeated, complete with the short smile, greetings, and wave, except now they all gathered at the boat. "Like peas in a pod, getting back into the pod. That's nine."

One more came down and stepped in behind the controls and methodically fired up each massive outboard engine. Anderson recognized the moment: he took a long boathook from the deck alongside the wheelhouse and stepped onto the dock to where he could push off the stern of the go-fast boat to make it easier for them to back into the bay. One of the men – the only black man among the nine others – stepped to the stern after the boat was clear and said with a smile: "Thank-you, Frank Anderson. Take care."

The elongated boat backed clear of the docks, turned slowly and awkwardly until it faced out of the bay and disappeared in a cloud of noise, exhaust and spray. It took off almost due north, obviously headed for the river and the canal and locks at Maple Falls.

"I sure hope he slows that thing down before he gets into that narrow river," said MacLeod.

"Well, I assume whoever was driving it two days ago brought it up the river alright."

"Suppose so. Geesh it goes fast. Do you know that other guy?"

"The black guy? Sure. He's the guy I talked to yesterday to broker our solution to the gang war."

"But he never saw you..."

"Just a thing, I guess. I respected him, and offered to trust him. He returned the favour."

"I guess. Worked out well.

Then their conversation was interrupted by a preppy looking young man in tennis shoes, shorts and a short-sleeved polo shirt.

He jogged onto the dock then along to where they were still tied up and said, "Good morning gentlemen, my name is Jayden, Jayden Wilson and I am the duty steward today. Mr. Karlsen has instructed me to invite you to join him at the main lodge for coffee. Things are still a little messy, as I am sure you will understand, but you are welcome to join us."

"Thank-you, Jayden Wilson. You may tell Mr. Karlsen that Staff Sergeant John Macleod and Captain Frank Anderson will meet with him shortly – perhaps in ten minutes."

"That would be perfect, Sir," and he nodded to each of them, turned and jogged back up the path.

"Queen Victoria would squeal with pleasure," chuckled Anderson.

"She certainly would, along with Emily Post. That was quite a display of class. Seriously overdone class, but I guess it beats him calling out "Hey, assholes." which I believe he was actually thinking."

The two of them walked along the wooden dock and up the moss-covered path toward the buildings. There were a number of small and medium sized cottages scattered along the island's rocky shorelines and in amongst the trees but they headed for the shingle-sided old mansion that obviously served as the main lodge. They could see people cutting grass and working in the gardens, and one small group of guests sitting outside on the south side of the massive verandah that surrounded three sides of the building. The peaceful atmosphere this morning seemed to Anderson as somewhat incongruous, considering that only yesterday three helicopters had burned and four men had died.

"People forget quickly, don't they."

"I guess if they had good memories, cops eventually wouldn't have jobs."

They mounted the wide set of wooden steps onto the verandah and were greeted at the door by Christopher Karlsen. The only sign of his ordeal yesterday was a small Band-aid above his left eye, where he had evidently cut his forehead when he was knocked to the ground by the first helicopter explosion. He was wearing khaki slacks, a matching polo shirt and a smile that oozed self-confidence: "Good morning, Frank. I remember you well from when you stopped by with Tony Barker a couple of weeks ago. And this must be Sergeant MacLeod from the Ontario Police Service... pleased to meet you, Sergeant, and I want to say how thankful we all are to you and your fellow officers for your skill in managing the events of yesterday."

Handshakes done, Karlsen led the two men down the pine-panelled hallway to his office, where a small octagonal boardroom table was already set with small coffee mugs and a decanter of coffee. There was no sign of Jayden Wilson, but a young woman in tennis shorts and a white blouse arrived at the door with a plate of muffins and a smile. "Thank-you, Ashley," Karlsen said. "They look delicious. You can put them on the table."

Once they were seated, with coffee mugs in hand, Karlsen looked across the table and said, "Sergeant MacLeod, I understand some of your people are out here again today. We have events going on this week and next and I am concerned about how long this will go on. Official-looking people with uniforms and guns are not exactly a perfect mix with our agency's brand."

Frank Anderson was probably half an inch shorter than both MacLeod and Karlsen, but he appeared to grow several inches in his chair. He held up his hand to silence MacLeod and began: "Christopher, we need to get a couple of things straight between us as neighbours on Awan Lake. First, my colleague John here is properly known as Staff Sergeant MacLeod when he is on official business. In this case, he is on a courtesy visit to the manager of a property which is now a crime scene. Second, all the OPS officers investigating this crime scene have every right to carry their weapons when they are on police business, which they most certainly are. And, I'll take this opportunity to point out that not one, but two, groups of your guests yesterday were carrying lethal weapons and were engaged in activities which were illegal at the time. And third, the New World Mission is not an agency, it is a private association with no rights at all except those of any private citizen. Now that I can see you fully comprehend these local matters, I defer to Staff Sergeant MacLeod to continue his investigation on behalf of the Crown."

"Thank-you, Frank. Mr. Karlsen, Captain Anderson has pointed out to you that this is indeed a criminal investigation. Today we have been joined by representatives of the Transportation Safety Board of Canada as well as our own personnel who are following up on a preliminary forensics investigation yesterday afternoon, at which time OPS and RCMP personnel were present. I am in charge of the investigation as a whole, but my particular function at this moment is to obtain from you the guest registry for the last 60 days and to learn in particular the whereabouts of Dr. Frederik Marcusson who is reported to be still here on the island today, and another gentleman, "

"Very well, Staff Sergeant. I meant no offense. I assume you will want a print-out of the guest registry?"

"More than that – I will need a digital copy of the data as well. I have a flash drive in my briefcase and some paper for a print copy. We can attend to that after we finish our coffee. Tell me about Dr. Marcusson... where is he?"

"He's here. He has his own suite in one of the guest cottages, where he writes. He receives very few visitors, although he will be meeting with a small group coming in this afternoon. The spiritual leader of the Mission, Rev. Andrew Jackson, will be arriving with a couple of European dignitaries. I think all of them will be shocked to have learned that our Canadian delegate, Minister Adams, has stepped away from government and gone home."

"Yes, we heard about that," said Anderson. "When did he leave the island?"

"He had been booked to stay over last night and tonight, but he caught a ride with the RGI helicopter on its second trip back last night. I hadn't heard anything about his resignation until the news this morning."

"How are the Mission delegates arriving in Maple Falls this afternoon?"

"Charter plane. Dr. Marcusson has arranged all that. There are now only four delegates coming in now, six if you include Rev. Jackson and Dr. Marcusson. Dr. Marcusson and I will go the mainland by boat after lunch and go to The Falls by car. We'll be staying overnight."

"What is the relationship between RGI and the New World Mission?"

"There is none, really. RGI is an industry partner of the Mission, that's all. One of many."

"Gotta be something more substantial than that," said Anderson. "You don't usually have government ministers, E.U. diplomats and corporate miners all gathering for a love-in at a resort in northern Canada, media invited."

"Well, if your name is Marcusson, you do. Dr. Marcusson is

a networking genius and an insanely hard worker."

"What brand of Kool-Aid does he drink?"

Karsten was silent for a long moment.

"Well?" It was an impatient-sounding Anderson.

"Okay. Dr. Marcusson and that Rev. Jackson are true believers, and they do seem to get high on their own Kool-Aid.

"And you're not a true believer?"

"Not that way. I am pleased to be playing a leadership role in the Mission for developing a New World Order, but only because I know intellectually that we need a better system of government to replace democracy, which we all know doesn't work. But it's not a religion – we all know that religions don't work either. So to me, Dr. Fred and Reverend Andy are just distractions. But they make a pretty good sales team to convince the ordinary people that we need change. Especially the tens of thousands of young people in the USA and Canada who are fed up with Sundays in Church, or Saturdays at Synagogue, or Fridays at the Mosque. They are excellent targets to build our ranks of young people looking for a better future."

"So McKinley Island is really just a youth mission, not the seat of a future government or something."

"Well, it is the Mission's first *owned* geographic footprint, but of course the location of the World Capital can't be revealed until the United Nations in New York and the Vatican in Rome are eradicated."

"Okay, thank-you sir." Staff Sergeant MacLeod stood up. "That's all very useful information. I think we should go to your office and get that guest registry file, then Captain Anderson and I will check on the progress of our officers, then go to have a quick chat with Dr. Marcusson. Don't worry, Mr. Karsten, we won't divulge any of our conversation this morning."

• • • •

Awan Lake, ON:1520: Nobody in the Ontario Police Service would probably have ever dreamed that sending Staff Sergeant John MacLeod or Auxiliary Sergeant Frank Anderson to transfer digital files from a desktop computer to a flash drive was a sensible thing to do. Nonetheless, using a fifteen-minute recess to go outside and bring in the ever-helpful Sergeant Dawson, they were able to quickly master the task and return to *The Beaver* with the required data.

The thirty-minute conversation with Dr. Frederik Marcusson was much less satisfactory. The good doctor raged on at length, claiming that Anderson, his big grey workboat and the provincial police had been harassing McKinley Island and its inhabitants for months and he was not at all pleased. Of course, he had also been aware of the takedown and arrest of his security team yesterday. Most of all, though, he was furious that his moment in the sun as the co-host of an event celebrating the expansion of the exotic-sounding Awan Lake tantalum-processing facility, along with a deepening relationship between Robertson Group International and the New World Mission, had all gone up in smoke, fire and crashed helicopters.

Marcusson blamed communist do-gooders, left-wing environmentalists and fascist provincial police, almost all in the same sentence, and he threatened lawsuits and an investigation by the federal government, although of which country he was unclear. The Staff Sergeant was unable to get coherent responses to his queries about who exactly had told Marcusson's security team to light the two passenger helicopters on fire, to steal Hanson's motorboat, or to open fire on police personnel.

As they strolled back across the lawn from Marcusson's cottage to the dock, Anderson said, "What I'd give to have collected a tape-recording of all that."

"So, he isn't the only one who didn't notice I was wearing a body-cam. Cool."

• • • •

On their way back to the village three-quarters of an hour later, complete with Sergeant Dawson and the two TSB personnel, Anderson's satphone started chirping. It was Marjorie, saying Wendy had called on her new burner phone to report that she would be boarding a flight from Kinshasa to Paris in half an hour. She had told Anita not to pick her up at the airport, but that she would find a hotel and call her to come and join her so they could fly out together.

"That has to be a huge relief for Marjorie."

"Yes, John. It ain't over 'til it's over and they are both sipping wine and nibbling nachos at the Inn, but it sounds hopeful, anyway."

"Not feeling very optimistic today, are you."

"Optimistic? Expecting positive results when dealing with governments in Africa, the US, and Canada along with the Robertson Group would be nothing but dumb. It's like dealing with a centipede and waiting for the next shoe to drop... it just never seems to end."

"Maybe don't tell Marjorie that?"

"Well, not today maybe. But now I'm also wondering about Giselle. Do you think she'll be okay?"

"Normally I would assume she'll just head back to Washington, where I'm pretty sure she won't have a job with RGI anymore. They might try to make her life difficult for awhile but really, from their perspective all she did was screw up her assignment – by doing it too well, maybe. She so impressed the Minister that he quit being the Minister - not what RGI intended, I'm pretty sure."

"The Ministry of Natural Resources is having a really bad summer, with the deputy minister and a former minister both murdered and now the new minister – a star at that – has up and quit. Don't imagine for a minute that the opposition parties aren't having a field day with all that."

Anderson paused to check his phone for texts, then continued: "I don't think we're done with McKinley Island yet. There is nothing about what Christopher Karsten was telling us that makes me feel very comfortable and I find him a lot scarier than Marcusson. I expect Marcusson's craziness has plenty of traction in some circles right now, but once Karsten started down that political science rabbit hole he sounded away more dangerous than his boss."

"I couldn't agree more, but I am at a loss to think about how we can do anything about it. The laws that protect free speech apply equally to saints and crooks, to say nothing of idiots. I'm really surprised that nobody in our government – or in the US for that matter – has shown any leadership by calling them out, trying to force them out of the shadows."

"I want to spend some time with Tony Barker and his wife – particularly with Joan – because she has done a whole lot of study into these guys. And I say *guys* deliberately because I haven't seen any sign at all that there is a female within a country mile of the New World Mission, except to bring the sandwiches and drinks."

Sergeant Peggy Dawson had joined them in the wheelhouse and had been listening in: "Sergeant Anderson, I'm curious to hear you make that observation. Having spent a couple of days working with you, I have learned that you are, well, *spiritually* a feminist, but I am a little surprised to hear you articulate that viewpoint so pointedly."

Before Anderson could answer, MacLeod broke in with a chuckle: "There's something about travelling in company with your cousin Anita and the two Webster sisters – you know Marjorie already – that is like taking a graduate degree in applied feminism."

"Thank-you, Peggy," Anderson added. "I will happily take that part about being a spiritual feminist as a compliment, although I really hardly understand the word. I've always been a guy who simply loves women – all of them. As a matter of principle, I have also long recognized that women are about fifty percent of humankind and likely represent the most useful fifty percent. And your boss here is right to point out that when our lives get entangled with women like those three ladies, there is no possible retreat to our dim Neanderthal past. Hell, it was only after we met those gals that we started carrying Glocks and C-8s instead of wooden clubs. Both of us are now fully-civilized twenty-first century males."

As he had been talking, Anderson had been nudging back the throttle to approach the dock. He interrupted Peggy's laughter to direct her and MacLeod to take the mooring lines and tie *The Beaver* down to the village dock. The Transportation Safety Board representatives were already standing at the rail and ready to leave. They were polite but pointed out that they had a three-hour drive to Ottawa before their day was done. Importantly, one left Anderson a business card with an address where he should send in his invoice "for professional marine services".

After they left, MacLeod asked Dawson if the TSB had reached a conclusion about the crash of that little yellow-and-purple helicopter: "You spent most of the day with them... did they have any reasons why it crashed?"

"Absolutely. They told me that it had been flying too low, allowing the rotor to strike a pine tree which likely caused the helicopter to turn on its side and descend rapidly until it made contact with the ground."

"Well, that'd do it. And why was it flying too low?"

"They assured me that the underlying cause of the accident was almost certainly an inexperienced pilot who was unfamiliar with the altimeter on that model of helicopter."

"Brilliant. I just love it when the experts show up and dig out the real issues behind a disaster. I wonder if the insurance will pay out."

"Of course, they were not in a position to reach any conclusion on that, but they did suggest that since the owner's rental agent had failed to qualify the pilot, they said it was highly likely that the insurance company would insist on taking the owner and the agent to court."

"Ah, Sergeant Dawson. Thank you for the clarifications. You are indeed a master sleuth."

"I know. Happy to please."

Marjorie had just joined them at the dock: "What's up with you guys? You're all giggling like a bunch of kids."

"You had to be here, you just had to. Peggy was doing her impersonation of the TSB guys doing a crash-scene report. It was hilarious. What did you do with Giselle?"

"She's gone. First thing after breakfast she used our computer to write a hard copy letter of resignation to RGI, which we sent by registered mail – using her name – from Maple Falls early this afternoon when I deposited her in a rental car. She planned to drive all the way to Washington, crossing the border early this evening before her letter reaches RGI. Incidentally, I did print off a copy of her letter, John, assuming it might be a good thing to have for your files."

She came over to Anderson and gave him a hug. "I missed you, and I missed *The Beaver*, and it looks like I won't have either one of you to myself for a little while yet... here comes Charlie Morrell. He must have seen you coming back across the lake... he's called me two or three times earlier today and now I see him driving down to the dock. He's frantic to learn what was going down out there yesterday, and I've been playing dumb except to say you were on the lake and out of range all day. And I certainly didn't want him to know about Giselle."

Anderson whispered in her ear: "Think Lockmaster's for dinner. You and me." Then: "Hey Charlie, how are you doing? I thought we'd have seen you out at McKinley yesterday. You know Marjorie, of course, and this is Sergeant Peggy Dawson. I think you know MacLeod already."

"Hello everyone. I have to be the only person in Ontario who has no clue about what's been happening out at McKinley Island. Roger Larsen, whom I've only met once or twice, told me last week he had arranged for me to be picked up by helicopter yesterday at about ten thirty, and to wait for the chopper at the Spirit River airfield. Crickets. I waited until noon and went home."

"Well, they kinda ran out of helicopters out there, Charlie, so I'm not surprised they didn't pick you up. I assume you have been watching the news?"

"Yes, I turned on the news last night and it looks like the whole thing was a total disaster. Were you-all part of it?"

"Sort of," said Anderson. "I mean, we were there because the OPS and the RCMP had received information from a third party about a possible threat. As it turned out, the third party was correct and there was, in effect, a bit of a gang war between security teams hired by individuals out at the island. That, and a news helicopter crash to liven things up a bit. I don't think your company ever did get its media announcement done yesterday."

"No, it seems the announcement wound up being made on the noon news from Washington today. The only reference to Awan Lake was a couple of lines about the existing facility. There was no mention at all about the resignation of Minister Adams, although there was a pre-recorded clip from the Prime Minister welcoming the new expansion. I had heard about the resignation on the morning news while I was out at the plant this morning. What can I tell Bonnie? She is pretty upset. To her it's all a repeat of the fire and all those people killed a month ago, and I guess I can't blame her for feeling a bit paranoid."

Anderson was thoughtful for a moment: "I wish I could be comforting to her – or you for that matter – but speaking as a friend and neighbour and not in any official way, Bonnie is not wrong. Robertson Mines, or at least the parent company Robertson Group International, is up to its ass in this and a bunch of other bad stuff including an assassination in Africa that took out a friend of ours. No need to panic, just keep your heads down, ears closed and mouths shut and things should be just fine."

Morrell stared hard at Anderson, then at Marjorie and then across at MacLeod: "I have to say I have been wondering. The Manville thing – I heard that he was assassinated – and recently the visits I have received from people my mother used to refer to as *unsavoury gentlemen*. That reminds me, have you heard anything about my old boss Maurice Bonner and his wife Vivienne? All I know is that he was fired and they disappeared. There's been no sign of anything at all at their house, which is pretty much next door to ours.

Anderson chuckled. "He fared much better than your old friend the late Thomas Manville. Marjorie and I had drinks and supper with Maurice and Viv last week on the coast - near Nanaimo on the Island, actually. He's got a casual gig as a lecturer at the University and they are living happily onboard their very elegant little sailboat."

"Oh, wow. Finally some good news for a change. I know they used to sail out there a lot. I take it they are happy?"

"Happy as clams. Talked about coming home for the summer... they really enjoy their house here and she loves her garden."

"That's great. Thanks." He noticed that Marjorie was setting the mooring padlocks and locking the wheelhouse: "I'll let you folks get back to work, and thanks for the information." He stepped off the boat and walked back along the dock to his Robertson Mines pickup.

• • • •

Maple Falls, ON, 1845: After the two sergeants had left the dock to go home, Marjorie and Anderson had a quick shower and drove to Maple Falls. Before going to The Lockmaster's

House, their favourite restaurant for a relaxed night out with good food, Anderson couldn't resist driving by the Maple Falls Motor Lodge. As he expected might be the case, John had arranged for two police cruisers to be parked outside, one in front and the other in the parking lot at the rear of the building.

"So, why are we here?" asked Marjorie.

"Sorry about that – I did miss you on the boat today, and if you had been with us you would have known. McKinney Island is still a crime scene and off-limits to visitors, so John made them take that meeting for the bunch of crazies involved in the New World Mission to another location. They set up at the motor lodge, I guess, although I don't suppose there are very many of them in there. And I see that John has arranged surveillance, for their safety of course."

"Of course."

"Let's go eat. I told Richard we'd be there by seven."

SEPTEMBER 13

Spirit River, ON, 0615: Anderson had been up for ten minutes or so, wanting to wait until close to 0700 to wake up Marjorie for her phone call from Arthur Brighton. He had let the coffee finish brewing before he put his hand on her shoulder and kissed her cheek. "I hate to do this to you," he said, "but it's almost time for Brighton to call."

Dinner at the Lockmaster's House had been as delicious as ever, and Marjorie and Anderson had taken their time to run over the events of the last few days, do a little future planning about the house (Marjorie wondered if they could put a washer and dryer into the workshop because they could both find better things to do together than sit in the laundromat.) And there was planning to close up Wendy's and Marjorie's cottage at their tiny island southeast of the village, and Wendy needing to decide what she wanted to do for the winter.

They had just finished coffee and cognac when Marjorie's telephone buzzed. "Geesh, who calls me at ten o'clock at night?"

She stabbed the answer button and said, "Hello? Anita – how are you, sweetie?... She hasn't?... What the hell, she told me when she called yesterday ... The airlines? No, you'll never get any information from them. Have you been to the Canadian Embassy?... Good, go there again this morning. Before you go, buy yourself a burner phone, turn yours off, take the battery out and throw it away. Never use it again until you get home... Yes, tell the embassy everything. And book yourself the next flight to Toronto. You need to get out of there, so call me just before you get on the plane... Yes, of course if you hear from Wendy, but only on the burner... Frank sends a hug with mine... Bye."

"That does not sound very good at all."

"No. She never arrived in Paris. According to Air France,

she was not on the flight manifest from Kinshasa and had never boarded."

"Is Anita holding it together?"

"Very well, very clear-headed, thank goodness. I have to get back to the house, where I have the contact information from Wendy's boss at Envirowire. He needs to know as soon as possible... I expect he has the best connections to get information."

They had gone back home immediately and found the number for Arthur Brighton at Envirowire. She needed to share with him the backstory about why Wendy had to leave suddenly and of course the information about Giselle and RGI. Brighton was shocked and intensely angry to the point of tears that he had put another journalist's life in jeopardy. Marjorie had to snap him out of his emotions so he could bring his focus to bear on the need to find out why and where she went missing. They agreed he would probably need to wait a few hours to find open offices in Kinshasa, where he needed to start. He was to call Marjorie at 0700 Toronto time.

He was as good as his promise. Marjorie's phone rang at 0659 and it was Arthur Brighton saying that he had at least a little good news. Through his connections at Reuters he found a consultant in Kinshasa who said a lady matching Wendy's description was already on the ramp to board a flight to Paris when she was directed to another gate and put on a flight to Bujumbura, in Burundi.

"Arthur, I was hoping she had simply missed her flight and was waiting for the next one. What you say sounds like kidnapping and that is not really very good news."

"Actually, in that part of the world that is pretty good news," he replied. "It means she is alive, and her kidnappers will likely work very hard to keep her that way, at least until they get their money or make their trade."

"Make their trade? What do you mean?"

"This has been well organized but I am pretty sure it is not about money. After all, it's not like she is with a big corporation or part of a wealthy family. I think it's about influence, maybe even in government. There is no money in murdering journalists, especially print ones, and no advantage... you can find murdered journalists almost everywhere. She's worth away more alive... we just have to figure out the connection. I'm waiting for the offices at the Department of State to open up... it's pretty early, and in Washington even the ones who are working this early don't answer their phones until office hours. Marjorie, I'm on this, honestly I am. I'll call you as soon as I have talked to a few people. This must not end badly."

Marjorie sat still for a few moments after Brighton hung up. She turned and looked at Anderson: "I was thinking we should go out and work at closing up one of the cottages, but I guess I don't dare get out of range of the cell tower today. Any ideas?"

"How about a washer and dryer at a washer and dryer store in The Falls?"

"There is such an animal?"

"Ya think?"

"Okay, I'll buy you a sour cream glazed donut and coffee."

"Deal."

• • • •

Ottawa, ON, 0935: Former Minister of Natural Resources Dale Adams had worn blue jeans, a hoodie and sneakers this morning. *I need to go somewhere and clear my head,* he had told himself when he got up so he texted a message to his constituency office to say he was going for a private trip but that he'd see them Thursday afternoon or maybe Friday morning if he got hung up somewhere. He packed his usual backpack with one change of clothes and a rain jacket, left his apartment and walked to the depanneur on the corner near his townhouse and bought two pack of cigarillos and a lighter and stuffed them into the backpack before going to the parking lot and retrieving his black Traverse. He drove northeast to the Canadian Tire near where Monte Paiement crosses the Autoroute and bought four twenty-litre plastic jerry cans and an inexpensive sleeping bag. He stopped and filled the jerry cans before heading out along the Autoroute to the airport where he had reserved a four-seater Cessna 172.

This was not the first time he had rented a small plane from this agency, and in fact, it seemed to him this was perhaps the same unit as he had rented earlier in the summer to fly over Awan Lake after that fire that had consumed Robertson's copper mine and smelter. It didn't take long to finish the paperwork and sign the rental agreement. He filed a flight plan that would take him to Orillia at the north end of Lake Simcoe, then drove the Traverse over to the C172, transferred all his gear and parked the SUV in the parking lot before walking back onto the tarmac and over to the little plane. He unearthed one pack of cigarillos and the lighter from his backpack... he would be airborne in minutes and he only smoked when he flew. Never at work, and certainly never at home.

· · · ·

Spirit River, ON, 1106: Anderson had emptied his slip tank, pulled it off his little truck and set it on the ground, which was a good thing because otherwise he would have had to make two trips to The Falls to bring back the washer and dryer. He opened one of the huge doors on the front end of his workshop and was able to back in past two ski-boats being repaired and almost to the walk-in door that led into the house. There, he and Marjorie were able to unload the machines along with the extra wiring he would need to connect the dryer and some plumbing supplies to reach the drain and supply lines further along the wall.

"Do you need my help to put the tank back on, or shall I make us some lunch and we can do that later?

"Nah, I'm feeling lazy. I'll just use the little excavator and a chain. Off was easy... on will be harder. And I guess I should do it now because *The Beaver* needs lunch too – we've been burning lots of fuel going back and forth to McKinney Island faster than I normally go. I'll load up and be back before lunch."

Marjorie ran over to the truck as he was getting in and kissed him on the nose.

She went back into the house and flipped on the television in time to catch the noon news from Ottawa. The first visual was of McKinney Island, complete with burning helicopters, then a shot of Dale Adams announcing his resignation from Cabinet. The news item was based on information leaked from the Prime Minister's office that Adams had been identified as having an illicit relationship with an employee of Robertson Group International, so therefore the Prime Minister had accepted the resignation with regret. Adams was unavailable for comment, and the RGI employee was not identified other than as being a female. The reporter went on to say that the former Minister of Natural Resources represented a constituency in southern Alberta where he lived with his wife and two teenaged daughters.

Marjorie turned off the TV and went on preparing lunch, but when Anderson arrived back with the diesel fuel and stopped at the house, she started to tell him and then almost collapsed into his arms with tears of rage, sorrow and frustration. "Why do people insist on tearing each other apart. And the goddamn media is like the picadores at a goddamn bullfight, trying to tease the last drop of blood out of every decent human being and make them dirty. I hope Giselle never sees this. I know she did wrong, but at least she fucking cared. These nasty-minded chicks in front of their TV cameras are only interested in their next promotion for telling dirty stories. They're not real reporters, not like Priscilla and Wendy who actually try to tell truth to power and get killed for their efforts."

Anderson folded her into his arms and took her to the sofa, where he cuddled her until the tears and the shaking subsided. "You haven't heard from Arthur yet, have you?"

"No. No. It's nothing that bad. But yes it is, it is that bad. There was a news item on the TV about Adams and they just destroyed everyone. Giselle wasn't identified. It's just the way they did it, those little bitches. It's not their duty to destroy people, it's their job to reveal truth behind the story, not the other way around. Oh crap, there I go again. I'm sorry, let's have lunch."

He smiled and kissed her, on *her* nose this time. "I understand, and I'm on your side."

Lunch was simple... fresh tomatoes and cucumbers, cold roast chicken sandwiches and cold beer. It was also delicious, and they enjoyed it together as – for the moment anyway – the outside world retreated beyond their home. After lunch, they finished refuelling the workboat and checked all the engine and transmission fluids. While in The Falls buying the washer and dryer, Anderson had brought measurements so he could replace the recently broken glass on the back door of the workshop and on the starboard side of the focsle. While they were working on the boat, they repaired the window glass in the focsle. At 1330, Marjorie's cellphone buzzed: it was a government number and after a short pause, she found herself talking to a François Le-Seigneur, Deputy Minister of Natural Resources.

"Ah," she said. "You have replaced the late Leonard Hamilton-DuBois?"

"Yes, Mademoiselle Wilson. You knew Leonard?"

"Not well, but he was a good neighbour. I know his sister-in-law better."

"Ah yes, Florence. Fine lady. Mademoiselle, you have a sister named Wendy who is a journalist currently stationed in Africa, I believe.

Marjorie felt her breath catch in her throat and stared wide-eyed across the cabin at Anderson: "Yes, sir. I do. We are trying to find her and bring her home."

"Mademoiselle, our department's international business associates in Africa have located your sister alive and well just outside Kinshasa and they will be flying her back to Canada on the first available flight. As I understand it, the next flight out of Kinshasa and its international connections to Canada will have her arriving in three days. Your sister will be transported from the airport to your home at Spirit River by government limousine... I will provide you with the exact time in due course."

"Mr. LeSeigneur, you can only imagine how relieved and grateful we are. I hope she is well and has not been injured?"

"Yes, Mademoiselle, that is correct. I also need to tell you that our business associate – Robertson Group International – is taking care of all of this at its own expense as a goodwill gesture. Our government has been told it will have to guarantee that your sister maintains the terms of a non-disclosure agreement she will be required to sign as a condition of her repatriation when she arrives in Canada. We – Canada and her business associates – would like to remind you and your sister that she has fared better than another friend of your sister's, because of government policies in our country. It has always been our understanding that Canadian journalists need to check with the Department of Foreign Affairs to avoid undue interference with corporate investment activities in countries which are less supportive of our liberal outlook on freedom of information."

It felt like the blood in Marjorie's veins had turned to ice. She paused long enough to regain composure before responding: "I understand fully, Mr. LeSeigneur, and assure you of our cooperation. Out of curiosity, was my sister's other friend named Priscilla Morgenstern?"

"Mademoiselle, it has been a distinct pleasure chatting with you. I can tell that you are an astute lady. Have a pleasant day."

He hung up, and Marjorie clicked off her phone. "I need a drink, Mr. Anderson," she said. "Now."

Anderson fished around in the locker under the berth in the focsle and took out a half-empty bottle of over-proof rum and a couple of plastic tumblers. He poured two short glasses and handed her one: "This is Wray and Nephew White, a Jamaican overproof rum. Do not, I repeat do not, inhale. Very small sips only."

"Geesh. Holy cow. Well, actually, right now it slides down just fine. That LeSeigneur guy has to be the most ice-cold son of a bitch I have ever talked to. But he is sending Wendy home, on the next connection from Kinshasa. It appears to me that she never left there... her kidnapping was staged. It's all about our frickin' government in Ottawa slapping nice little female journalists on the wrist and sending them home so they don't interfere with Canada's business partners. God forbid we should interfere with Robertson Group International."

This time it was Anderson's phone ringing. "Hello? ...Tony?...Yes, indeed, we need to give you a debriefing. I have Marjorie here with me, how about we come out to your place, pick up you and Jean and sail out to McKinney Island and back? ...Yes, now... Well, as long as it takes, probably forty-five minutes... Great, see you soon." And he clicked off and turned to Marjorie: "Sorry, I kind of jumped on that but we really do need to fill him in on what's been happening – especially this, with Wendy."

"Yes. Should we take anything?"

"This time, just jackets and go. I'll grab them from the house and lock up if you want to fire everything up and take off the locks."

"Absolutely."

• • • •

Awan Lake, ON, 1515: The slight wind of the morning had fallen flat and the afternoon was sunny and bright. *The Beaver* ambled southward from Tony and Jean Barker's cottage home, through a nest of small islands and onto a large stretch of open water toward McKinney Island, still some two miles ahead. Marjorie had assigned the task of maintaining the ship's course to the autohelm. The four people onboard were behaving in a highly illegal fashion, sipping on bottles of locally-brewed dark beer while munching on what seemed an endless supply of Jean Barker's cold roast beef sandwiches.

The autohelm took care of the direction of forward travel, but knew nothing of what might be lurking behind, so the four friends didn't see the white Cessna 172 with its green markings until it shot by them a scant twelve feet above the cabin top. The pilot waggled his wings as if to invite a race and continued on the same course as *The Beaver*: straight toward McKinney Island. They stood up and watched as the pilot boosted the engine speed and gained altitude to pass over the island.

And didn't. Forty-seven seconds after passing them overhead, the Cessna disappeared in a flash, followed by a quick puff of smoke, at the centre of McKinley Island.

PETER KINGSMILL

THE END

EPILOGUE

The Transportation Safety Board ruled that the crash of a Cessna 172 on an island on Awan Lake in northern Ontario was caused by pilot error. The Alberta pilot, a Member of Parliament and former cabinet minister in the Government of Canada, was survived by his wife and daughters who were at their ranch home south of Calgary at the time. The crash unfortunately caused the death of seven staff members at a resort on the small island north of Toronto. Damage on the ground was confined to the resort's main lodge, which was fully destroyed by fire. Fire inspectors have suggested that improper storage of gasoline in the building may have been responsible for the extreme heat generated by the fire.

PETER KINGSMILL

...and yet, here we are...

Thankfully, the Awan Lake experiment was short-lived. On reflection, fewer than twenty-four hours spent on an island on a remote lake in northern Canada changed my life forever. People died during that time, but I lived. When your life story begins anew with something like that, what you did beforehand was clearly a waste and what follows becomes – for me anyway – a calling. *Giselle Matthews, Staff Writer, Envirowire*

ABOUT THE AUTHOR

Peter Kingsmill is the author of the Awan Lake mystery series. Peter is a recipient of the Governor General's Conservation Award (Canada) and the founder of the Redberry Lake (UNESCO) Biosphere Reserve in Saskatchewan. When he is not writing novels, he serves as publications editor with the Alberta Society of Professional Biologists and works as a consultant on regional development projects. Peter joined Crime Writers of Canada as a Professional Author Member in 2018.

Peter has been a frequent writer and editor since leaving high-school in Montreal and college in Vermont. He recently retired from many years as a riverboat captain and owner of a small-waters marine services business, and has worked at an eclectic mix of tasks which include logger, trucker and cattle farmer. He is passionate about Canada's rural spaces and has served two terms as Mayor in his home community of Hafford, where he lives with his wife Valerie, an artist and the author/illustrator of the *Redberry Tales*[1] series of gentle children's books.

Like most authors (maybe all authors?) Peter always appreciates reviews and comments from readers, whether they are posted on retail websites like Amazon or Kobo or Goodreads, or directly by email (author@peterkingsmill.ca).

Other novels by Peter Kingsmill:

SUNSET at 20:47

NOBODY DROWNED

Learn more at:

www.peterkingsmill.ca[2]

1.　　*https://www.kobo.com/ca/en/ebook/redberry-tales-muskrat-lodge*

2.　　http://www.peterkingsmill.ca